The Red Triangle

By

Eric Magliocca

Sire-Corridor

Sire-Corridor
Pittsburgh, Pennsylvania

ISBN-13: **978-0692029176**
ISBN-10: **0692029176**

First edition Charles Towne Publishing February 2013
Second edition Sire-Corridor April 2014

Manufactured in the United States of America

The Red Triangle

CHAPTER 1: THE ATTACK

Peter Mayday had seen his wife, Evelyn, hammer her arms against the waves of San Sino beach every evening for two years, and every time he watched her, he grew nervous. She liked to swim out very far, a good seventy yards from shore until her feet could no longer touch the sand. What worried Peter were the obvious accidents that ritually found themselves in the newspaper: *Boat Propeller Kills Swimmer; Rip Tide Drowns Local Twenty Yards from Shore.* They were the stories that made him reluctant to watch her swim. In his mind, she was just asking for an accident, but for Evelyn, giving up swimming meant giving up an identity. She was the best swimmer in the state for two years in high school, and it was the ocean and a strong evening tide that made her the swimmer she was.

If that didn't make Peter nervous enough, the sight of his parents on the beach made his stomach a corkscrew. They had flown all the way from Rochester to celebrate his becoming a board-certified vascular surgeon, and it was their last night staying with him before they flew back. Little did they know that he was going to give it one last try to convince them to move out to California and live with him. They were adamant about staying on the east coast, however, and his dad could become very combative about the subject. This was his last chance.

Standing in the kitchen and peeking through the blinds like a child, he watched them closely before his eyes localized around his five year old son, Conrad, playing with a plastic red shovel a yard from where the last wave sapped the sand. It was time to join his family.

He dropped his coat on the kitchen table, opened the nearest door panel, and walked nimbly down the steep stone steps to the rock-infested beach. Peter was careful not to run toward them with the black-jagged rocks and shards of glass sometimes lying just beneath the waves in the sand. He had seen bare-footed runners drench the sand with blood because of them. You never knew how deep they were in the sand's waves.

As he approached them, he could tell by their wary posture that they had been on the beach some time and were agitated that Evelyn was both swimming rather far out and seemed to leave them to babysit Conrad. "She stuck us with him again," he imagined his father, Ned, had already said. Ned could be irascible, sometimes deliberately difficult for the sake of it.

His mother, Clare, on the other hand, made pleasantness her religion. "Peter, it's so good to see you!" she said as she walked toward him. He could tell her knee, now void of most of its cartilage, had been bothering her all day, and yet she stayed down there to make the most of her time with her grandson.

Peter kissed her on the cheek. "Sit down, Mom." He pulled a lawn chair over to her, and she took it, surprisingly.

"How are you, Dad?"

"All right," he puffed. "Isn't she a little too far out?"

"Peter, I don't like her swimming that far out like that,"

Clare said. "You let her do that?"

"What am I going to do?" Peter replied. "She's been doing it all her life."

"Is it safe?" Clare asked. Concern ruled the creases in her face. Old age had hit her hard since Peter moved across the country three years ago. Greys were all over her head now, and her skin had made room for age spots.

"It's safe," he confirmed to calm her down. "She swims horizontally there from our house down to the end of the street. About a quarter of a mile and back until she is tired." Peter sat down in the sand next to her, watching Conrad build his sandcastle a few yards from shore. The beach had a particular appearance to it that evening, as if varnished and all the sand lay perfectly wavy despite beachgoers trod. While the red sun was firmly on its way into the ocean, the clouds took on a putty color as they absorbed the last glares of amber sunlight.

"So, overall, what'd you think?" Peter asked proudly with a smile, looking back at his enormous, three-story beach house with twin decks on both stories wrapped from the front of the house to the back.

"Beautiful," Clare said smiling, her blue eyes searing in the diminishing light. "Absolutely beautiful."

"Dad?"

"What are the taxes like here in San Sangre?" Ned asked. While his mom had aged, Peter noticed his father had barely aged a bit.

"Is that all you care about?"

"What are the taxes like?" Ned asked again. He walked in circles, kicking his footprints of sand.

"Better, okay?" Peter said. "They're better. Everything out here is better than the East. This was a good move."

Ned got defensive. "I'm not saying they aren't. What about resale value? This town borders San Francisco. You know how bad their resale value is on homes?"

Peter continued to watch Conrad who was still digging up sand with his red shovel, building a sandcastle in such a concentrated way that he still hadn't noticed his father. "I know you'll never move out here," Peter said shaking his head. "You'll be content to live across the country from me because taxes might be an extra fifty a month."

"They'd actually be less than that," Ned said.

Peter was stunned. He looked up at him. "You actually looked into this?"

Ned turned back to him. Clare was smiling. "We're thinking about moving out here," Ned said.

Peter immediately stood up. "That's great! I mean, when did you make this decision?"

"I haven't yet," Ned said.

"There's a condo up for sale right down the street – "

"Not yet," Ned stopped him. "We can talk about it at dinner. Now when is that wife of yours coming in?"

"I took the lamb out of the oven fifteen minutes ago," Clare said. "I hollered out to her then, but she didn't hear."

They looked out to sea where they could see Evelyn's arms swooping in and out of the water at a strikingly rapid pace.

"Should we call her?" Clare asked.

"No, she wouldn't hear us," Peter said. Something propelled him forward. He didn't like the look of the water out there, and he was sure that was the farthest from the beach he had ever seen Evelyn swim.

As soon as Peter made his way to the shore, Evelyn's head emerged, and she began heading back to shore. It didn't take her long before she could stand in the surf.

Noticing her soon arrival, Peter called to Conrad. Conrad dropped his red shovel and looked to Peter with his big black eyes all shiny and stark. "Come on, Conrad. We're going

8

to go up to the house to eat." Peter began picking up towels and Conrad's toys.

"Okay, Daddy," he said while slapping his hands together on his pink bathing suit to rid himself of sand. He then stood up, still wobbly at the age of five, and walked toward them. As he felt comfortable on the wet sand, he began to run lightly. He looked back to the sea to observe how far he came when something curious struck his eye: a sharp, gray protrusion penetrated softly a foot above the water, thirty yards from shore. It was thick on one side and narrow on the other, and Conrad likened it to a floating gravestone, like the gravestones he had seen when Evelyn would take him to see her parents' markers every Sunday. Then two balanced, long, gray, and slender beams shown above the water and were equidistant to the gravestone, which now, as Conrad's vision cultivated the image, resembled a huge knife. The beams were each five feet from the vertical spike.

Conrad understood the shape to be an airplane that flew in the water. He looked worriedly to his father, but Peter was busy collecting Conrad's toys, and his grandparents were talking. If adults weren't worried about the shape, then why should he be?

When Conrad turned around again, the object submerged. He felt less nervous now. He headed back toward his family.

"Did you bring your shovel?" Peter asked him. Conrad shook his head and began to walk back to where he was playing when he saw that it had drifted out to sea, a little red dot in massive blue. "Come on, Conrad," Peter said, staring at the floating shovel. Evelyn was waist deep when he pointed behind her. "He left his shovel!"

Evelyn turned around, slightly losing her balance in the waves, and turned back with an exhausted expression.

9

"Don't worry about it," Peter said. "It's just a toy."

She saw it drifting slowly with the current about twenty yards from her. "I'll get it." She submerged, and a few seconds later, when she broke the surface, she had already cut the distance between her and the shovel in half. With a few more swift strides, she possessed it.

In that moment, her surroundings seemed to darken. There was still plenty of light on the coast as the sun had thrown up a sublime sunset with mixes of pink and orange and light blue swirls. The water, though, had a darker hue, and Evelyn could see nothing despite her hands just an inch below the surface. The water was also growing louder and the waves were smacking the beach farther up the sand each time. Conrad's half-finished sandcastle was soon drowned in the waves.

"Why don't you guys head up to the house now," Peter said. "Especially you, Mom, with your bad knee. I'll get Evelyn. Dad, can you take him?"

"All right," Ned replied. "Come on, Conrad."

"I want to stay with Daddy," Conrad said with severe puerile parlance.

"It's okay. I'll take him up," Peter said. "Sometimes he doesn't like to go up without me." Ned held his palms up in acquiescence then headed up the sand toward the beach house, holding Clare's forearm to help her balance herself.

"Hey Daddy," Conrad said tugging Peter's black pants. "Why was there an airplane in the water?" Peter was still ignoring Conrad, for most of Conrad's comments were naturally unappealing. But Ned did not hesitate to stop dead in the sand, leaving his wife to walk hob-legged six yards until she realized she had lost her aid for good.

"Is something wrong?" Clare asked.

Ned came back and looked at Peter to see if he had heard his son correctly. He squatted near Conrad, his heartbeat

10

a loud tick. Conrad's eyes opened wide and his pupils darkened when he saw the distressed look on his grandfather's face.

"Conrad, what did you say you saw?" Ned asked slowly. Conrad hesitated. He was still afraid of strangers and it had been a year since he last saw his grandfather. "It's okay. You can tell me. Did you say you saw an airplane? Was it an airplane?"

Peter was worried by his father's sudden alarm. "What's going on?"

Ned rose slowly while looking out to sea. "He said he saw an airplane…in the water." They locked worried eyes and looked up and down the coast. The ocean was dark and choppy blue.

Peter felt there was something wrong about the sea. It was by no means a scientific explanation he offered except that he didn't like the way it looked. It had a strange energy to it, a frantic, busy energy in the way the waves were proceeding over Evelyn's body, denying her presence on the beach. It seemed almost deliberate.

"Evelyn, hurry up!" Peter screamed. He turned to Conrad and asked, "Conrad, what did this plane look like? Was it gray?"

"Yes."

"Was it big, like a plane?"

"It was smaller."

"Not like one in the sky. Was it in the water? Actually under the water?"

"Yea, it was down that way," he said pointing his little finger down the beach where his red shovel used to lie stamped in the sand. There was only blue water and white sand and no one in sight for half a mile.

Evelyn looked up and noticed Peter standing in the surf. The water was soaking his suit pants and she knew he would

11

never allow salt water to touch a thousand dollar suit. She sat up, her arms beginning to tremble, partly from the cold and partly from the scared look on her husband's face. She saw his family pivoting around the beach, looking out to sea, then up and down the coast.

"What is it?" she asked back to shore.

"Evelyn, come quickly!" Peter said.

"You don't think there's a shark, do you?" Clare asked as she walked hob-legged sideways down the beach.

"I don't think a shark would ever come this close to shore," Peter assured himself. "She's fine. She's already in the surf. Dad, you've got to stop doing this!"

"He said he saw an airplane in the water!" Ned snapped indignantly. "What do you think that could be!"

Peter was being driven mad by the uncertainty. "She's still so far out," he said to himself. "Did it look like a shark or not!" he hollered. Conrad began crying. "You can't cry now!" he screamed and picked Conrad up under his armpits and lifted him to his face. "Did you see a shark or not!"

"He doesn't know what a shark looks like!" Ned hollered. "Put him down!"

Conrad rolled his tiny hands around his eyes and pushed hard into them as if he were trying to stop a large wound from bleeding.

"What did you see?"

"A-a shark," he stammered. He had spoken the truth. Peter believed him. Somewhere out there was a shark.

Evelyn was thirty yards from shore now but moving slowly. She was standing in sand, tiptoeing in six feet of water and fighting the tide and waves that seemed to pick up power. Even the wind was flying faster.

"He's just telling you what you want to hear, Peter. He's five years old," Ned said.

12

"Peter, what's the matter!" Evelyn shouted to shore, her arms thrashing through the waves. "Why's he crying!"

"Just come in!" Peter screamed. The waves, with a sudden decrescendo, made the ocean flat.

A rumbling sound suddenly filled the air. It was coming down the coast. Everyone looked left to see what it was. It was a helicopter. Bright red orbs, which attached to the skids and the tail rotor, began fluttering. The helicopter started blasting siren music akin to a fire truck's din.

"Oh God, what's happening!" Evelyn screamed.

Peter had no doubt the coast guard made its appearance because of what it could see that he couldn't, and he was sure it was a shark. "Evelyn, look at me," he tried to say calmly. She did as she was told but couldn't be misled by the doom in his eyes. "With all your might, swim directly to me."

Peter's mother, watching the waves and anticipating a gray fin, felt like she stepped out of her body when she finally saw an irregular movement beneath the water. "Oh my God," she gasped, covering her mouth. It was as though the thought of the fin conjured it.

Evelyn saw their faces and stopped moving. She turned white and her arms dangled at her shoulders. Her family was no longer looking at her, but slightly above her where a small gray line sawed through the pink sky directly above her head, growing larger and larger. When Evelyn submerged again in a final effort, a huge dorsal fin paved through the water like a tractor in mud, spitting water on all sides. Peter had trouble understanding what he was seeing.

The gray, amorphous creature turned on its side, its white belly facing the sky, and inclined unseemly bright, fat red lips. Pearly triangles hung like shingles as it swallowed sea water, pulling Evelyn's body toward it. Its mouth never seemed to stop inclining. The shark was large enough to swallow her.

13

Then the bite came. Flawless. The jaws clamped down on her waist and the lower jaw followed through cleanly with the upper. Bright red mist spurted in the air.

Evelyn never saw her attacker. Her head jolted backward and her neck declined into her chest as if she had had the wind knocked out of her. Her chin collapsed in her face as she fell like a cut tree trunk forward into the blue. Peter flung himself into the shoreline, far enough where he could see the shark chew through half of her body then spin upside down where its white stomach shown. Its tail kicked high and slapped water all the way to the sand. Peter looked into the shark's black eye just below the surface as it headed down the coast – its dorsal fin disappearing.

Her legs were taken back into the ocean by the tide and a dark purple drifted over the surface of the water. The helicopter roared over their heads, taking some of their hearing with it in the process to land on the beach.

Peter, reacting only on instinct, jumped into the shore. Ned, preparing for this, grabbed his arms and forced him back on the beach. He wrestled his son to the ground and held his arms funereally into his chest. The waves still kept coming, only now they were red. They capsized on Peter's face, and he spit up the red saltwater.

"I can still save her! I can still save her!" he screamed.

"She's gone!" Ned screamed.

"Get off of me! She's not gone!"

"Yes she is, Peter. She's dead!"

"You have to let me up!"

"She's gone, Peter! She's gone!" But Ned knew she wasn't. She was staring at them from the sea, her body and face paralyzed in a doll's stare.

"Let me up! I'm a doctor!"

"It's gonna come back, Peter! It's gonna come back!"

Peter stopped his struggle and began crying as his legs bent up in a fetal position. "It's waiting for her to die." He sat on the beach, watching his wife as she watched him. He was sure his heart, which felt like it was shaking and spinning around in his chest, was about to explode.

The helicopter finally landed, swiping sand and sediment rocks across their eyes. But nobody blinked.

"Get out of the water! The shore is pulling you back in!" Clare screamed as she covered Conrad's eyes. They had already receded a yard into the shore and were now in a foot of water. "It's coming back!" Ned dragged Peter from the shore to the beach and pushed him into the sand there, still guarding him as they watched the large gray fin breach again, this time slowly circling what remained of her. The shark made an abrupt U-turn, and without showing its head, pulled Evelyn down.

"Don't look!" Peter's head was pushed into the sand.

One of the coast guard officers sprinted from the helicopter and uselessly threw a life vest into the water. Realizing his foolishness, he turned and screamed, "Get the family into the house! An ambulance is on its way!"

The other officer stepped from the helicopter but did not run. He instead looked intently at Conrad whose eyes were so big from alarm they were entirely black. Conrad looked up at the man. He saw the name "Briggs" on the man's jacket. It didn't make sense to him that the man's name was Briggs. He only saw letters from the alphabet in a particular order. He kept staring at them until they were a permanent part of his memory.

Briggs, just twenty-five years old and his first year on the job, lifted Conrad from the beach and carried him up to the house. Conrad looked over Briggs' shoulder and saw his mom gone from the sea, it now just flat and dark in the disappearing sunset.

CHAPTER 2: THE INTERVIEW

Conrad Mayday spent most of his waiting staring at a small American flag attached at the end of a pencil in the secretary's pencil holder. It was billowing because of the air condition vent directly above the secretary's desk. He tried to keep his eyes on the flag while moving his chin forward and backward to an internal beat. *Second chances, second chances,* he kept convincing himself. *America is the land of second chances.*

When his attempt at persiflage was rebuffed with a faint smile from the secretary, he grew very nervous. He was sure she and what seemed like all of Northern California had heard of Donny Locks, the man who cost him his job three months ago. But he suspected she also knew what happened to his mother, Evelyn Mayday, the poor mother who met her demise at the hands of a great white shark twenty-two years ago. Reporters said it was the most grisly attack in California history, largely because after the body was bitten in half, it was consumed. It was the story that made the rounds on the news for weeks after, and every so often, popped up when another attack occurred. And then just a year later after Evelyn's death, Conrad lost his father, Peter Mayday, who walked himself into the Pacific and never returned.

As a result, the name Mayday followed him wherever he went. People always recognized it, one way or another. Despite the tragedies, he found that people saw him as a freak – as damaged goods. How could someone who saw the demise of both his parents still be normal? The Donny Locks incident three months ago made sense to some people. They saw him as a ticking time bomb.

As Conrad was thinking about the responses to the questions he was sure to be asked, he would sometimes mutter to himself and cause the secretary to look up at him. Each time, though, he would simply treat her to a quick smile. She seemed cold. Her hair was bobbed black and spiked at the top and her slender face sat atop a particularly long narrow neck. Conrad spotted trouble with her immediately. By appearance alone, there was no reasoning with this woman.

He heard a chair creak and louder commotion inside the office as the managers finished up their interview. In a few moments they would be coming for him. He didn't know what to expect. It was an entry-level position in sales at a small supply company, Malton's. A far cry from being a former supervisor at one of California's largest fishing companies, but a job he had to take. He had been on interviews for months now, and no company would hire him.

As he waited to see the candidate, one of the six he heard was left battling him for the position, he looped his wife, Micker's, wisdom over and over in his head like a recorder: *Don't bring up Donny Locks unless you are certain they know about it. If it comes to that, you made a terrible mistake and are hoping for a second chance. It will never happen again.*

Rather than burst through the door, the managers and the candidate gathered at the foot of it to continue their banter. They hovered around there for three minutes, the timbre in their

17

voices changing the more they moved back and forth in the office. Conrad's heart was ticking. He needed to urinate and he was thirsty. He kept trying to swallow and sat with his butt just on the edge of the chair to relieve his bladder. Then the door opened slightly, stopped, opened more, stopped, and then swung open.

Don Frowler, the Manager, and Michael Full, the Assistant Manager, were both in the doorway with their candidate: a skinny, short man of no more than twenty-four – most likely on his first job interviews. His hair was prematurely thinning and his shoulders were steeped into his neck like a cat, but his face was lively and his Armani suit – a gift of his father's probably – made him appear bankerish. Frowler dropped his hand from the young man's shoulder, and the young man walked decisively to the secretary's desk and shook her hand. "Have a good day, ma'am."

"Good luck with your career," she delivered automatically, smiling as the last syllable rolled off her tongue.

"Try to stay out of the sand Tuesday!" Full hollered. Immediately, Conrad recognized such banter meant the candidate was a "seed," planted in the candidate pool most likely by a powerful parent or relative. These types of candidates were ever popular in business. Conrad's hope sank.

The young man let off a splintering, ostentatious laugh before replying, "I will, I will. My stroke is definitely improving. Maybe one day I'll be challenging you down there."

"Not if I have a say in it!"

The laugh continued untrammeled by the candidate. "All right. Take care and thank you again for this opportunity!"

Frowler opened Conrad's folder gently. Full stood squinting over Frowler's shoulder, his stout and portly body appearing all the more inept with the tie he wore that barely passed his pectorals. His dress pants were also unbecoming as

18

his belt hung halfway down his butt, giving the impression that his back and legs were linear. He swung his arms back and forth, his left arm made into a tiny fist that was hammered into his right palm. He glimpsed Conrad's brown dress shoes and smiled softly when he saw Conrad staring back at him.

"Okay, sales as well," Frowler began, still reading Conrad's folder. "Miiiister Maaaaayday," he intonated as his long, stabbing blue eyes jumped up and completely changed his guy-next-door perception. They were deep, hypnotic crystal blue eyes that called everyone to take him seriously. "Come on back."

Once the interview got going, Conrad felt his answers were getting better and better. He already had three years of sales experience under his belt and a year as a supervisor of sales, and he had been through the interview stage before, so it was hard for managers to throw questions at him for entry level positions that caught him off guard.

"Why do you like selling so much?" Frowler asked, his first tough question.

Conrad didn't hesitate. "I enjoy selling because I love to work with people and help them arrive at a decision that will solve their problems and better their lives. In my three years of sales, my customers were always satisfied because I gave them all the needed information about the product I was selling, I explained how the product would affect their lives and their future, and I arrived at an agreement with the customer with honor and integrity. I was always someone they could trust, and that is why I had such a large repeat customer base in my years of sales. "

Frowler and Full looked at each other briefly. His answer was spot on.

Frowler then closed his folder and went for the question

that always seemed to make candidate's sweat. "Conrad, what do you think is your greatest weakness?"

Conrad didn't budge. He and Micker had spent an hour hammering out the right response to this question. The key was to keep it short. The longer you talked about it, the more trouble you could potentially cause. "I have trouble controlling the feeling that I have to do a million things at once," he said confidently. "After identifying this problem by asking for feedback from colleagues, I have taken proactive measures to try and see my life from a spatial perspective, so I can suppress the feeling that everything needs to be achieved at once. Now, when I have a lot on my plate, I do a little bit at a time. There's still room for improvement, but I feel like I'm on the right path."

They traded satisfactory glances. Frowler's folder opened again, and he scoured his notes to find his toughest question. And then it came, like they were trying to put an end to the interview. "Why did you leave your last job?"

It was a tough question for anyone, but Conrad knew how they were trying to trip him up. They wanted to see if he would refer to Donny Locks, the intern he allegedly pushed down a flight of stairs. It was a story that had somehow grown legs all over Northern California, and even found its way into the newspaper. Most companies wouldn't touch him because of it, and the one's that had he was sure dismissed him because of it. But this interview was different: it had been set up by his wife, Micker, and Bran Hall, his former manager, had put in a good word for him. This question was expected, and an answer had been planned.

"I think that whenever you leave a company, you are sure to have different emotions. You will be leaving behind friendships you forged and successes you made, and you'll always remember a part of your history as a professional is going

20

to be left behind. But I truly believe in change as an agent of growth, and change is a critical element to my success as a professional. I am excited to create new friendships and new successes with a company that will offer new opportunities for me, and I can't wait to bring my skills and my experience to your company if I am given the chance."

The managers were impressed even though he was slightly indirect with his answer. He had that gift: he could answer questions in such a way to make the interviewer feel he answered it when he did not. But all Conrad was worried about was being safe with his responses. His only hurdle now was Donny Locks. If they could look beyond what had happened three months ago in June, the job was his.

Conrad felt good, and he learned in his experience that when bosses liked you, they rarely hesitated in expressing their interest in hiring you. He waited for them to ask if he was available to start immediately. It was early September, and the position needed to be filled by the end of the week.

Frowler and Full made eye contact once again, and Full did something that made Conrad's stomach tighten. He looked away dismissively. Frowler seemed to take a cue from that. He smacked the folder with his hand a few times as if thinking what to do, and then he said, "Okay," and wheeled his chair to his Mac. He typed in his password then looked over the computer, his blue eyes searing right above the screen.

Conrad noticed that Full wouldn't look at him. He hadn't even asked a question the entire interview. Those were telltale signs. Conrad knew he had lost it. It was good, but just not good enough for a guy who just got fired so publicly.

"I need to review your demographics, and you're out of here," Frowler said before pinching his declivitous nose, a jittery gesticulation Conrad had noticed throughout the interview. "You were born on Halloween?"

Another bad sign for Conrad. Halloween wasn't the best holiday to be born on when you're trying to rehabilitate your reputation.

"Yes, I was."

"All right. Mr. Mayday, we will be in touch with you after our deliberation. We should know by next Friday which candidate we have chosen to fill the position." Conrad dropped his head and pushed his tongue severely into his right cheek. The feeling was absolute. He had lost it. "Do you have any questions?"

Conrad rose slowly, catching the same American flag pencil on Frowler's desk, only this one was wilted. "Look," he said. His voice was dry and his forehead perspiring. "What happened with Donny Locks…that will never," Conrad let his lower teeth show like a Tusk Boxer, "ever happen again." He sighed and looked Frowler in the eyes, the blue now drastically lighter and less severe, almost deadened like a blind man's. "We have all been bosses here. We've all had that employee…"

"What employee is that?" asked Full for the first time, now intrigued to see what Conrad would admit about the situation Full was briefed on hours before the interviews started.

Conrad felt the need to be blunt. They seemed to want that from him anyways.

"A guy you just, you knew was going to do bad out there. He was bad news – a danger to people. He just, agitated me, would try to make me lose my temper every single day. I – I waited; I kept my composure all the way to June when he was going to leave. I had just one day to go before…." They were holding onto his every word now. "I lost my cool. Now there isn't a day that goes by I don't regret –I don't wake up thinking about it.

"This is my last interview of the summer. I have no other offers. Everyone knows about Donny Locks. They're all

22

ready for me the moment I walk in. I've thought of moving, but this is my home. It's where my wife is." His black eyes met Frowler's steel blue. "I believe in redemption, and I'm looking at you guys, and I'm hoping it's available."

Full folded his arms in dismissal, but Frowler appeared fully immersed in Conrad's plea. His blue eyes were bristling again.

"And that's all I'm asking for here." Conrad's voice grew coarse. "The saddest truth of life, for men in my situation, is that if you're going to get anywhere, you're going to have to depend on your fellow man every step of the way. Life is dependent on that principle. No gate is without a man before the latch."

Frowler closed his folder. His right hand covered his mouth while his index finger softly pressed his nose. He had made his decision. "Thank you," he said coldly. "We'll keep your file under advisement."

And just like that, Conrad knew he wouldn't have a job that fall.

After the interview, Conrad parked his cobalt blue Jetta atop the coastal bluff overlooking San Sino beach, the place his mother was killed. The beach was empty because the wind was too strong for swimmers and because it was evening, the time of day most marine life moves into the shallows and is invariably followed by predators.

The last time he had been to this beach was right after he was fired for pushing Locks. It was September now, and he noticed that in those months since June the beach had eroded further. It was like meeting a balding uncle once a year and noticing the hairline slowly abating with each shower and comb. It was a haggard, forlorn looking beach with brown sand plastered with grime and lumps of decaying seaweed. The trees

23

were rustic and abused by the heavy winds and not a single palm tree sat atop the bluff. With the sun firmly ensconced behind the foreboding clouds, the sea turned gray with the sand and the separation was hard to detect.

Conrad's head rested on the window. He couldn't remember the beach he had grown up on any longer. His parent's home was bulldozed. A brief boardwalk was added before the bluff. The military ships were all gone, but the *Palo Alto* – to the south of the beach, that still hankered for its twenty-foot pier.

Usually Conrad came to the beach because he believed he could speak with his parents. But times had changed. Now it was the memory of his childhood he was after, longing to associate the sand and the smell to better times. Sometimes he could still see himself walking with his father atop the bluff along where their house stood, picking out those heavy black stones that hid under the sand, placing them into buckets with the same clank as if he were dropping a coin in a piggy bank. But then his memory would turn sour and he could see his father placing those heavy black stones in handfuls into his pockets before heading out to sea.

CHAPTER 3: MICKER

Conrad sat at his kitchen window watching the lights from the San Sangre boardwalk reflect off his window in the dying sun. There were bursts of green and red lights from the top of the Ferris wheel, and large blue and white spotlights outlining the track of the Giant Dipper. The sound of children's laughter and joyous screams permeated the house. If only he could feel like them.

He was feeling depressed, maybe even hopeless, and once Micker arrived, his feelings would grow even worse. She expected him to land this job, and the prospect of living off one income for God knows how long never entered her mind. Failure was not something she understood. The more Conrad thought about it, he wasn't sure if she had ever failed at anything.

Though Conrad weaved in and out of foster homes for much of his childhood, he always managed to stay in San Sangre, giving him the fortune of being in the same school as Micker, though she was two grades ahead. For as long as he could remember, his wife had seemed pubescent since the third grade.

Her manner was precocious yet subtle, confident yet vulnerable. Boys were intimidated by her in high school, not only because of her superlative mind and refined, long-matured manner, but by her mysticism. There was a sense that what you didn't know about her, what was hiding beneath that perfect, Barbie-doll face and that brilliant mind, was dark. It radiated from her and could never be stripped from her like the glow of the moon. It was one of the chief reasons Micker ironically had very few friends in high school. If fellow alumni were asked to characterize her, they would undoubtedly attribute popularity to her angelic face. If they were then asked to name her best friend, they would submit to silence.

Even Micker's physical dimensions appealed to the mutability of the moon. She had moments of utter pulchritude. Then there were days when she would show up dressed like a Goth or a maiden to hide a physical frame that increased twenty pounds. Even her height would appear to change without the effects of shoes. Sometimes she would look tall and statuesque, other times short and susceptible.

Often Conrad's high school buddies would designate names for Micker's shifts in appearance. There was 10 Micker, office Micker, Grandma Micker, Gothic Micker, I'm-better-than-you Micker, and cute Micker. But her chameleonic propensity was never observed by other students because whenever one of Conrad's friends would mention it to someone they would always provide a confounded squint.

Consequently, it was Micker's demeanor and way with people that Conrad felt made her a star. People loved to watch her, be it simply her walk or the way she maneuvered in a conversation, words coming so naturally to her and always fitting the mannerism she chose so perfectly. She was the kind of person who could approach someone and sell his day with a greeting. She was that charming. It had something to do with

26

her perfect, highly feminine, baby-soft face and her low, forceful voice that was so contradicting that any other combination was a failed recourse. She was firm with her speech, an erudite with a fortune of words at her disposal that, inexplicably, always sounded perspicuous and never pedantic. Teachers loved her certainty and students admired her wittiness and effortless ability to provoke thought.

Graduating summa cum laude from Berkeley, Micker made the decision that was so becoming of her character: to become a lawyer. An English and philosophy major, she seemed destined for law books. She had scored wonderfully on the LSAT's, one of the few in the country to ace the Games Section, and she graduated fifth in her class at Stanford Law. New York wanted her, and major firms along the California seaboard offered her outrageous pay, but she did what was so enigmatic of her being: she went to work for the prosecuting attorney in San Sangre. She fought to prosecute the cases most lawyers shied away from. She wanted battery cases, domestic disputes, rape cases, and cases of child abuse. That was what appealed to her: she hated the idea of someone bigger and stronger taking advantage of the weak.

She spent three years there, losing her first case but winning all the rest, and built a sterling reputation. Then came an opening. Bran Hall, her then boyfriend, persuaded his father, Gilbert Hall, the CEO of Walker's Fishing Corporation, to offer her a job as a corporate lawyer in their newly opened offices in San Francisco. Despite her tenuous grasp of tax law and contract law, she took it. The pay was twice as good, and she didn't want to stay hooked to the unpredictability of the PA's office the rest of her life.

She suffered that first year. She missed being a prosecutor, the smell of the courtroom, the voir dire process, the sound of the gavel, all of it. Most of all, she missed winning a case. In the corporate world, the wins were much more abstract.

She soon grew apart from Bran, then the Regional Manager of the branch offices in San Sangre. Her decision to terminate their relationship was sudden and vague, even to Bran. Lonely and feeling her work insignificant, she rode an elevator with a newly hired sales representative at the San Sangre branch – Conrad Mayday. He had traveled to the San Francisco offices for an important conference meeting, and on his way back took the same elevator as her. The elevator happened to stop at every possible floor on the way down. After nearly ten minutes of waiting, they walked away talking about it. He knew who she was, the beautiful attorney that worked for corporate and had just broken off her relationship to Bran Hall. She had no idea who he was; to her just a cute, inexperienced guy. He wanted to ask her out, but he had heard the horror stories of her infamous dismissals. But he didn't have to. She asked him out, and he happily obliged. When Micker began asking him to dinner routinely, their relationship started, and a year later, around the time Bran Hall got hitched, Conrad popped the question and they were married. It shocked a lot of people, most of whom felt Micker was too good for Conrad, but they seemed to have strong chemistry. Where most men failed with Micker, Conrad succeeded. He was happy to play second fiddle to her, and she enjoyed strutting her authority in their relationship. The next year, Conrad was promoted to supervisor of sales at the San Sangre branch, and everyone knew Micker had everything to do with Conrad's promotion.

And now their relationship felt turned upside down.

Conrad heard her car pull up behind his in the driveway and he turned to watch her enter. Her high heels were clopping along the cement steps leading up to the front porch, a crescendo that matched a nervous heart. He walked to the

28

kitchen table, which took up a third of their kitchen, plopped his elbows on the table and folded his hands and placed them over his mouth, resting them on his nose.

She entered slowly, not yet seen by Conrad because of the stairway wall before the entrance. He could tell by her stillness that she was looking for him. He could barely think of how to break the bad news, and few things scared him more than disappointing her.

She came through the living room and stopped before the entrance to the kitchen. She was wearing an ivory suit and shoes and adorned white, donut-shaped earrings and a pearled necklace. Her hair was arranged in a ponytail so far back that the perfect, circuitousness of her face was on display. Her jade eyes peppered with ivy green spots like a bloodstone immediately caught him.

"So, what's the news?" she asked.

He lowered his head like a scolded puppy.

"What's the news?" she asked again more forcefully.

He sat up and rubbed his right hand on his forehead. "I didn't get it," he said breathlessly.

"You're kidding," she said. Her body sank back against the wall and slanted like she was made of putty. "This is unbelievable."

They both spent a minute of silence. Conrad was feeling pitied and for the first time had nothing to resist such a loathe feeling. Tears began falling from the inner corners of his eyes like a winning slots machine and he immediately pinched them with his left thumb and index finger.

"Don't cry," she said. "We'll figure everything out."

He knew that if he tried to speak he would explode. He had not cried since his father's death and his first night at the shelter. The orphanage taught him better. Crying didn't solve anything, and sometimes the pent up anger it tapered was needed for future rejections to make one more resilient.

He held on, and soon the tears passed.

"What did they say?" she asked.

"They didn't say anything."

"Then how do you know you didn't get it?"

"You know."

"You know?"

"When you get a job, you know."

"I had no idea I was going to be hired after my last interview," she said, her eyes large and intense, a signal she had intentions of dominating their conversation.

Conrad smiled flatly. "That's because your presence doesn't demand another's assurance."

She disregarded his comment and asked, "Did you bring up Donny Locks?"

"Yes."

She walked to the other side of the kitchen, angrily biting her lower lip. "Why did you do that, Conrad?"

"They knew."

"They didn't know!" she screamed, her voice terrifyingly loud. "I had that ready-made for you!" she said, slapping her right hand into her left palm. "Even Bran put in a good word. This company is just fifteen miles away!"

"I'm sorry."

"You can't keep screwing things up, Conrad. Sorry is not enough anymore."

He bowed his head. "Micker, what should I do?"

"Maybe it's time to change careers."

"I can't. I have my major – all my job experience is in business!"

Before she could respond their eyes turned to the ceiling as they heard stiff creaks of movement like freezing glass cracking. Conrad's eyes lit up as the creaks led to the top of the staircase. "Don't bring him down here now," he said. "I can't deal with him."

She waved Conrad away so he would be silent. "Dad, are you okay?" she shouted to the ceiling.

A croaky, old-aged voice cried out, "I need my pill."

"I left it for you on your nightstand!" she shouted back.

"On my nightstand?" her dad, Joe, repeated in painful slowness.

"Yes. It is right there on the corner of the table for you." Micker looked down at Conrad as she spoke to her father. "You need anything else?"

A faint "no" whirled around the second floor.

Micker smiled and pointed to the ceiling while whispering, "He came down because you swore. He knew where the pill was."

Conrad said, "He's always a Catholic priest again when there's swearing. Wait, I didn't even swear." Micker didn't hear him.

She leaned her elbows back against the counter as her back slouched beside it. She was staring at him, admiring the blackness and thick dilation of his eyes when he was scared and sleep-deprived. Then something triggered her thoughts: "The docks."

"No," Conrad responded convincingly.

"Bran could get you on. You could do it for a year."

"I'm not going back to that life, Micker. That was in high school."

"You'll make $40,000, maybe more if it's a good year. That is more than you would have made at this company. It is not like they were going to start you off at $60,000."

"I'm not going back there. That's a past life. I am a supervisor. That's what I want to do."

"You were a good fisherman. That is a skill that few

31

people have, Conrad."

"I have more promise than that."

She didn't respond.

"You don't think so?" he asked.

"If you couldn't get this job with my help and Bran's help, then there's no other job out there for you around here in the business world."

That hit him hard, but he knew it. He didn't fight her analysis.

"I'll be humiliated."

"Maybe so, but you need a job. And you know what else, Conrad? Since you stopped going to church –"

"Please don't start with that."

"Nothing good has come your way since. It's been a year. Prove me wrong. Has anything good happened since then?"

He brushed sweat from his forehead and sat silently as she lectured him.

"You need to go to church," she said, invoking her strict-Catholic upbringing. Then something her father always said: "Mend your relationship with God."

"My relationship is fine."

"There's anger in you. You never used to be this way. You assaulted one of your staff."

"He set me up."

"I don't care what he did to you. You can't do that in the business world where every action has consequences." She clenched the counter with both hands. She was not going to let him feel sorry for himself. That equaled quitting in her book. "You're friends with Bran," she continued, her voice precise and hypnotic. "You play tennis and racquetball with him all the time."

"I would die before I asked him."

"You have too much pride to ask him for a job?"

"I'm not doing it."

"Bran Hall comes from one of the best families in this town," she affirmed. "Believe me, you want him on your side."

"He's been handed money his whole life."

"Bran's not about money. Trust me. He's about making a difference."

"He's not about money? He's Vice President of Walker's now."

"And one of the youngest vice presidents there is. He knows how to ascend the ladder. That's what I'm telling you. He's a great contact to have. In ten years he will be the company's president."

But Conrad wasn't hearing her. He was thinking about what she said earlier. "You're right; he's not about money," he told her. "Never was. He's about power. There's a difference. I'm just not sure which is worse."

She stared at him as if her eyes were trying to burn through his obstinacy. "What went on between the two of you that makes you so…" she looked at him inquisitively then stood up straight, her back leaving the counter. "Whatever. I know him better than you. I will ask him. I helped Marjorie get her job with the PA. He owes me a favor."

"I'm not doing it."

"This job isn't even guaranteed, Conrad? I'm going to ask him for help. If he does me the favor, he will have to ask his father to let you on at Walker's. You think his father hasn't heard about Donny Locks?"

Conrad appeared disconsolate. "Don't do this, Micker. I'll find a job. We'll pay off the month's mortgage and…."

"What about the car bill, the electric bill, the student loans? I don't make enough to pay all of those and support you right now! Just take the job if he offers it to you, and you work

33

your way on the boats for a year and who knows. Maybe he will give you a second chance there and move you inside. You build up from there, and in a few years time no one will even remember Donny Locks. Maybe we will even think of trying a move East."

"We should have done it already."

"We can't move yet, Conrad. The East is harder out there. I'll be making more this year. That should buy us time. That's what we need to do: just give it time. Time solves everything, every wound; and it will heal yours. You've just got to make changes. Start changing yourself. Begin networking, building relationships."

Conrad peered up at her, his feelings too tired to find a reason to use the strength to hold his neck straight. "I will," he said, but even he wasn't convinced by his own words. "But let me ask Bran."

CHAPTER 4: THE MATCH

When the weekend arrived, Conrad and Bran Hall met at the public courts in San Sangre to play tennis. They played tennis there once a week, but occasionally they would go to a local gym to play racquetball for the variety. They hadn't played each other in tennis in nearly two months, though, because Bran had slipped a disc in his lower back. Now that their rivalry resumed, Conrad felt this was the best time for him to break his losing streak to Bran. He hadn't beaten him in twelve straight meetings. The losing streak ate at him.

This match, however, proved no different. Conrad had a lead, had two match points to boot, and despite a rusty and slightly out of shape foe, he lost. He lost because he played not to lose, and he lost because Bran Hall was just that good.

After the match, they sat on the bench outside the tennis courts, listening to the bullet-like shots coming from the players dueling two courts down. Tired, they both wiped their arms and faces down with towels.

"What is that, eleven, twelve in a row now," Bran said smiling before letting out a jubilant cackle. Conrad sank on the bench; he knew the statistics too well. It had really been thirteen. Thirteen straight losses. The fact that Bran didn't know his own streak led insult to injury.

"Yea, it's been a lot," Conrad said, feigning a smile. "You played well today. I just don't know what I was doing out there at the end."

"No, I just made the shots when I needed to," Bran said assertively. "It was a question of when is my time. Up until then I couldn't make a shot to save my life."

Conrad's face tightened. "Yea, you played well. It was a good match."

"Ya' know what, I'm half of what I was when I was at Stanford," Bran replied. "My junior year, I could have hit any shot I wanted to. And then this," he said with his hand rubbing the small of his back. "Put me right out of business."

Conrad wondered if Bran even knew how arrogant he sounded. "Yea, a back injury will do it to ya." Conrad tried to change the subject. "So, how's being a vice president?"

"Not what I thought, but, you know, the pay is incredible and I oversee almost every operation. I'm still in shock my dad gave me the position right after my brother –" Bran hesitated. He almost brought up Donny Locks. That was the reason his brother, Kevin Hall, was demoted from Vice President of the company to Regional Manager of the Sacramento branch because of his mishandling of the Locks situation. The brothers essentially switched positions. He continued, "What sucks, though, is the travelling. Going back and forth between branches. But the pay is so much better now that I'm not the Regional Manager. It's practically double. I can't go back to what I used to make."

Conrad found his arrogance suffocating.

He watched Bran reminisce for a moment, then sniffle over and over because of his allergies. Right then a fleet of old

36

memories Conrad thought he had pushed deep into the recesses of his mind came back. He was back on the tennis team during his senior year of high school, watching Bran win the California Regional Tennis Conference as he sat in the stands, just a few yards away, failing to qualify. And every morning that season he remembered waking up and reading the newspaper to see a number one singles ranking next to Bran's name; his name was always just below Bran's in the number two spot. Despair now resurfaced as he remembered wishing Bran would lose. But Bran never lost. The worst was when he saved seven match points to clinch the top seed for the Regional tournament as Conrad sat watching like a prisoner, like Sisyphus, his rock rolling back to his starting point.

Conrad's resentment had more to do with the fact that while he had played tennis since he was seven, Bran didn't start until he was thirteen, and he only played for fun. Within two years, Bran tried out and made the high school team because of a friend's dare. Most remarkably, he became the number one seed, easily surpassing Conrad.

Conrad couldn't understand it. He had more experience, better technique, and a better understanding of the game, and yet Bran came along and wiped all of that away. He made the game about power and athleticism, which he had more of than anyone else. And the truth that Conrad had trouble accepting was that Bran really was better than him in every way.

The more Conrad studied Bran's characteristics, the more he affirmed that Bran was his foil, a clever machination of God's to punish him for unknown reasons. Bran, in Conrad's eyes, was an improvement of himself. They looked alike, as if they came from the same litter despite a few disparities: brown hair, brown eyes, and anfractuous, thick, unavoidable eyebrows that rendered all other features secondary. They were the same person except that Bran, when truly compared, was more masculine and chiseled than his counterpart. He was two inches taller than Conrad, his shoulders much broader, his neck thick like a linebacker, and his chest a protruding strongman's. His legs were denser too, like two timbers. Bran's voice was also coarser and crisper than Conrad's subtly effeminate pitch.

"Micker called me," Bran said as Conrad was jolted back to focus. "I just wanted to be upfront about it. I hate when people circle around everything."

Conrad dropped his head dejectedly as Bran waited for him to respond.

The wait was awkward, so Bran kept talking: "There is a job opening up on the docks. It is third tier though; you'll be working the same job you were in high school: 5 a.m. to 4 p.m., boat inspection every two weeks, overtime if the season's bad." Bran tilted his head to see Conrad react in pain. "It pays well. You'll make fifteen dollars an hour, plus incentives if you break the monthly quota. And...."

Conrad stood up, unable to look Bran in the face. But Bran rose too, standing two inches above him.

"Look, Con, I know that's not what you want to do. Micker told me about what happened, and, it's really no big deal. I'll give you the job. I mean, you have a college degree. It wouldn't be that big of a transition. Besides, most of those guys down there never graduated high school."

Conrad found little use in facing Bran. He muttered, "I appreciate it," then headed toward the water fountain.

Bran was irritated. There was nothing he had more disdain for than someone who didn't show him appreciation when he offered a favor. "So do you want it, because I can give it to someone else?"

Conrad turned. He was ticked off, mainly at Micker. "I have to think about it."

"How long will that take?" Bran asked, his voice

assertive and loud. "It's not like I don't have people lined up."

Conrad turned to the courts, squinted his eyes, and then turned back to Bran more confidently. He felt like he could actually see his pride scurrying out the door. "I'll take it."

"Well, you'll have to go through the interview process first with my dad."

"Your dad? The CEO wants to conduct an interview for a fishing position?"

Bran walked up to him, scratching his face. "It's Donny Locks. He's scared to bring you on, and it was the only request he had."

Just that name placed Conrad on his figurative heels, where it's mentioning drained all confidence, all autonomy from him. His posture was now in surrender mode.

He offered a light, deflated response that had become his trademark when Donny Locks was dug up from his own history of hell: "I understand."

CHAPTER 5: THE SECOND INTERVIEW

Bran's father, Gilbert Hall, was a curmudgeon who stood 6'2 and was built long and strong. His arms stretched down to his knees and his hands were ape-thick and badly calloused. He was a balding man who grew spider-thin pales of hair out down to his shoulders, making it seem like he had two foreheads piled one atop the other. His nose was badly crooked, the bone's shape showing under the skin to be bumpy and rigid like a broken finger.

He sat a desk-length apart from Conrad, hovering over him as he deliberately gave Conrad a smaller chair. Bran sat to the side of his father's desk. Apparently, his father wanted him to sit in on the interview. Bran's hair was combed sideways and his bulky figure appeared ready to burst open his dress shirt and unravel his red and black striped tie. He gave a smile to Conrad before they all shook hands, then stayed quiet and kept his eyes centered on his father.

They met in a conference room a ways away from Hall's

actual office. On the way to the interview, Conrad felt like he was on display. While riding the escalator to the lobby with the backdrop of San Francisco and the blinding sun that pierced right through the glass walls, people stared. It was either because he was out of place or because they had recognized him from the papers. On the elevator up to the top floor, the same elevator he used when he first met Micker, he cowered in the corner as eyes seemed to hammer him down a few feet.

The interview questions generally regarded Conrad's previous job experience. It was hard for Conrad to stay enthusiastic, but he tried nonetheless. After nearly ten minutes perusing his resume and application as though he were hoping to catch a mistake, Gilbert Hall set his resume to the side and said, "You'll start work next Monday, the 12th of September."

"Thank you, sir," Conrad replied. He looked around the room, noticing the bevy of framed pictures of Gilbert Hall standing with people who seemed pretty important players in the town, and this wasn't even his office.

Gilbert Hall sighed. "I'll be honest, you wouldn't have this job if you didn't know my son," he said. "I don't like what you did to that guy, and I don't care how bad he was. I believe in second chances, but I'm not sure I believe in them for stuff like that. So let it be known that your track record precedes you. You make one mistake with me, or if I hear of any problems out there, you're back on the job counter. Do you understand?"

Conrad was shocked by the old man's directness. "Yes sir, and again, I thank you for this opportunity. I won't let you down."

Gilbert Hall rose like a giant and he shook hands, sighing once more as Bran winked at Conrad.

Conrad left the corporate offices having paid for the parking and the drive into the city. He felt Gilbert Hall made him come all the way to the corporate offices to make Conrad

41

feel as small as his reputation was.

And there wasn't a thing Conrad could do about it.

Conrad could not sleep that night. Each time he peered up, he could see Donny Locks' freckled face grinning back at him, that large, red bass-like mouth showing those tiny gapped teeth that horrified him. It was the same twisted grin he remembered in the office, as Locks would sit far in the back of their team meetings and smile during his presentations. When confronted, Locks would say nothing – just smile.

It was 5 a.m. and Conrad could tell his tossing and turning had kept Micker up. He gave sleep one last chance, closed his eyes, but sure enough he opened them, and there he kept imagining Donny Locks standing in his doorway.

Conrad walked downstairs to the kitchen and sat down by the window. The lights to the boardwalk Ferris wheel and rollercoaster were gone. The window was just a reflection of him in his kitchen. He began thinking about Bran and their talk after the tennis match. "Micker called me," he had said.

Rising from his seat, Conrad walked to the kitchen counter and turned on the faucet. It sounded like pouring rain. He opened Micker's white purse and took out her red cell phone. He stared at it awhile before opening it. She had no text messages. He checked her phone history. No dialed calls to Bran. He checked her received and missed calls. Bran was absent there too. It was just what he expected.

Now he was fully awake.

CHAPTER 6: WALKER'S

Walker's harbor was a bantam series of fishing houses and gray office buildings that led to the San Sangre harbor. The office buildings were distended and protruded over the harbor like overgrown trees. Walker's harbor, the name inspired from the hundreds of "walkers" that used the two-mile boardwalk it oversaw for morning exercise, had an unusual position to the sea and the highway. First, it was boxed in by fishing houses and gray office buildings that were mostly rented by real estate agents and mortgage firms. The buildings were fifty to sixty feet high and built on the parking lot that used to belong only to the harbor, completely ensconcing the small fishing houses. Second, a series of palm trees were planted out in front of the buildings. The problem was they were planted just a couple feet apart so that they looked almost like a wooden fence from the sea. Standing twenty-five feet high, they blocked the view of the fishing houses and the first few stories of the buildings.

Gilbert Hall, who owned some of the smaller buildings that were half-shielded by the palms, was constantly complaining of how the unseemly architecture and landscaping had made his building offices a secret. He was unauthorized, however, to cut down or even transplant the palm trees in front of his building. When he asked city council why, they told him the palm trees were city landmarks, and that there had been a statute carved into law restricting any palm trees from being cut down in San Sangre. With the especially tricky terrain of San Sangre, which compounded of sharp hills and plains with embedded rock formations, few palm trees naturally resided in the city. Therefore, palm trees could not be cut down in San Sangre. If they were, it became a criminal offense.

"There's yours," Conrad's burly manager Will Brosnan said, pointing to a red trawler pulled up on the sand by a long rope tied to the boardwalk. Brosnan was a stout man with a husky beard and mustache, long frizzy brown hair that hung over his ears and past the back of his neck, and a round pink bald spot directly atop his head the size of a fifty cent coin. He wore thick-rimmed owl glasses, and his eyes were surrounded by black circles and sagging wrinkles in the skin that wrapped around his eyes before blending into his cheeks. "We keep it tight," he said. "Only seventeen fishermen here. Each man has his own boat and net." He popped the collar to his long, dark-green slicker that made his shoulders look broader than they were. He talked fast and perspicuously, a baritone voice that kept each word succinct and punctual. He was pointing around the harbor like a navigator, concerned that his every point was explained with proficiency. Conrad knew immediately that he was someone he could trust.

"Mr. Hall does pay us according to quotas, which can seem inhumane at times, but you'll manage," Brosnan said, grabbing Conrad by the shoulder and directing him down the boardwalk. "Most guys in here have little trouble hitting their quotas. They'll be on the bulletin board the fifteenth of every month. You'll be after shrimp, mollusks, mackerel, cod, rockfish, squid, Halibut, and anchovies. Anchovies and shrimp

44

will be easiest to hit. Mackerel take time, and they're harder to get. I want two from each of you every day, but there will be days when no one can get one." Brosnan began to lower his voice. "They'll also be tough to get because you can't use benthic trawling anymore. Are you familiar with benthic trawling?"

"Yes, the lowest trawling," Conrad responded naturally like his fishing days had never passed.

Brosnan was impressed. "Well, we have to use what they call Demersel trawling because the government says we are polluting the sea the Benthic way. I think it's because the nets scrape up the sediment along the bottom and murk up the waters, and kelp need light to survive, and, well, you know the rest of that green bull crap. What I'm saying is you're gonna have a tough time with mackerel. They live far near the bottom, and we can only stay within a foot of the bottom of the water column. So it can be difficult, but I'll show you some tricks." The fog was running out to sea and the sun, a bright white orb, snuck up above them and its gilded rays coated the ocean waves like a varnish. Brosnan blocked his eyes from the sun with his hands. "You know what, you start tomorrow, September 12th. I forgot to tell you – you will probably be after Dungeness crab starting tomorrow. Hall likes us starting early. You've met him? He did your interview?"

"Yes."

"Awful, ain't he?"

Conrad's shoulders stiffened. He was shocked an employee would admit such personal scorn. In a way, though, it made Conrad like him all the more. *It is natural*, he thought, *to like someone who goes against the boss rather than someone who serves as their advocate.*

"Me, I'm too old to care, so don't worry about my lip. Gilbert Hall likes to come down here a few times a year, show he's a CEO of the people. It's his way of reminding us that he got his start as a fisherman. Like he gives a damn about us or what we do around here." Brosnan could see he startled Conrad. He shook his shoulders. "Hey, you can trust me out here. I can tell you're gonna be good for us. Everyone here gets along real well. Usually in the mornings one of us will take turns hittin' a Starbucks on the way in. It's just like an office job, really. Here a little earlier though. But you'll probably be able to see everybody on the water. We're usually spaced a half-mile apart at all times. All the ships are color-coated."

Conrad asked, "What happens if you don't meet your quota?"

"You'll make it." Brosnan poked his tongue in his cheek. "If you don't, you just try not to make a habit of it the next day. Honestly, it's rare to see a guy miss his quota if he knows what he's doing. I won't evaluate you for the first two weeks, and by the time I do start to evaluate you, you'll know what you're doing. You worked on the sea before, did ya?"

"Yea, but that was fifteen years ago."

"Eh, it's not that different...except for the boundary lines."

"The boundary lines?" Conrad asked incredulously. He hated dire restrictions to a job because they made him uncomfortable all the time, like a nervous tick.

"It wasn't one of our guys, but a couple miles up the coast near San Francisco, a fisherman went out too far near the Farallon Islands. You'll see the boundary lines; we've got red buoys out there set up an equal distance apart out about five miles. Anyways, he was alone, it was near nightfall, wasn't pulling his load so he continued far out into Farallon waters, and a white shark, probably mistaking his boat for a seal, smashed the boat from the bottom and flung him overboard. His boat sank, and they never found him. Officially, it was ruled an

46

accidental drowning, but everyone around here knows he was eaten alive. These are the deadliest waters in the world. From Point Reyes, Point Sur, and the Farallon Islands, they call it the Red Triangle."

Conrad instantly began thinking about his mother. He grew a little sick at the thought, but as he thought about the tale for a while, he wondered how much of it was true. Brosnan, while apparently trustworthy with important stuff, was a good raconteur, and raconteurs tended not to let the truth get in the way of a good story. But Conrad had caught this tale before. He finally replied, "I think I heard about it."

Now Brosnan grew more excited, the way someone does when they have privileged information and are about to share it. He was like an old man in that way, carrying a bit of haughtiness in him that he always had a story to tell that no one had heard before. Conrad could see he was just warming up. "Just don't ever cross the boundary lines. I know you don't think it will ever happen to you, but trust me, those things could sink just about any boat they wanted. They circle around the Farallones, waiting for elephant seals to go in after fish. There could be thirty or more whites at once circling the island. You ever hear the old mariner's tales about the old timers who used row boats and the sharks would wait for them and would flip their boats?" Brosnan asked, his eyes growing wide.

Conrad found no need to interject as the answer was coming with or without his confirmation.

"When the fishermen wouldn't come back from the inlets, the commoners blamed it on bad tides. The sharks got away with murder for over a hundred years.

"Sharks are not stupid. Remember that. They might be fish, but they do not behave like fish. When it comes to killing, there's no better assassin. It must have been good for them back then. They made their own fast food joint out of us."

47

Conrad looked intriguingly at the sea. It was impossible for him not to think of his mother. It saddened him to think of the terror she must have felt when it happened. But he had trouble remembering the incident. It was a long time ago, and he held no grudges against the great creatures. He asked, "You ever see one?"

"Oh, yes. And you'll see them too," Brosnan answered positively. "Maybe not this year, maybe not for five, but one day, when you least expect it, you'll pull up your net and one will be starin' back at you through the bottom. It will scare the hell out of you, and I'll guarantee you he had been trailing your net for hours."

It surprised Conrad how definitely Brosnan spoke about this moment as though he knew it was going to happen. Brosnan then became animated with his hands, painting a picture of the creature with them on his own face. "They've got these sunken, black eyes and skeleton faces. Ugly beasts. They're so big it's unbelievable. You'll think it's a whale at first. Then it might swim up by you, and when it does, you'll realize how truly helpless God made you."

That comment scared Conrad a bit, but that wasn't Brosnan's intention. He was a man who loved to excite people, to get them interested in something. He was married and divorced once, had no children, and had a strained relationship with his family. Without attention at home he had grown accustomed to over amplifying his anecdotes to compensate for his quiet nights. But his nature was good-hearted, and Conrad could tell that when you made a friend of him, you made a friend for life.

CHAPTER 7: THE RED TRIANGLE

The Red Triangle, which stretches from Bodega Bay in Northern California down to Point Sur in Southern California and forms its triangular tip at the Farallon Islands, was not always the shark attack capital of the world. For a hundred years bathers in California were safe. Even when the numbers of people proliferated because of the Gold Rush, attacks were absent.

That all changed when the surfing culture of the 1960s took hold of California. The reasoning seemed simple enough: surfboards are shaped like seals, a great white's favorite meal. The attacks that started happening in the 1960s, even then, were linked to causes of mistaken identity. Scientists were sure the surfers brought the sharks to the coast. Little did anyone know that surfers had nothing to do with the attacks.

The slaughter of seals had been a habit of the Indians for thousands of years. Their destination from the Pacific coast was a rock formation ninety miles from what is now San Francisco Bay. Great seal populations inhabited the islands.

Nobody knows how or why the seals made the Farallones their home. The Indians weren't concerned; they traveled to the Farallones biannually on huge canoes where they stocked seal meat, blubber, teeth, and fur after the slaughter.

The waters in the Farallones were different, though. Even on that first voyage, the Indians lost men. Their canoes seemed to capsize and their members were ravished by something under the water. Only the culprit's grey snout was seen along with the accompanying red that signaled their member had died. Over the centuries the region had been known as something of a gauntlet: get by and you reap the rewards of meat, warmth, and weapons for the year. The water beasts that lay under the water had, by the time the Indians were pushed out of the Pacific region, become folklore. The paintings and drawings of the huge beasts, however, were destroyed by the Spanish, leaving future colonies the experience of learning about the sharks on their own.

Spanish explorer Sebastian Vizcaino named them the Farallones, meaning rocks out of the sea, in 1603. His people used the islands to slaughter seals for three centuries until the Russians took it over in the 1800s. Neither the Russians nor the Spanish ever inquired about sharks. They had seen sharks before, even great whites. What gave the area a dangerous reputation was the unusually high number of shipwrecks in the area. Between 1600 and 1800, eleven ships were sunk. To this day no one knows how the ships sank. The evidence pointed to the abrupt shallowness of the islands and the rocky edges of the seabed below. What was truly a mystery was the high number of sailors who didn't make it to shore once the ships went down.

With wildlife concerns becoming a major political issue in the 1968 election of Richard Nixon, congress made the Farallon Islands a national Wildlife Refuge in 1969, and the slaughter of seals illegal in the U.S. Marine Mammals Protection

Act of 1972. During the 1960s, there were never more than fifteen of one species of seal in the Red Triangle area. By the end of 1973, there were a thousand. By the end of the 1970s, there were 10,000 seals swimming in California waters. It was then that the shark attacks began.

Before *Jaws* ever lured bathers back to the sand, California residents knew what a great white shark was. In June of 1973, Robert Jydell was swimming in twenty feet of water off South Moss beach in Monterey before bathers and spectators saw him lifted out of the air by a huge shark that had latched on to him at the waist. Jydell was kept above water in a freakish way before the shark pulled him under. Spectators swore Jydell was swallowed whole. The body was never recovered.

The murder of Jydell sent shock waves down the California coast. From that day it seemed surfers and bathers were attacked or gobbled up twice a year. The scientists continued to link the appearance and aggression of great whites to the popularity of surfing, seemingly disregarding the unique rise in pinnipeds.

The Red Triangle moniker originated in the early 1980s and stuck after *Time* magazine did its first cover story on the lethal stretch of water. Then, the Mayday attack occurred. It was the kind of story that fueled water-cooler talk and made magazine covers and news episodes. The reasons for its notoriety were found in the details: *Wife Is Bitten in Half by Great White; Family Watched Attack from Shore; Only Victim's Legs Recovered; Killer Great White Largest Ever in California Waters; Coast Guard Had Lost Track of Shark; Mayday Shark Had Been Tagged by Scientists."*

That last detail gave the story considerable running gear. It was learned that Mayday's great white, named Victor by the scientists, had a camera attached to its dorsal fin. That camera, which collected video footage of the shark's voyage through the

51

seas, also captured the entire attack on film. While the camera was rescued after the shark died a few days later out at sea, scientists and news reporters agreed the footage was too brutal to show televised audiences.

Victor gave scientists the first evidence of great white shark migration patterns. For one year the camera was attached to Victor's dorsal, and in that time the shark had travelled over twenty thousand miles, to South African and New Zealand waters, to depths of 2,000 feet. When the body of the shark was autopsied to find the torso and head of Evelyn Mayday, marine biologists, who tentatively estimate the lifespan of great whites to be around forty years, estimated that Victor might have been alive for more than ninety years, putting him in waters before the twentieth century.

After the Mayday attack, the Red Triangle became a myth. By 2010 there were 110 total attacks with twenty-eight being fatal. In that same year, the Red Triangle had become responsible for half of the world's great white shark attacks.

CHAPTER 8: FATHER AND DAUGHTER

Knowing Conrad wouldn't be home before four, Micker's father, Joe Raeden, came downstairs and sat at the kitchen table to wait for his daughter. He looked like a surly man, and if looks revealed personality, he would be a poster-child of the rule. He was short and skinny with a round, ruddy face and big, blowfish eyes that made him look like he was serially sick. His pale hair was scattered at the top with long strands combed over his looming baldness. He sat drooping low on the chair, his head set back against the wall like it was pasted there, his breathing languid and sounding like someone had stuffed newspaper up his nose.

When he heard Micker's car pull up, he brought his hands together above the table in a triangle with his body and began rubbing his fingers together. He needed to talk to someone.

Now at sixty-eight, Joe was someone who could no longer sleep for more than five hours or rise with that fresh eagerness to start a new day. He had reached that stage in old men when sleep was no longer the antidote to fatigue. He acknowledged reaching that stage a few weeks before, and realizing it scared him because he was not ready to enter that last chapter of his life.

Micker entered the house in a peach-yellow chiffon dress with her now mahogany hair wrapped in a French twist. A smile lit up her face when she saw Joe sitting at the kitchen table. "Hey Dad!" she exclaimed. "What made you come down here?"

"I hadn't seen you in a while," he said with his voice very light. His left index finger twirled around the table. "I wanted to check in on you, see how you're doing."

She laid her purse on the counter, opened it, and slowly pulled out an orange dispenser for pills. "I filled out your prescription today." She handed the new container to him. It was filled with dime-sized white pills. "The doctor said these are the best to fight psoriasis." She grabbed his old beige corduroy shirt and wrapped it above his elbow. His entire wrist was covered in crusty white scabs with a red flowering deeply engraved in the skin like burn marks. It worsened the higher up on his arm.

She rubbed her forehead. "It has gotten worse..."

"I don't care. Not doing any modeling this week."

She smiled and sat across from him. She raised her arms, felt her hairpin, and clenched it with both hands and leaned back in the chair. Her arms were fully extended as she watched the carriage on the Giant Dipper reach the top of the hill. "You can feel fall coming out there."

"Is it chilly?"

"No, just the air. You can smell it changing."

Joe turned to look out the window, but there were only the tops of the Ferris wheel and Giant Dipper. He frowned and said, "He was walking around down here all night last night."

Now Micker knew Conrad was on his mind. "I know,"

she said. "He has been having nights like that ever since June."

"Because of that guy?"

"Because of a lot of things," she said rubbing her lip with her finger. "He never really tells me much about it."

"And this new job he's got? He's back on the docks?"

She nodded, visibly perturbed by the questions. "Well, he needs something for now, and he has done it before."

And then it came, like a lightning bolt: "I still can't believe I let you marry him."

She responded quickly. "You didn't." That let him know just how much authority he had ever had on the subject. "I'm in a good place, Dad," she added with an affectionate nod.

But he was still uneasy. Feeling she ended any civil conversation about Conrad, he pushed it. "I never wanted this for you."

"I am in a good place."

"What is it that you see in him?"

"Dad, leave it alone," she snapped, her right arm chopping the air to emphasize her irritation.

He folded his arms. "I can't have a say?"

"What's to say? I've heard it before. I don't need to hear it again."

He shook his head and turned back to the window. The Ferris wheel had stopped and he could see the carriages shaking in the wind. "I'm gettin' old, Micker." He sighed and leaned back, sinking his shoulders to ruminate. "When I was younger, I could never understand how my dad would say he was tired of living. I could just never come to understand that, because if death was all there was…well, I suppose he believed in heaven. I'm not sure actually. But now I'm starting to understand why he said that." He looked at his legs. He was too tired and dejected to even speak in complete sentences. "Muscles have completely atrophied. Try to contract my quad, or tighten my hamstring,

55

and there's nothing there – no feeling even if I punch it. Shrunk three inches. I can practically grab my stomach to wash my face in the morning."

"Everybody goes through it," she added coldly.

"Everybody goes through it? That's how you respond?"

She put her elbows down on the table and tightened her hands in balls and balanced her chin on them like a child trying to win affection from her father. In that moment, he cherished her. She was his little girl again.

"I'm sorry," she said, now rising from the table, the child-like innocence gone. She was in deep thought now, trying to figure out her own ways. "I sometimes wonder myself why I am with Conrad, and I think it is because things were going so well whenever I was with him. I know that sounds strange, but – well, there are many reasons some women find certain men. But with Conrad, every time we would grow closer things outside our relationship would get better. Things have just always been good when he's around."

"You married this man because he was a good luck charm?"

"I cannot pretend to justify it. And of course that's not the reason. I do love him," but she hesitated, and tried to wax over the mutual recognition of awkwardness by continuing to talk. "Who knows why people do the things they do. The explanation is as simple as that, and yet it is as complicated as that." She smiled at the incredibility of her omission. "And now, I – he is hopeless without me. And I know that if I leave him, he will fall apart."

Joe was not about to let pity for Conrad Mayday steer into a conversation about it. "I think that's best for both of you, before, God forbid, you might have a child."

"How can you say something like that?" she asked. "You know, Conrad has done pretty well considering what God

56

has put him up against.   He was orphaned at five; his grandparents put him in a taxicab and sent him to a shelter. They didn't even tell him where he was going." Micker's voice became faint. "To think what must have been going on in his mind. He was left with nothing. Every time I look at him, I realize how lucky I am." Her eyes grew tepid. "So, I think Conrad turned out all right, considering where he landed."

Joe didn't want to say something he would regret. He had pushed the bar far too high already. He rose from the table, kissed his daughter on the head, and went back to his room upstairs.

CHAPTER 9: A RETURN TO THE PACIFIC

Conrad met Will Brosnan at the top of the pier at 5:30 a.m. The stars were big white clusters over the blue night sky, and the air was thin and cold. Though it was on its way up behind them, the sun gave no hints of its appearance in the darkness. The sea below it was passive and welcoming. It was going to be Conrad's first trip over the sea since high school.

Brosnan let Conrad start the engine and lower the trawl. They set out around 6:00 a.m. after a quick breakfast of bagels and coffee. The night looked unusual just before dawn. It was as if the sun had the stars on strings and slowly pulled them back behind the black slip so it could make its appearance. As dawn approached, the sun's first rays sprayed over the gray office buildings with accompanying red and purple splashed clouds, and the sea returned its usual equanimity for their trawler.

The dock's colors seemed to break apart then turn barren-brown as the fishermen dispensed in opposite directions. The sun looked as though it had struck a deal with the night as it road in an arc over top of them, gilding the tops of the waves and causing an opalescence of blue and glinting gold below.

When they were out of the shore's sight, Brosnan asked Conrad to reel the trawl in. This was supposed to be his shadow work, but reeling in the trawl was very amateur and could be seen as slightly insulting to a man who previously sweated on the sea. Nonetheless, the surprised but acquiescent Conrad reeled in the trawl and found the net without a foundation. It was just a huge round hole at the bottom. Brosnan returned from the pilothouse while Conrad was standing near the stern as the boat teetered now. He had an orange net in his hand and tossed it to Conrad.

"Crank it back out," he said. Conrad stood holding the hundred foot long net with a bemused gaze. Brosnan peered back at shore like a child who stole something. "We don't have time for initiation."

Conrad understood Brosnan perfectly. He was flouting the rules of training because he found them useless. The net was supposed to be a tester net with a hole in the bottom preventing a novice from catching something in the trawl that might be illegal. Brosnan felt he didn't have time for that. He trusted Conrad's previous years of experience, and Conrad respected his trust in him.

As the sun peaked atop them, signaling it was near or after noon, Brosnan allowed Conrad to steer the trawler. He seemed to have total trust in his apprentice. He fell asleep a few times under the sun, and when he woke, he found no issue in quickly going back to sleep. After an hour steering, Conrad saw the red buoys Brosnan was talking about floating in a line two hundred feet apart like huge gumdrops. They were seventy feet away, so Conrad decelerated. They came upon him fast, as if they were moving toward him in the water.

Brosnan flew forward, pressing his gray flat cap to his head as if he were held upside down. "What's happened?" he

59

snapped.

"The buoys," Conrad answered, pointing to them.

Brosnan made his way around the pilothouse to the bow. "Turn around. We'll head back."

As Conrad made a faint U-turn, he looked hard in the distance and could see what appeared to be a formation of brown mountains atop blue flames, at least that was what the ocean looked like far in the distance. It seemed so mysterious down there, so permanent, the place you went to have things settled. He was sure it was the Farallon Islands, and he imagined the sharks were well below the boat. He expected them to be picking up the scent of crab insides that entered the current and streamed out west toward the inlet as the tiny crustaceans mangled and smashed each other in the trawl.

Steering back toward the mainland, Conrad turned the engine off as instructed and sat across from Brosnan by the stern. Brosnan's eyes were half-closed as he watched the gray office buildings and the large red sign, WALKER'S, appear in the sky a mile away. Conrad clenched his hands and heard all of his knuckles pop. He was more nervous, though, about Brosnan. He had not spoken a word to him, and he was wondering if he misjudged the man.

"Mr. Brosnan?" He finally interjected. "Will you be out with me tomorrow?"

Brosnan tilted his head slowly. "No." Then he leaned back, looking up at the sky. "You know what you're doing."

Conrad had gotten the seal of approval. It made him feel good. "What will I be after?"

"The crab."

"I've never fished for those before."

"It's all right. I'll give you some pointers when we get in. Best you learn on your own, develop your own methods."

60

"Okay."

"Will, by the way," Brosnan said as he investigated the relationship the sun had with the sea. "Call me Will," he repeated. "I hate that gentlemanly crap."

"Yes, sir."

Brosnan gave him a stern look.

"Some humor."

Brosnan smiled.

A tiny, white fishing boat roared past them. "That idiot!" Brosnan said, holding his cap against his head.

"Who's that?" Conrad asked as a fishing boat of fifteen feet in length made its way past the boundary line.

"Hall."

"Gilbert Hall?"

"He meets with the scientists once every few months, drives out each time with that. Thinks he's the Indiana Jones of the sea."

"Why would the CEO be riding out like that?"

"Macho-head case, that's why. He wants to prove to everyone that he's not scared of the waters out there. It's an age thing too. He's pushing seventy and doesn't want people to think he's washed up. Hopefully one day he won't come back."

A rounded crab of purple texture flopped weightlessly atop the waves. Brosnan watched it. He rose, knowing the crab was injured and had somehow maneuvered its way through the tiny holes in the trawl. He reached down and snatched it from the water. He held it above his face, safe from its pincers – its arms and claws an inch from his nose.

"This is Dungeness Crab," he declared. "This is what you're after. They are famous for having a human face."

Conrad, sensing Brosnan was asking him to come forth and observe the anomaly, stepped forward and looked deep in the dying crab's face. Though its eyes were parallel to its nose,

61

the mouth, a stretched triangle of tiny, hair-thin yellow teeth accentuated the smashed look of its face. Conrad noticed its eyes were tangible – as if the human eyeball lay atop the skin of the face and were small white dots in a purple basin before the shell. They resembled, uncannily, a turtle, and their legs and body structure, a tarantula.

"They are the most sought after crab in the world," Brosnan said pridefully. The creature came to life, struggled, opening and closing its pincers. "We all try to hold on, no matter what," Brosnan said austerely. He tossed the crab back into the sea.

Conrad watched the creature, despite its efforts to fight, slowly descend below the waves.

"The guys are going to Lou's after work. It's a bar a few blocks from here."

"I don't know," Conrad said. His head was pounding and his body was fighting exhaustion. It had been a tough first day and he wasn't in the swing of things yet.

"Conrad, the worst thing you can do is not come tonight. The other guys will feel it's a slight. Come."

He didn't want to, but the warning was clear. "I'll be there."

Conrad saw his phone had little strength left, so he turned the power off. Little did he know of the attention his phone would receive. He had a dinner party to attend at Bran's, and he didn't have the faintest clue that it was in two hours.

CHAPTER 10: THE FIGHT

Conrad drove home with a massive headache. He had stayed at the bar as long as he possibly could before leaving would seem rude. It was an awkward time. He didn't know anyone except Brosnan, and Brosnan could talk to him for only so long.

Micker stood in the doorway, her arms folded and her head already shaking in disapproval. He hadn't the slightest clue of what was to come.

As soon as he reached the door, she let him have it. "Jesus, Conrad, where in the hell have you been!"

Conrad's face ensnarled. "What do you think I've been doing!"

"Look at you. You are not even dressed. Go up and throw on a sweater. We were supposed to be at Bran and Marjorie's at seven. We're thirty minutes late."

"When were you gonna tell me this?"

Micker screamed, her voice strong and dominant. "I told you on Wednesday!"

He pulled his cell phone from his pocket. He was going to ask her why she didn't call when he realized he had turned the power off.

He powered it back on and quickly twenty-one missed calls popped up. They were all from her. "You called me twenty-one times!"

"That was over the last two hours, Conrad."

"So you called me every five minutes?"

"Get upstairs!"

"Don't complain to me about the cell phone bill then."

He walked swiftly through the kitchen to the hallway, his temper raging. Joe had just come downstairs to meet Conrad at the steps. He challenged him immediately. "You leave my daughter waiting like that! Who the hell do you think you are!"

Conrad walked by him, clashing with his shoulder and nearly knocking him down. "Get out of my face!"

"Excuse me!"

"Dad!" Micker called as Joe limped to Conrad's bedroom door. "Dad! Let it go!"

Conrad slammed the door on him.

Joe turned and stared at Micker. He was furious. "I want him out of here," he said. "You hear me! I want you out of here!"

"Dad!" Micker screamed, hoping to repair the situation fast.

Then Conrad opened the door, the last thing she wanted to happen. "You know what? You get out! This is my house, not yours!" he screamed in a raged panic. He had no filter any longer. He was screaming whatever he felt and was so angry he was prepared to resort to physical altercation if the old man dared. "This is my house, you get the hell out of it you alcoholic mutt!"

Joe nearly fell backward.

64

It felt good to say it, and good to see it got the old man where he lived. Then the guilt found its way into his cerebrum, telling him to stop talking. But he was pumped for the fight. It had never happened and he had wanted it to happen for years. The old man was abusive toward him; he never showed him, nor even considered showing him, respect. Joe thought of him as too low class for his daughter, yet he lived in his house, ate his food, exercised his utilities, and still saw him with contemptible eyes. Enough was enough.

Micker, however, hadn't expected such a rebuke. "Conrad, what are you doing!" She raced between them, her green eyes bristling. "Get in the goddamn room! I want to talk to you. Now!" She pushed his back. "Go!" She slammed the door behind her. "What is wrong with you!"

"I want him out of here!"

"That is my dad! He has nowhere else to go!"

"So he's got to make my life a living hell!"

She held up her hands. "Did something happen at work?"

"No, it's what happened when I walked in the doorway and that slob got in my face!"

Her voice suddenly more effeminate now, "So you are trying to scream and make matters worse?"

"I don't care how loud I scream! I hate him and I want him out of my house – or he gets a job and starts paying rent! I'm sick of this!"

"You listen here –" Joe said behind the door.

"Go cheat on your wife! Go cheat on your wife, you hypocrite!" And Conrad had said it. It was the one thing that was off limits. Joe had cheated on his wife years ago, and he did it while his wife was dying of cancer, even invited the mistress to the house on several occasions. The news, which got out almost instantly, caused his immediate defrockment from the Catholic

Church. He was no longer a priest, something he had spent his life doing.

Micker forgave him for what he did to her mom, but years were traded in the process.

Micker held the walls as if ready to puke. She held her stomach too, then turned away from Conrad and placed her hand on the door, as if she were patting the destroyed feelings of her father. Then she said lowly, "I want you out of here, Conrad."

Conrad's head slowly rose. "What?" He was surprised, not shocked, for he had heard this before multiple times from foster parents, usually when he found trouble and broke weighty promises. "Did you just say that?"

Her voice was low and dominant again, her back still to him. "I don't want to see you again. Get out."

Conrad moved toward the closet. The last thing on earth he was prepared for was moving out and finding a hotel. In just ten hours he would be expected back at the dock for a new day with new clothes and plenty of sleep. This would cut into all of that. He needed to remedy the situation fast. "Forget everything I did. Let's just go to the party. Here, I'll put on my sweater."

He threw off his shirt, put an undershirt on and pulled a blue sweater over his head. "Everything's fine, everything's fine!" he repeated nervously.

She opened the door, grabbed her father's hands that were pressed against it, and closed the door. Conrad ambled across the room, mumbling to himself. "Fix it, fix it, fix it, fix it. Oh please, God, fix it." He grabbed a pair of pants and threw off his soiled jeans. He put on a pair of dress shoes as he heard Micker's Acura revving. He made one knot in the shoes and sprinted toward the bedroom window, opened it, and jumped out, landing firmly on his feet. He raced down the steps to the

66

car as it was leaving the driveway. Micker stopped the car and had to admit to herself that he looked awfully attractive jumping desperately from that window just to curtail her anger.

She stopped, considered what she would say if she arrived at the party without him. It would eat up too much energy and cause too much worry. It wasn't worth it. Maybe she overreacted too. After all, it was Joe who provoked him.

She unlocked the door and let him in, but despite his several attempts to apologize, she refused to acknowledge him. Tears welded in her eyes but wouldn't drop, and Conrad, his heart racing, was praying the party would go well to ease her current disgust with him.

Bran and Marjorie Hall's home was a three-story Queen Anne style home painted orange and yellow with a two-story porch that extended across three sides of the house. A small turret grew above the gable and ornamental brackets and spindles covered the façade in an admirable fashion.

Bran answered the door and noticed immediately that something was wrong with Micker. Despite his prying, she disclosed nothing.

Dinner was befitting a Syrian food fair: lamb, wild rice, grape leaves, and Greek salad. It was already set when they arrived and two other guests, Randall and Kelly Furnas, were seated on the opposite side of Micker and Conrad. The dining room had a cathedral ceiling, was painted crimson red, and still had no paintings on the wall. The Hall's had just moved in two weeks ago, and unopened cardboard boxes were scattered in the sunken living room off the dining room.

"The place is beautiful," Micker said as she entered the kitchen built in the traditional style of cherry wood with an island in the middle.

Marjorie slammed her hand on her chest as if she were

trying to catch her breath. "Oh, Micker, do you mean that? I was so scared of what you might say?"

"Marjorie!"

Marjorie's bulb-like brown eyes bulged. "No, Bran said you can be brutally honest?"

Bran walked in laughing. Micker looked at him and smiled. "You told her that?"

"Yea," he confirmed playfully.

"Don't listen to him," she said casually. "Now I wonder why people are scared of me."

"Okay," Marjorie said, her mouth still agape as if she were in awe of Micker.

Marjorie Hall was a tiny woman of twenty-seven years. She held a sophisticated bob-weave where her raven-black hair curled around her ears. Her cheeks protruded slightly and her face was as white as chalk. Her nose – a button, and her eyes big and rounded with sketched eyebrows that wrapped around her eyes, almost importuned one to look into them.

"Do you have some water, Bran?" Micker asked, holding her throat as her body seemed to grow tighter in her white suit.

"Yea. What's wrong? You thirsty?"

"I've been thirsty all day for some reason."

Bran poured some water in a white cup and handed it to her gently. She leaned against the counter so her belly button was facing it, and stared out the window over the sink, standing more erect with each gulp like it was giving her strength. Conrad poured a glass of Chardonnay and watched the counter. A slow red pool of cranberry juice from a saucer of recently boiled cranberries broke off into a stream and headed right for her suit. Conrad sat motionless. There was something unbecoming to warn such a keen person of trailing cranberry juice. Once it hit her suit though, it built up a dam and stained

68

the entire front side in a line before fusillading over the counter. Bran heard drips of the cranberry juice on the hardwood floor and sprung from the counter. "Micker!" he cried.

She looked down and awkwardly stepped away from the counter with the cup still in her hand. "Oh my God." The cranberry juice had stained her so that it looked like she had been bitten in half when turned to her front. The juice was still perforating the suit and expanding into a round ball the size of an orange. Conrad stood up quickly, rushed to the counter, ran the faucet, grabbed a washcloth, and handed it to Micker. She rose vigorously and headed toward the bathroom with Marjorie holding her arm.

Conrad and Bran stood with the stained washcloths in their hands, staring at each other. "Marge will have something for her to wear, don't worry," Bran said.

The Furnas' walked in. "What's going on?" Randall asked while wiping his mouth with his handkerchief. Conrad and Bran looked at each other and their mouths began twitching as they were forcing back laughter. At the same time they burst out laughing. It was laughter not just at Micker's shocked face, but the fact that Micker had never been caught gauche before.

Micker returned to the table a half hour later after all the food had gone cold. She appeared skittish when she returned, wearing one of Marjorie's black velvet dresses that fell short a few inches above the knees. Randall sat across from her next to Kelly, who sat directly across from Conrad and diagonal to Micker. The Hall's sat at the ends of the table: Bran to the right of Conrad and Marjorie to the left of Micker, unnoticeably disrupting the conventional gender alignment reserved for formal dinners.

Micker inched her way into the dinner talk that soon fell on the resuscitation of nebulous parables and fables. The

Furnas' were both teachers, so they had some at their disposal. Kelly was a kindergarten teacher and Randall was a high school chemistry teacher. After Bran and Marjorie had summarized a few of Aesop's less known fables, Micker began with a parable by an unknown author of an unknown time. She began after finishing her third glass of Chardonnay:

"There once was an old peddler woman who was traveling through an agrarian village looking for someone to buy an old flask with an indistinct liquid inside, having never found use for it. She happened upon a young man in his early thirties who was struggling economically. After scouting him through the village and realizing his hardship, the old peddler woman approached him.

"'Do you believe in magic?' she asked.

"The young man inspected the old woman's look, alarmed at her grotesquely large nose, slumped back, and witch-like countenance. 'Yes,' he said, for he was a fervent believer of the Old Testament.

"'Would you believe that in this flask holds the power to stay human forever?'

"The young man looked deep in her blue eyes and found belief in her. 'Yes.'

"'Would you want to live forever?' she asked.

"Sensing urgency, the young man shook his head and answered, 'Yes.'

"'Have you thought it through?' she asked. 'If not, you shouldn't take it.'

"'I can find nothing bad in choosing it. There is no guarantee in death.'

"'You are the first person to say that.' She handed him the flask. 'Take it. It will give you that power. But with power comes less choice. Remember that,' she warned. The young man drank it and threw it to the ground as the peddler woman

70

sauntered down the hill in the road and disappeared."

Bran stood up, walked into the kitchen, and returned with a bottle of wine. Conrad found it odd that he would leave the table like that. It seemed like he had already heard the parable before.

Bran began filling up their glasses with Chardonnay.

"The young man quickly found that while his body never changed, he still had to live like a human. He got tired like a human; he grew hungry like a human; and he grew thirsty like a human. After watching his family grow old and die, and suspicions aroused in the town as to his ageless appearance, the young man decided to do something drastic. He decided to rob his fellow villagers and take off to another town. When their bullets failed, the young man felt invincible. He robbed as many towns as he could, living mightily as he moved town-to-town before the news spread.

"Having finally found the town he wanted to live in, and with a fortune at his disposal, the man felt happy again about the prospects of living forever. But one day he was surreptitiously caught by a band of townsmen at a bank. He had his rifle pointed at them, but when it came to firing, despite knowing he would never have to face the uncertainty of death, he could not fire. The bandsmen kidnapped him and took him to a nearby garage. They tried to kill him; they drowned him and hanged him and while the young man felt the pain of dying, he wouldn't die…his body would just recuperate like magic.

"Eventually, the townsmen got to talking. Considering him an abomination but understanding their inability to kill him, they decided upon a way to silence him, a way that would be worse than death: bury him below a lake that had been dug two hundred feet deep but had yet to be filled. Stuck in a coffin molded to his own body, the young man still resides there, his mind running, his heart still beating, way down below the

71

bottom of an unknown lake."

"The moral?" Marjorie asked.

"Death is a privilege."

People had always been accustomed to Micker either telling the last story at a social assortment, or the only story. Topping her was impossible. Conrad, though, for whatever reason, was feeling more confident around her than he usually did. Maybe it was the accident in the kitchen or the fight with Joe. Whatever it was, it prompted him to tell his own parable. This was one he had known for a long time. He felt comfortable with it, so comfortable he knew it could stand up to Micker's.

He lifted his left index finger above the table. "I have one," he said.

Micker looked at him impassively. She figured he would only look comical trying to equal her.

He began confidently, quickly finding the story-telling groove. "In the 1800s, during the last year of the Civil War, there was this man – the same one who invented walking the tightrope – who informed the country that he was going to walk across Niagara Falls. People naturally thought he was crazy, so they gathered by the thousands to watch what they thought for sure would be his death. When they got there, all they saw was a taut rope tied from one end across the falls to the other. Then the man began, without any mention, walking across the tightrope at an alarmingly fast pace; and when he got halfway across, he planted his feet, and his arms fell to his sides. The crowd was stunned. They could hear and see the falls rumbling loudly a hundred feet below and knew any hesitation and he would die. The man balanced himself suddenly and did a back flip, landing safely on the rope. He then walked across to the other side and the crowd roared. As he was about to begin another crossing, he grabbed a wheelbarrow from a young

72

farmer and told him he was going to take it across with him. Just as he was about to step out on the line, he turned around and asked the crowd if they believed he could cross pushing the wheelbarrow.

"They all answered 'Yes.' Then the man pointed to a teenager and asked, 'Do you believe I can push this wheelbarrow across on that tightrope that's just an inch wide and thick?'

"The teenager enthusiastically answered, 'Yes.' The man then asked him if he was certain, and the teenager smiled and confirmed his faith in the man. The man then asked the teenager if he was 'absolutely certain.'

"The teenager did not hesitate. 'I am absolutely certain you can cross with that wheelbarrow.' The man then walked forward to him, pushed the wheelbarrow forward, and said, 'Then get in.'"

Each guest sat back in their chair and smiled. Conrad was surprised by the reaction, for it was the same positive reaction he got whenever he recounted the tale. He had sold the story, and sold it well.

"And the moral is…," Kelly said, her mouth ajar in wonderment.

"Trust is stronger than belief."

The Furnas' sighed with smiles wrapped gently across their faces.

"That's a good one," Randall said.

Micker's eyes moved to the right and locked with Bran's. She smiled at him and he smiled back. Little did she know that her face was reflecting in the China cabinet, where Conrad had focused his attention. Though it was only for a second, Conrad turned an unhealthy pallor when he saw her and Bran's eyes. It was the look two people give when they are in love.

Micker, sensing she was being watched, looked down at

her plate without seeing if Conrad was indeed watching her. But Conrad had seen her and he had seen how she looked afterward. She wore the look of wrongdoing, the look of implication, the look of deceit. She was breathing heavily.

Curious if Conrad had caught her, her eyes slowly rose. Her reflection was bright in the china cabinet and stabbed by white rays from the chandelier. Conrad was looking the other way. She was not relieved, though. She spent the rest of the dinner trying to configure a scenario where her eye lock with Bran was caught, and at times she wished Conrad had caught her – for she found more fear in wondering.

The car ride home was quiet and tense. They both seemed to be feeling each other out, trying to decipher how the other was thinking behind their impassive veneers. It had crossed Conrad's mind that the look Bran and Micker shared, though only for a second, was suggestive, but he wasn't willing to put much stake in it. Bran and Micker had been high school sweethearts, and they always carried themselves like ex-lovers in social situations: always conscious of the other despite pretending not to be. Conrad had seen plenty of eye-locking between the two of them before, and though this one appeared unique in that it seemed they were trying to communicate something passionate, Conrad weighed the context of the moment: It had occurred when he was telling a story that succeeded Micker's, something that rarely happened to her.

For that, Conrad assumed they were exchanging sarcastic comments nonverbally: *Who does the idiot think he is?* He knew neither of them considered him on intellectual footing with them. They had always condescended to him. They had better grades, went to better schools, stuff like that. It was a lousy feeling, but something he could never overcome. It was with these thoughts that he casually pushed the stare out of his

74

mind. He was feeling good about the night, and he didn't want skepticism to ruin it. "Tonight was one of the few times this year where I felt myself. Honestly, Micker," he said.

She looked stolidly into the lifeless darkness as she drove around the sidling cliffs above the ocean. Conrad suddenly grew fearful she would bring up their fight. He tried to avoid any references to it. At the moment, he was simply trying to get her to engage him. "What'd you think of Bran and Marjorie's place?" he asked timorously. There was silence again. "Micker?"

She gave him a grave stare and said, "This does not change what you did tonight, Conrad."

He replied instantly. "I'm sorry. I will apologize to him. I blew up and it was my fault, and I promise I will make him feel better. He has every right to stay."

"It does not change the way I felt. You do not get second chances."

"Yes, you do," he said. "That's all life is."

"No," she retorted condescendingly.

He pushed back. "Yes it is. Yes it is. We screw up because we're human, but it's the better part in us that corrects the mistake."

"This is not a parable, Conrad. You cross *me*, and you don't get a second chance. That was a personal thing you did back there, and I cannot forgive that." There was sincere anger and disappointment in her voice.

"Listen – "

"No – "

"Just listen." He sat up in his seat and turned to her. "Things are looking up right now. I'm starting to get used to this job. I'm even enjoying hanging with some of the guys. I think I've got a lot of potential there. Bran and I are hitting it off well, and I'm starting to learn how to deal with my own

75

demons…because of your help, Micker, because of your help. Don't do anything drastic." He looked hard at her, but her face was intransigent. His eyes rolled around in their sockets as he pondered, searching for something more to convince her. Then it sprang in his head like a light bulb turned on. "I thought it was wrong that you *called* Bran. I didn't want you to do it. And now I don't know how to repay you."

Micker's eyes subtly widened. He had emphasized "called," like it wasn't true. And it wasn't. She had spoken to Bran about it in person.

"I'll talk to Joe," he continued. "It wasn't as bad as it could have been. I know I can change things for the better. If there's anything I know, it's that I can change for the better."

He grabbed her hand and caressed it. Micker, after waiting a few seconds, clenched down on it, but it didn't have the feel of authenticity. It seemed she did it for the sake of moving on. They drove on into the night, and while Conrad was convinced he had handled the situation well, something didn't seem quite right. He started thinking about the rumors that always existed about Bran and Micker. He never took them seriously. He was practical about the whole situation. They were in love at one point in their lives, so naturally some feelings surely still existed. And they always had good chemistry, but they were just friends now. He kept repeating it in his mind. *They're just friends now.* People just misinterpreted their friendship.

And then he remembered what Donny Locks had said to him. It was the comment that changed his life.

CHAPTER 11: THE DONNY LOCKS INCIDENT

From the moment Donny Locks was hired on as an intern at the Walker's branch office in San Sangre, Conrad knew something was off about him. He was hired by Kevin Hall, the Vice President, under the advisement of Bran, then the Regional Manager of the San Sangre branch, as part of a support program to give people right out of high school a paid internship experience. The move was supposed to give Walker's positive exposure in the community. Ten interns were placed in the San Sangre branch, and Conrad drew Donny Locks.

Just nineteen years old, Locks had no plans to go to college. Conrad was surprised by how poorly he spoke and how unknowledgeable he was to win such a position. The rest of Conrad's sales staff was turned off by him too.

Locks was assigned typical internship duties: run errands, make copies, file papers, stack boxes, and deliver forms and necessary documents to the Walker's warehouse. Things ran smoothly that first month until one of Conrad's more loyal staffers, Elsa Miles, approached him. She said she had caught Locks in an obscenity-laced tirade while dropping boxes in the copying room. When she asked him to watch his tongue, he threw her some choice words.

She was shaken. "Conrad, in all my sixteen years, I have never heard anyone talk to me like that." Conrad assured her he would speak to Locks when he returned. Locks was only part time, and he had Thursday through Sunday to himself.

Conrad called Locks into the conference room on Monday and asked him to set the record straight about the allegation. A smug smile on his face, Locks called Miles a liar. When Conrad read him a few pages from his *Standards of Etiquette in the Workplace*, Locks confidently told him he was wasting his time. "You're just a pushover," Locks said, those half-rotted teeth delivering the smile.

Conrad slammed the book down. "You're out of here." He left Locks in the room. The staff took notice of his agitated pace and red face through the hallway. He marched into Bran's office.

Bran agreed the situation was dire. He sat down with Locks to a rather long meeting without Conrad's presence. When the meeting adjourned, Locks kept his smile and went home for the day. Bran told Conrad that Locks held a very different version. He agreed to using inappropriate language in front of Elsa, but he said Conrad blew his lid and called him "white trash" and "a low life."

Conrad couldn't believe it. He denied it vociferously. Bran told him he had his back, but Conrad could tell Bran wasn't a hundred percent sure Locks' account was untrue.

"Just ride the storm," Bran told him. "I don't want to fire an intern like this. He's out of here in June. That's three months. Just give it three months."

"Can't you transfer him from my department?" Conrad asked.

"He's needed in your department. You're low on staff

as it is. I've talked with him. You won't have a problem again."

And that was how it was left. A month went by with no issues. In staff meetings, Locks never spoke. He just sat by himself with that perpetual grin on his face. The staff couldn't stand him. The kid was a snake, and that sentiment permeated the department. But Conrad kept his distance. Besides, he had better things to worry about than Donny Locks.

A deal was in the making that could propel Conrad's career. Hillmard foods, a small food store in San Sangre, had agreed, after years of indecision, to sign a contract agreement to sell Walker's seafood in their store. While the deal didn't include a huge monetary gain, it was enough to keep Walker's ahead of its competition as the preeminent seafood company in the region.

On the day of the deal, Conrad tried to hide his excitement. Everyone was complimenting him on the achievement, being he spearheaded the deal. The contracts needed faxed, signed, and returned, and it was done. The contract signing was done upstairs with Bran, Kevin, and the Hillmard owners. Conrad waited for the congratulatory call.

After two hours went by, he grew concerned. Contract signings rarely took this long. The call came. A cacophony of shouts and frustrations over a speaker demanding his presence. Two pages of the contract were missing during the signing and numbers prior to the arrangement had changed. The Hillmard owners had nearly pulled out of the deal until Bran rescued the correct paperwork.

Bran said he had never been so embarrassed, and Kevin lashed out at him. Conrad hadn't the slightest clue of what was going on.

He called Elsa in the next day.

"Sorry to hear about what happened yesterday," she said.

Conrad got right down to it. "I don't think it was an accident."

She knew what he was thinking. "Locks?"

"Was he working the fax machine that day?"

"For a short time, yes."

"Is he good with computers?"

"I've heard he is. Very good, in fact. Not much upstairs with him, besides knowledge of computers. Why?"

"Good enough to manipulate documents?"

"Maybe."

"Keep your eyes open. Report to me each day what he is doing."

She wanted to do one better. "Where did he go to school?"

"San Sangre High."

Her eyes grew acute. "I know some people over there. Might be worth it to find out what kind of record he has."

Conrad didn't stop her.

Elsa came with a rap sheet by the end of the week. Conrad looked at it intently. Sixteen suspensions and thirty-two detentions in four years, problems with the law, poor grades, and frequent absenteeism. Conrad felt vindicated, yet scared. Half of the infractions involved fights, but they could never prove that Locks had provoked any of the altercations.

"Is that enough?" Elsa asked.

"We need to cross check this with the application he submitted."

Elsa swung the application in front of her face. "Already did," she said gleefully. "He lied."

Conrad juxtaposed the documents. His grades, his apparent accolades, all of it was a lie.

Elsa smiled. Her eyes glowed behind her glasses. "That

80

should be it, right?"

Conrad didn't feel right about it. "How could they miss this?"

"I don't know," she admitted.

He wanted to ask Micker for advice, but she told him not to get involved in petty happenings around the workplace. "You can't hire or fire anyone," she told him. "So don't worry about it. This is all on Bran's plate, not yours." But that wasn't necessarily true. Kevin Hall was remarkably stubborn, so stubborn, in fact, that he made sure any decision, hiring, or firing had his sole authorization.

Conrad told Elsa he wanted to think it over before he brought it to Bran. She was confused but trusted his judgment. *There must be more to this than meets the eye*, she thought.

"One last thing," she said before she left the room. "Some staff members were talking yesterday at lunch, John and Rachel, and Locks was in there. They were talking about the 1st of May this year, when all the power went out in San Sangre. When they asked Locks if he remembered it, he kept saying that he *definitely* wasn't in San Sangre on May 1st."

Conrad didn't get it. He squinted.

"Why would he say that he *definitely* wasn't around here that day?" she asked. "It was weird. He said it pridefully, like he was doing something else worthwhile."

Conrad though about it. "I'm sure he was."

May 1st. What was going on May 1st? Conrad surfed the internet for hours. Many things happened on May 1st. He was trying to find something, anything suspicious on that day. And just as he was about to quit, he happened upon an incident in San Sangre National Park, a patch of wilderness of nearly four square miles. The incident wasn't reported until after the 1st, but a recently married couple on their honeymoon reported having their belongings stolen. They saw a man walking from their tent at night as they returned from an evening walk. Their wallets and goods were in a garbage bag over the man's shoulder.

The husband ran after him but couldn't catch him. The sketch artist did what he could from a fragmented account of the man's face. He was young, 18-21, about 6'1", skinny, 180 pounds, and had a very recognizable face. Freckles and a crew cut with dark, menacing eyes. It looked a lot like Donny Locks.

The article mentioned that it was the second incident like that in the park, which had little security besides park rangers. On March 25th, a woman's belongings were stolen. She didn't get a look at the man, but some witnesses said they saw a young man in the park traveling alone without camping or hiking gear. The description of the man matched the May 1st description.

Locks was 6'1" and about 180 pounds. Conrad checked Locks' work schedule. Sure enough, he was off both days the robberies occurred.

Conrad couldn't sleep that night. He wanted to tell Micker about what he found, but he wasn't sure what her reaction would be. If Locks were a criminal, he could be putting her life in danger with the information. He went into the bathroom to throw water on his face. The blinds to the window were open. A red pickup truck was across the street. Conrad found that odd. He had never known anyone to own a red pickup truck on his street.

He watched it. Looked it side to side. Someone was in that truck. Conrad went into the bedroom for a better view. The blinds were down. He pulled a few back slowly. He let his eyes adjust. Enough light from the street lamp trickled through the window to illuminate a face. Freckled and deliberate, staring right back at him, smiling ear to ear, was Donny Locks. Conrad

82

grabbed his cell phone from the dresser and held it to his ear. Locks' head turned back toward the street, and the truck started. It drove off slowly into the night.

Conrad's hands shook the blinds. He waited there, kept them open, and stared into the street waiting for that red pickup truck to come riding back to his place.

Conrad didn't tell anyone what had happened. There wasn't a doubt in his mind that Locks was dangerous. *He must have found out I was searching for him on the internet,* Conrad thought. He needed to be careful. Elsa had told him that Locks was some kind of computer whiz. She wasn't sure how good, but people she had talked to said they remembered he was able to build his own computer. They also said he was dangerous.

Conrad kept the incidents in the National Park quiet for the time being. He had a meeting scheduled with Bran, and this time Kevin Hall would be joining. He was going to show them the application and the inconsistencies. That would most likely be enough. Then he could send the police a letter informing them of his suspicions of Donny Locks. Maybe it was Locks, maybe it wasn't. He just wanted to make sure the people who found that out were law enforcement and not him.

Bran was livid that background checks weren't conducted and resumes verified. Kevin kept quiet. Conrad knew right then that Kevin Hall was the one that made the error. He did the checks personally.

"I didn't take the time," he said angrily. "This could blow up in our faces if we fire him now for this."

"We have to fire him," Bran insisted.

Conrad was relieved.

But Bran continued to talk as his brother massaged his forehead dejectedly. "Worse would be the publicity if this were discovered though. If we fire him now, and the *San Sangre Star* got a hold of this – this kids' rap sheet is two pages long! They would have a field day with our screening process."

"That newspaper hates us," Kevin said.

"He has two weeks," Bran said. "Let's just ride it out. Once he's gone, no one will know. No one will care. And we just go on about our daily business. Let's cut his hours in half. Kevin, this is your call, but I don't see any other way."

Kevin didn't hesitate. Bran always had the better forethought. "It will be like he was never here."

Conrad was shocked. He hadn't expected this. He handed them the San Sangre National Park burglary incidents and explained his theory on Locks' involvement.

Bran and Kevin gave him a cold stare.

"This will require some investigating. Thank you, Conrad," Bran said.

"What are you going to do with it?"

"Take it to the police, obviously," Bran said. "I'll take care of it." The meeting ended like that – without much closure.

A week later, Bran approached Conrad with news. "I talked to the police and sent them your findings," Bran said. "He's clean. He has alibis on both days."

"He does?" Conrad said.

"You sound upset?"

"No."

"Anyways, they have a suspect in custody. You can check it out online."

As soon as Bran left, Conrad did. A suspect was in custody. He was denying the crime, but the article said some pretty incriminating evidence was found.

So that's that, Conrad thought. *Locks is only a violent, lying, computer genius.*

Now Conrad only needed to prepare his department

goals and objectives presentation to the San Francisco offices in a week. He also thought it would look good if he followed orders and didn't mention anything about Locks again. The day of his presentation would be Locks' last day.

Conrad had prepared incessantly for his department presentation. It was only to be about twenty-five minutes, and then Bran would come in and talk about regional changes. An email came the night before from corporate pushing the meeting back two hours. Conrad was delighted. Not only would he be getting rid of Donny Locks forever, but he could sleep in.

Conrad drove into the city forty minutes early. He felt refreshed. The sun lit up the windy San Francisco streets, and the green sea met the blue sky like in a painting.

When he entered, the lobby was clear. *Odd.* He climbed the escalator, took the elevator to the conference room, and could hear a voice penetrating the walls because of a microphone.

Fear and sickness struck him. He opened the door gently. Gilbert Hall was giving his closing remarks. In fact, he was thanking all the interns that made the program fulfilling, and Donny Locks name was up there on the screen along with all the other interns.

Conrad had missed his speech.

He caught Bran's eyes. Bran's tongue moved inside his cheek, and he looked away. Donny Locks was sitting a few rows behind him. His head was clean shaved. He smiled dismissively, as if it were all too easy.

The meeting soon ended, and everyone filed out. Conrad approached Bran, but Bran walked right by him. Conrad wasn't sure of his future.

He found a kiosk in the lobby. He logged into his email. The email from corporate, notifying him of the meeting being pushed back, was gone.

Conrad was fury and rage and everything else but a clear mind on the drive back to the San Sangre offices. He didn't know what he was going to do, but he knew he had to get even. He hadn't even fought back.

He took the stairs with the glass windows on both sides. The entire department could see him as he arrived. As he ascended the stairs, He heard footsteps behind him. He stopped and turned, knowing it was Locks without even having to look.

"It's the last day – for both of us," Locks said smiling. Even his shaved head was freckled.

Conrad's hands were making fists. He was wrestling back all of his anger. He was near the top of the stairs. *This guy just won't leave me alone.*

"I've never seen anyone take as much abuse as you. You're so easy to play with. I guess what I don't understand," Locks said, "is how you deal with knowing your wife is really Bran Hall's?"

Conrad was trembling because of his anger. He couldn't think. He turned swiftly with the intention of taking Locks by the shirt and pulling him to the side. But his anger allowed too much force in his arms when he extended them horizontally, and as he moved, Locks did something so cunning that it took care of everything.

Subtly, Locks skipped a step so that he could meet Conrad's arms. Peripherally, Conrad could see the people at their cubicles stand up and take notice. It looked like a push, and there was impact, enough to make Locks' flop backward legitimate.

Locks took everything with him, tumbling down the stairs, scraping skin away from his face. Everyone saw it. Conrad couldn't protest it. If he didn't know better, he would have thought he just pushed Locks down a staircase too.

Locks rose to a fountain of blood from his nose.

Conrad was reprimanded by a few in his department. As he was taken to Bran's office, he walked by Elsa, who held a tissue to her nose. She was crying.

Bran showed him sympathy, said he would do everything he could to fight for him, but that he had to put him on administrative leave until the investigation was over. He was escorted out of the building by a police officer, and Locks had them charge him with assault.

It didn't matter what Conrad said about the set up. No one believed him. The witnesses were many, and they saw an enraged man push an intern down a flight of stairs.

Bran held off the pressure, but Kevin Hall found it too much. Conrad was summarily fired by Kevin Hall before the investigation concluded.

The Locks incident didn't prove damaging to everyone, however. The newspapers covered the story relentlessly, mostly those who hated the Halls for past, petty squabbles. The blame seemed to fall squarely on Kevin Hall. It was discovered later by the press that Locks had a violent history and had lied on his application. When Gilbert Hall caught wind of this, he demoted Kevin Hall and reassigned him to the Sacramento branch they were opening.

Bran, having been the one to notify Kevin of Locks' history, came out unscathed. He moved into Kevin Hall's position, becoming one of the youngest vice presidents in the region.

CHAPTER 12: THEIR MEETING PLACE

"We still have time," Micker said anxiously. "You don't have to go." She studied the motel room and wished she could be somewhere else. Pale strands of sunlight obstructed her view of him. She muted the television. "I said you don't have to go."

"I have to," Bran replied calmly and began straightening his tie.

Micker put her legs up in mountains. She was already starting to feel alone.

"Are you sure he doesn't suspect anything?" Bran asked while fixing his collar.

"With him, I can't tell. The only time he's ever asked questions about us was after Donny Locks. I held him off then."

"He worships you, like a little puppy dog."

Her eyes widened to confirm it.

"What has it been, a year now?"

She corrected him. "Ten months."

He was taken aback by her quickness.

"We met here, ten months ago, in this motel," she remembered.

"You're worried?"

"Of course. Who wouldn't be?" she said, looking for dirt under her nails. "There's no instructional manual out there for having an affair."

He turned and tugged his tie. "Good point."

"I think I'm ready to ask for a divorce," she said, looking up quickly to see his reaction. He walked to the foot of the bed while fumbling with his tie. His consternating stare begged her elaboration. "He finally went after Joe the other week. It was awful. I think that's ammunition enough, don't you?"

"Could be. Do you think you could get him to do more?"

"I could, but I don't want to use my dad as a guinea pig," she said, visibly frustrated. "He's weak enough as it is."

"What if I had my dad lay him off? Just tell him he had to make cutbacks. You could cite in a divorce hearing that he's unemployed and has poor prospects with his reputation."

She responded sharply. "No. We need the money to pay the mortgage. We're thousands in debt as it is."

"How? The both of you?"

"We are a month behind on the mortgage. We are incurring hundred dollar late charges every month. We have an adjustable rate, and that went up with the credit hits. And last year I cosigned with him on the Jetta."

"Why would you do that?"

"What was I supposed to do? He needed a car. We were sharing mine. How was he going to pay for his own car?"

Bran stood by the window, the white curtains sprawled, listening to the semis roar past the motel. His hand was on his chin. He shuttered when he heard one of the engine drones

89

break off a fire-cracking sound.

"What did you ever see in him?"

"I could ask you the same thing?"

"About Marjorie?" Bran sat on the foot of the bed. "You know, we've only got one shot at this."

"I know."

"Divorce is second nature nowadays. Your first marriage is like a test drive."

"Could you leave Marjorie like that?"

"I love you."

"But you care for her?"

Bran rose from the bed all perturbed. "I don't want to end up like Ethan Frome here. I got one shot at this. I finally found the person I want to spend the rest of my life with and I've got to sneak around? That's not how I've ever lived my life. If I can take it, I take it. No apologies. No remorse. I already lost you once to this low life. It won't happen again."

"But you have considered that this might be us one day, in a motel, having this same conversation, but with somebody else."

"That's the discipline that comes with love. You've got to be willing to pack your bags when the heart beats differently."

Micker rubbed her temples. "Bran, I'm with you, and then I'm not. If you think Conrad is going to go into the dark quietly…."

"Screw him. He's a waste."

"He's not stupid though."

"Trust me. He's plenty stupid."

He annoyed her now. "Really? You know he knows we never talked on the phone about you offering him the fishing job."

"So?"

"At tennis, you told him I called you," she said. Bran

90

still didn't understand what it meant. "We never talked over the phone. I asked you if you could get him the fishing job when we were together here, at this motel. He knows I asked you in person."

"So what?"

"He must have checked my cell," she mumbled to herself.

Bran was lost.

"He knows we never talked over the phone!"

"How do you know that?"

She sat up. "When I was coming back from your house, I was just about to ask for a divorce when he brought up that I called you. He brought it up deliberately. "

"So, he brought it up."

"No, that's the thing. He never asked me if I called you. He didn't even imply anything about us."

Bran sighed. "Come on, Micker."

"Trust me. He knows. It is the way he said it. He emphasized 'called' in a subtle way."

Bran looked at her skeptically.

"He is clever. He has always been clever."

"So, he knows. So what? We talked in person after work. That's all we have to say. It's just a mix up."

"Honestly, how can you mix that up? Talking over the phone is too different from talking in person."

"Just say you called me from our business line."

"When we work in the same building?"

"Yea. Just say you didn't want to walk down to my wing so you called my extension."

"But would I call you over a business line to talk about something personal like that?"

"Who cares! Quit looking into things so deeply."

"I think he caught us at dinner too, when you looked at

91

me."

"Jesus, Micker! What's happening to you! So what if he saw us staring at each other? We've been friends for ten years. We dated on and off again before you got married. That allows us to share a moment."

"Maybe. I don't know. There is no divorce if he finds out about us. I will lose everything. "

"How could anyone find out? We don't use phones; we spend an hour once each week on a different day. We drive one car and leave the other at the supermarket. And we spend one hour out alone each day in case there are suspicions."

Micker rubbed her hands through her recently dyed auburn hair. "How has he been at the job?"

Bran made a bloated face. "Actually, he's pretty good. They said he's already making his quotas. Only thing is…"

Micker grabbed her stomach. "What?"

"Did he hurt his knee? He said he hurt it carrying a fish crate."

"He might have. Why?"

"But you don't think he did?"

"He never mentioned it to me," she said. Then she smiled a wise smile. "Were you beating him in tennis?"

"Yea."

"Well, there's your answer. Conrad can't handle losing."

"Well, neither can I," said Bran. "That's why I don't even bother with it," he said sarcastically.

She smiled. "If only I had your confidence."

When Micker returned home, she found Conrad dressed up nicely with his hair gelled back, his face clean-shaven and unsullied by uncertainty and stress. He was standing above the liquor cabinet, looking clean in a just washed burgundy sweatshirt and jeans. Micker could smell the warmed detergent from the bedroom doorway.

"Did you just get back?" she asked, having changed into a black sleeveless shirt and blue jeans. She pulled out her hair tie and threw it on the bed, fluffing her hair high above her head as she walked to the bed and sat.

"Just a minute ago," he said, preoccupied by a bottle of Jack Daniels. He unscrewed the cap and smelled the top of the half-gallon bottle. The liquor was pale brown.

"What?" she asked restively.

Conrad turned to her. "It's watered down," he said observantly.

Micker walked to the cabinet and grabbed the bottle from Conrad's hands and placed it below her nose. She gave it a good shake. "Is it?" Her lips compounded austerely. She tasted it. "Yep," she muttered angrily.

The stairway, twelve wooden, degrading steps of a narrow passage, had creaking floors that played a crescendo the closer to the top. Micker walked them slowly, the bitter light in the hallway giving way to the coral pink walls atop the stairs. "Dad?" she called. There was a soft thud from downstairs. Conrad had closed their bedroom door and latched it. "Hey Dad?" she called again, still standing in the middle of the stairway. There was dead silence. Normally Joe would have responded by the first call. "Dad!"

She bit on her lower lip as her heart rate accelerated. Joe's bedroom door was opened slightly. When she noticed this, she turned around, facing the bottom of the stairs, and began panting. Slowly she fell to her knees, her butt just touching the hardwood step. She closed her eyes, tucked her head into her chest and held her hands to her forehead. "Oh please, God. Don't let him have died," she sighed desperately. "Please, don't let him have died."

She turned back to the top of the steps. The pink in the walls was like a thick gas around her. Trembling, she approached the final step and peered in the bedroom door. Joe was lying on his back, his arms sprawled out breast level, his legs in the shape of a tent. Aloe Vera plants were erect on the bedpost beside him. Each long shoot was a silhouette against the yellow drapes of the window. Six chromatic frangipani flowerpots sat above his lone dresser in the seven-by-eight foot bedroom of concave walls. She grabbed her neck and squeezed it before she saw his white t-shirt lift up ever so slightly like someone was blowing air into it. A relieved smile penetrated her face. Joe's eyes opened at once and he turned to her. He was startled. He sat up in his bed. The light in the door slid over his eyes.

He saw Micker had the whiskey bottle in her hand. His eyes drooped slowly like an old dog.

She looked around the room before speaking. There were Joe's pictures of the saints from years ago, pictures that hadn't been damaged and looked just as they had the day they were given to him to fix up his office in the priesthood. She remembered visiting him all those early years, how they would read the *Bible* together, how she was the first in her Sunday school class to know all of the commandments verbatim. And how all that affection they had for each other and religion and God slowly melted before them because of what he did with her mother before they were married. She resented him. She wanted to take him on. She held up the bottle. "How did you get into the liquor cabinet?"

"Oh, I'm not – I'm not gonna get into another discussion like this with you."

"How did you find his key?"

"I," he talked lifelessly. "I don't know what you're talking about."

94

"You have only one liver. Do you realize that? I know you are holding out hope that they will give you a new one, but an alcoholic at sixty-eight years old is not reaching the top of the list. You could live another twenty – thirty years. You could."

"Micker, I would prefer it if you left me alone for a while. Please?"

"You are all I have left," she said desperately.

Joe looked up guiltily. "I know."

"Then why do you do this? Why? You cannot keep thinking of yourself as a victim."

"I'm lucky?" he asked scornfully about his physical predicament.

"To be alive? Yes!" she said declaratively. "I would say you are privileged to have a surviving condition."

"Cirrhosis isn't a privilege, Micker."

"Being alive is."

Joe was discouraged. "Look at my arm," he said raising it into the faint light. It was dark red with patches of brown scabs and visible oozing puss running from it. There was not a shred of normal, human skin on his arm. "It's turned me into a monster. I bite my lip and I have to be rushed to the emergency room because my blood's too thin to clot. My eyes are yellow."

"And whose fault is that, Dad? You knew what could happen."

He grabbed his brows in submission. "I can't stop drinking."

"I need you to hang on," her voice sounding muffled like she was out of breath, "for me. Do you understand? With Mom gone, I cannot lose you. You have to fight. If not for you, then for me."

"I'll try. I'll try," he muttered morosely.

She walked toward him and kissed him softly on the head. A tear she didn't feel or sense dropped from her eye on

95

his head and quickly fell through the white threads and dried on his scalp.

She left the room and went outside on the porch. The street was teeming with adolescents playing a game of tag on their bicycles. She pondered throwing the key into the bushes below the porch, but she knew it would only create a hassle. She opened the mailbox, and as she was about to place the key at the bottom, she saw a crevice where the mailbox was attached to the panels. She slid it effortlessly into the crevice, stunned at how perfectly it fit. *Dad never comes outside*, she thought.

Back in the house, Conrad was lying on the bed about to fall asleep. She walked gently to him and whispered in his ear where the key was. His eyes jolted open, and he sat up. He was slightly disoriented.

"He is drinking himself to death," she said.

"Should we take him to the hospital?" he asked, still waking.

"No. It's up to him if he wants to live or not."

"It's just a relapse, Micker. It's just one time."

"I have caught him before," she admitted. "I just never revealed it." Conrad rubbed her back. She turned softly to lie on his stomach, her left arm sprawled over his chest. Conrad was frightened to touch her, to rouse her. Micker hadn't shown him affection like this in six months. "I don't know what to do with him. I can't stop him if he wants to go," she said softly.

He asked, "A liver is tough to destroy though, isn't it? It can regenerate."

"Why do you ask that?"

"He knows how much it will take to kill it. It shows how reluctant he is."

Micker thought about what Conrad said. She spun her legs around and planted them on the floor. After a few seconds she left the bed and went downstairs to the kitchen to pour a
96

glass of milk.

Something was wrong with her. Conrad, in all his years, had never seen her this vulnerable. Above all, he never quite understood how she still loved Joe, in some ways loved him more, after what he did to her mother. Conrad attributed it to the fact that Micker was a mystery. She always was and probably always would be.

A tiresome riddle.

He felt a big enough blow might send her over the edge.

CHAPTER 13: ANOTHER RENDEZVOUS

Bran held Micker in his arms as they sat on the couch in the motel. Without remembering how, their conversation soon turned toward admired politicians.

"Castro was making a speech to a large assembly," Bran said, his hair buffed up. "And he was going on at great length before a voice out in the crowd said, 'peanuts, popcorn, crackerjacks.' He went on speaking. And again the voice said, 'Peanuts, popcorn, crackerjack.' And about the fourth time this happened he stopped his speech, and he said, 'The next time he says that, I'm going to find out who he is and I'm gonna kick his butt all the way to America!' And everybody in the crowd said, 'Peanuts, popcorn, crackerjack!'"

Micker let out a soft laugh. She leaned in close to Bran's right shoulder and placed her head on his chest. "Who said that?" she asked. Her eyes darted upward.

"Reagan."

"Yea, but who wrote it for him?"

"Who knows."

She watched the dapper sunlight trickle onto the white

walls through the yellow drapes. He leaned back and asked, "What are you thinking about?"

Her face turned forlornly to the yellow drapes and the cloven sunlight. She asked, "You think we'll ever get out of here?"

"Yea."

"Where?"

"Back East."

"How?"

"Just pack up and go. Somewhere East."

"Can we really just pack up and go without our reputations haunting us? Word can travel faster from California to New York than we can."

"So what if it travels with us. Today, everybody has dirt on them. You walk into a room and everybody has a scandal they've been fighting for years. It's second nature."

"I have never had that. I have never had bad press."

"I have to get going," he said. He was frustrated by her, and she could tell.

She sat up. "I'm just saying that we have to think things through before we get ourselves in too deep."

He wheeled around. "Screw this. I mean, what are we even talking about anymore? We're wasting time!" he moaned.

"What do you want me to do?" she snapped back. The stress was mounting on her face.

"Just divorce him."

"I don't think I can do that."

"Why?"

"I don't think he would recover."

"You think he'd kill himself?"

She nodded, her voice starting to tremble. "It's possible."

"That's not your responsibility."

"It is. The fact that I suspect what he might do makes it my responsibility."

"It's his problem."

She looked up at him, disgusted by his callousness. "How can you be so cold?"

"That's how I am. That's what you like about me."

"Not that cold."

He smiled and pulled her into his chest. "I'm hot about you though."

"I'm all Conrad has."

"He can find another woman. People adapt. That's all he needs to do. Adapt."

"Do you know what happened to Conrad's father after his mother was killed?" she asked softly.

Bran rolled his eyes. He was tired of talking about Conrad.

She didn't take her eyes off of him. She felt Bran needed to hear it. "His father took him to collect stones on the beach. They were looking for those stones with the fossils imprinted in them. And when they collected enough to fill a bucket, His father sent him back inside the house to get another bucket. And while Conrad was gone, his father filled his pockets with those stones and walked himself into the sea, where his wife was killed. Conrad saw the whole thing. He saw his father struggle to come back. His father had changed his mind, but it was too late. He fell beneath the waves. Conrad saw this when he was just a kid."

"Again, it's a tough break."

She sighed away her frustration. "You don't understand."

He started kissing her forcefully. "You're the strongest woman I've ever known. Forever I've wondered what your weakness is, and here I've found it."

100

She looked up at him, waiting for a response.

"Your weakness is the weak," he said. "You feel obligated to them somehow."

She pushed him off. She was tired of him trying to psychoanalyze her. "I have to get back to my dad." She fixed her hair as he sat back and watched her.

Before she left she turned and said, "I guess you're weak because God knows I'm obligated to you." She slammed the door, and he laughed at how worked up she was.

CHAPTER 14: TEMPTATION

At the top of the garbage in the last spears of sunlight was a Coors Light beer can calling Joe forth. He rose from his kitchen chair and walked over to it. He bent down so the silver shine of the columnar would penetrate his eyes. He pulled it from the garbage very slowly, almost daring himself to lick the top. He looked out the window to make sure Micker wasn't pulling in. Conrad was still at work, but Micker was on her way and she would kill him if she saw him in such a pitiful act.

He held the can in his hands like he was receiving communion. The top of the can was dry. He smelled it. The malt scent of ale was so potent it was sweet in his lungs. The can shook when his arm rattled from excitement and he heard a gentle slush in the can. There was about a tablespoon of ale left. He studied the tin steadily and realized the stub had been ripped off to make the opening a jagged crag.

When he thought through the risk of puncturing his tongue trying to siphon the last droplets of ale, he sighed, bent down, and carefully placed the can back where it was at the very top of the garbage on a slant over a banana peel and a TV dinner tray. He could feel his taste buds enlarging as he gave the tin can one last feel. He crunched the can ever so slightly to hear that punching sound he loved. Then he set the can lightly atop the banana peel.

When he rose from his bent position, he turned his head and felt a snap in his neck. Instantly, his head grew dizzy and there was a flush of pain. He became very concerned. This was more than just a tweaked neck. He could hear his blood rushing back up to his head, sounding like a drainpipe after a flushed toilet a story above. Suddenly, his vision told him that he was moving away from the garbage at an accelerated pace. But he wasn't moving. He was still close to the garbage can. Now nebulous white blotches spotted the tops of his eyes. He could not breathe. His skin color was instantly wan. The power in his legs quickly left him.

He fell face first on the hardwood floor, and everything turned dark.

When Joe awoke, his vision was fine. He rolled over on his back and turned his neck to the left. Sharp, brutal heat shot up into his head. He moaned. Grabbing the back of his neck with his left hand to hold it in motion, he realized his neck was stiff and that he had pulled a muscle in it before he fell. He looked around and saw the floor was covered in drying brownish blood. He reached with his right hand for the back of his head to feel a wound. He pinched his scalp looking for wounds where there was sharp pounding but felt nothing. He wasn't wet either. His head was certainly not lying in blood. *So where was it coming from?*

He began feeling his forehead and then his temples. He moved his fingers down his face to his nose. That was when he felt wet paint: a light glossy substance jutting from his nostrils the more he rose from the floor.

His nose was bleeding, all right. It had bled for the hour he was unconscious. The floor was drying but still wet and thickening like syrup.

When he realized his white t-shirt was saturated in bright red blood, he was certain he would die. It was the clearest, most precise understanding he had ever come to in his life. He looked at the time and it was 3:47. *I'll die around 4:00.*

Joe didn't know what to make of it. The blood kept running from his nose, and it seemed futile to try and fight it. The bleeding could not be stopped, even if he were taken to the emergency room: His liver was too damaged and he was a hemophiliac.

This is it, he thought, so terrified he was calm. He made his way to his feet while holding his neck, blood still jettisoning through his fingers, light as water now. He decided to fight anyways. It was the right thing to do; it was what humans do, what animals do. He walked through the hallway looking for the phone, wasting a half-minute before realizing they had to disconnect the landline four months ago. His cell was upstairs.

He crawled four stairs, blood quickly saturating everything he walked above. The blood was in the back of his throat now, that bitter saline taste just like metal. By the fifth step he realized he did not have the strength to walk the stairs. He held his head in his hands leaning farther and farther to the right as his neck stiffened.

He turned and made his way carefully downstairs. Panic had robbed his body and he knew he was losing strength. His vision was slowly growing lighter in color and parts of his body were checking out fast now.

He walked out to the back patio door and raised his right hand. He stumbled into the neighbor's flower garden. The sun was bright and he was blinded within seconds but still able to walk in the whiteout. He grabbed hold of a juvenile peach

104

tree plant with his right hand, holding it tenuously, his very existence to that moment contingent on the sturdiness of the balancing iron. He could hear the dirt and roots deracinating and he toppled over and was covered beneath the green, sinuous vines that formed a surrogate grave.

Had Micker noticed that the peach tree in her backyard was no longer there, she might have been prompted to walk around the backyard first. If she did, she would have been able to feel Joe's faint pulse and take action. Instead, her surroundings were all a blur to her because all she could think about was the affair and the guilt she was now feeling about it. She looked right at the backyard, but it didn't register that the tree wasn't there.

The blood greeted her at the entry. She ran around the house looking for him, sometimes slipping and falling in her father's blood. Her heart didn't seem to pulsate. It was on a long vibrating string, and she was beginning to battle nausea.

Before she figured he was in the backyard, she sensed he was dead. No one could survive that much blood loss. Droplets she hadn't seen in all the commotion sat dried by the backdoor. She saw him through the window, his head a red balloon and his now blue hands locked around green vines.

The neighbors heard the most guttural, animalistic scream. It was unmistakably human, but a sound that seemed from another world it was so bombarded by sadness and violent anger. They came running, kicking themselves for not looking out the window before, and found Micker in an emotional frenzy trying to resuscitate her father who was now long dead.

CHAPTER 15: AFTERMATH OF THE WAKE

Micker refused to have Joe's body autopsied. "He's been through enough," she said to Conrad when he mentioned it, acting as if Joe would feel the scalpel even in death. Those were the only words she spoke to Conrad in the immediate aftermath.

When the coroner explained that Joe fell in the kitchen, right before the garbage can and broke his nose, Micker discovered the beer can sitting there. It was Conrad's from the night before, and she had told him repeatedly for years that when he had a beer at night he had to throw it away in the garbage in the lock box. She had embarrassed her father one time when she discovered him cutting open an empty beer can with scissors just to lick the insides of the can. Her biggest fear was that he would slice his tongue on the can. Once he started bleeding, it took mammoth effort from doctors to make him stop. When she learned he died of a nosebleed, however, she was enraged. It seemed too strange, too wimpy a way to die. Joe had been through too much to die that way.

In her silence, Conrad knew she blamed him. As a

result, he did all the right things in the aftermath. He helped her take care of the funeral arrangements. He paid for the coffin and the suit Joe was laid out in. He paid the funeral parlor for the wake and the embalming. He even paid for the luncheon at the church after the service. With all this paying, he had dried up his savings.

Micker continued to ignore him, yet despite her silence, no one had the slightest suspicion there was tension between him and her. They stood beside each other, and she allowed him to hold and hug her during the last prayer. She had tears in her eyes during the services. They were real tears and they brought her a vulnerability no one had ever seen before. Nearly a hundred people came to pay their respects during the afternoon and evening wakes, and Conrad could guarantee some of them were there to see if she would cry or not: if Micker could show weakness. They got their visit's worth.

Conrad was careful with how he approached dealing with the death of her father. He was relieved he was gone. He didn't fight those feelings. He did, however, do as much apologizing as a person could. He knew he needed to express the most sincere regret, not just for the beer can, which he apologized for throwing in the garbage when he knew not to, but for his vehement anger toward Joe the week before. He knew she could forgive, but it had to be on her terms after a lot of groveling.

He caught her one morning as she was preparing to leave for work. He had the day off because of a storm, but still woke at the same early morning time out of habit. He waited for her to fix herself up when he went into the kitchen to find her sitting at the table in deep thought.

"Micker," he began in a much-planned way, "I just wanted to say again how sorry I am for what happened to your dad. I wish to God I could take everything I said to him that night back, but I can't. I was angry, I let my frustration at work get to me, and I took it out on him. For that I will never be forgiven. I just ask that we try to work on getting back to where we were before this happened. I love you and I'm sorry and I will do whatever I can to help you get through this."

She licked her upper lip and turned to her side. She gave him a terrible look of disgust. "Go back to bed, Conrad," she said dismissively.

"I am so sorry for what happened, Micker," he said carefully. He knew what she needed to hear. "I am so very sorry."

"Yea, you're sorry," she said lowly. Her anger evaporated in her face. She rose, and without looking at him, walked out of the house. For anyone else it was a failed effort, but Conrad knew he did just what he needed. He needed her to talk to him, to say something in acknowledgment that he was living. Once she did that, he knew she would slowly rebuild their relationship. Such spouts of disappointment were common with Micker, and Conrad knew the anecdote was admitting guilt and asking for remorse. Once she spoke, her words were a symbol the healing was beginning.

That day she began asking him questions, still with reservations, and within two weeks they were back to normal. While not surprised she granted him penance, he was considerably taken aback at how fast she appeared to get over her father's death. There seemed to be a relief in his departure.

Perhaps she didn't miss him as much as he thought.

CHAPTER 16: THE CONFRONTATION

Bran continued to check his email during his lunch. For three weeks after Joe's death, he had been emailing and texting Micker, and not once did she respond to him. For the first week, he assumed Micker was shutting off the world as some people do when they lose a loved one. In consideration, he tried reaching out to her every other day. It was during the second week after Joe's death when she returned to work that he began to realize something was wrong. Because their schedules were completely different and neither of them had free time together, Bran was constantly trying to find ways to meet up with her in the hallways at Walker's. Everything he tried, arriving early, leaving late, walking by the conference rooms where the lawyers met, had failed. He never had a moment's time with her, and it was killing him.

By the third week, the paranoia, the not knowing, the wondering what she was doing was driving him crazy.

He needed to talk to her. It didn't matter what he did; he needed to talk to her and end the silence.

He had his secretary tell the members of the meeting

that he would be late because he had an emergency call. He found that saying you had an emergency call could get you out of anything without any worry of repercussion.

He walked down to her office. It was something he agreed never to do, but he had to see her. He tiptoed down the hallway. Her office door was open. She wasn't even working. She was just staring.

He entered the doorway. At first she thought it was Conrad. She looked behind him to make sure no one had seen him then treated him to a cold, biting stare.

"Come with me. I need to talk to you," he said.

Bran had asked Micker to walk down to the auditorium with him. The walls in her office were thin and he knew nobody was occupying the auditorium. She obliged, but he was certain now she was deeply disappointed in something he did.

She walked into the auditorium first and switched on the lights, each one flickering on and lighting the enormous room that had stadium seating. She walked quickly down toward the stage, looking behind it, then to the exits to make sure no one was there. They were alone by all accounts. She marched back up one of the aisles and said very sternly, "This is highly inappropriate! Do you not have a meeting right now?"

"I told them I had an emergency call. I have about twenty minutes."

"You have got to be kidding me," she said meanly, her lower teeth showing.

"Wait a minute," he said with equal aggression. "You have not returned a single email or text of mine in three weeks! Don't you think I have a right to know why?"

"My father died three weeks ago," she said scornfully. "And he died of a nose bleed." Her words echoed a bit in the auditorium. "Of a nose bleed! I cannot fathom that. A

110

nosebleed as an exit. A man who suffered and fought and battled a terrible disease and failed and got back up and failed and then doesn't even die of the disease? He dies of a freak accident where he gets a nose bleed? What a sissy way to die! What a cowardly thing not to die of the disease you go to war with everyday. It's like a terminally ill cancer patient dying from a bee sting."

"And this is why you haven't returned my calls?"

"I was with *you* when he fell. I was with *you* when the blood started pouring from his nose. I was with *you* when he tried to walk up the stairs to get to the phone. I was with *you* when he fell in a garden and died lying in dirt. I was with *you* – cheating on my husband!" Her words reverberated around the room, her voice, so intimidating. He wondered how clients survived that voice, the fear it spit.

"I don't understand this other than emotional angst causing you to say irrational things," he said. "Even if that's not the case, how could you hold such a circumstance against me?"

She stared at him. Bran wanted to move out of the darkness at the back of the auditorium and into the light, but something about her anger told him to stay put. She was standing near the stage. He was standing at the top looking down at her. The distance between them at that moment was about forty feet. Figuratively, it was much further.

"This cannot work."

He stepped in. "Yes it can. Stop treating me like you don't know me and think of all the time we have spent together in our lives. All the good times."

"You have compromised my life."

"Open your eyes, Micker! We compromised ourselves years ago when we were too stupid to realize we should have been together then. We have to stop playing games with each other and just do what feels right." He looked wildly around the

111

room, his eyes about to rage. "Let's just get out of here!"

She shuddered as his words reverberated around the room. "We can't."

"We could have a divorce finalized in a month. We – we could be on our way by Christmas."

"Where do you want to go?"

"Anywhere. Go East."

"We can't go East. We've got our jobs here."

"We'll leave them behind with everything else." His stare configured powerfully on the dappled gold and yellow carpet. He was now speaking powerfully. "We'll find us a white house in the suburbs. No noise or traffic. No ocean in our backyard. Just make a clean break. We'll be somewhere where it actually rains – where it snows and where the leaves fall and winter isn't just a week where summer takes a break."

"You're talking crazy."

"Let's actually go to a place where we can see trees grow. Hell, let's see what a drought feels like, or what it's like to be snowed in or flooded out." Desperation was alive in his face. "Let's just go!" he screamed. "I love you! I don't – life is too short and unpredictable not to do all that you can to capture what you love. I'm tired of feeling like a prisoner in that motel room. I don't want to hide anymore when I'm around you. We haven't been to a dinner on our own or seen a movie together. I don't want to live like that. I *can't* live like that. I need to get out of here."

She stared back silently. "I'm pregnant," she said, the last consonant trembling off. She studied him prudently. His hips moved slightly around, and his eyes seemed to get darker.

"You're pregnant?"

She sat down in one of the seats. The weight of façade seemed to fall from her shoulders. She spoke softly and directly. "You're the first one I've told. I found out yesterday."

112

"It's mine," he blurted with raw confidence.

His arrogance angered her and led her to do something that she did from time to time when she could. "No," she said with a subtle smirk. She liked to toy with him.

"It has to be mine."

She shook her head.

"It's his?"

She had him now. She wanted him to feel some pain. "Who else's would it be?" she asked unfeelingly.

"I thought you didn't like him anymore."

"No," she said.

Bran began biting his thumb. "What's this mean then?"

The façade broke. The reality of the situation was beyond childish mind games.

She shook her head disapprovingly. "I have to get back." She began walking past him for the exit.

He stood up and asked, "Are we going to meet on Wednesday?"

She calmly ran her hands through the sides of her auburn hair, and without turning to face him, said, "Let's take a breather for a while." She then walked out, the door thudding behind her and echoing in the auditorium.

Bran was shocked. For the first time in a long time, he had no control. She had done this to him the last time. Everything was going well, and then, unexpectedly, she pulled the plug.

His face wrestled back anger. He wanted to go after her, but he thought it better to give her space. He didn't want her to think she had that much of an effect on him. His anger, instead, started to direct itself toward Conrad. *He is the real reason*, Bran thought, *that I can't have her.*

That night, Micker sat on the bed listening to sounds of

Conrad's obstructed wails from breathing through the bend in his nose. It went on for hours. She didn't know what to do. She wanted to wake him and tell him the good news, but she wasn't sure it was good news. She didn't know who the father was. She kept thinking about it, but there was no way of her knowing. It was the one time in her life when she was disorganized.

She sat there for an hour, two hours, never moving. Guilt had come upon her now, a feeling she never had during the affair. And fear. Guilt and fear were walling her in. What if the child was Bran's? What if Bran told people? Thoughts of not having the child came to mind, but she quickly suppressed them. That was an anathema to her.

She walked into the bathroom and stared at her complexion. She was disgusted by herself. She ran her fingers through her auburn hair. Strands came off in her fingers. She needed a change. She grabbed a dyeing kit from below the sink. It was black dye. She stared at herself in the mirror. Her auburn hair looked wilted and faded. She clogged the drain, ran the faucet, wet her hair by submersing her head halfway, and began applying the dye chaotically all over her hair with both hands.

Conrad awoke to the sound of splashing water. He knew Micker was dyeing her hair again. It was the third time in six months. He was worried about her.

For the first time in his marriage, he was starting to feel like his wife might be losing it.

CHAPTER 17: MURDER IN THE FARALLONES

The next morning, Conrad awoke to a call from Brosnan asking him to come in again. Apparently he wasn't hitting his quotas, and Gilbert Hall had ordered Brosnan to call his subordinates and implore them to put in the extra hours.

Conrad had a bad headache. He didn't say much and didn't notice much.

Micker wasn't in bed as he dressed.

He found her sitting in the kitchen staring out the window at the Ferris wheel. Her hair was raven black. He had forgotten she had dyed it.

His eyes grew large, and she noticed. "Thanks," she said.

"I like it. I just didn't expect it," he said. "Do you think it's okay if you dye this much? Will your clients say anything?"

"I don't care what they think," she answered.

"Okay," he said. "I do like it."

She didn't react. Dark circles hid under her eyes. She clutched a cup of coffee.

"Did you sleep at all?"

"A little," she said, but he sensed that was a lie.

"What's the matter?"

"Nothing," she replied.

He noticed her voice sounding groggier than his.

"Back to work again?" she asked.

"Yea. Should only be a few hours." He studied her face. She seemed in a bit of a daze, and he could see that there was no coffee in the coffee cup she clutched. *Odd*, he thought.

As he walked out, she said, "Happy birthday."

He peeked his head in and smiled. "I forgot," he admitted. "It's Halloween."

She smiled at his forgetfulness.

There was a sharp ugliness in everything at Walker's harbor. The sky was overcast and the sea was gray. The green trees from the beach were dark and the sand was the color of dirt.

"Can't believe he made us come in on a Sunday, on Halloween," said Paul Snaley, another fisherman who happened to be the youngest on the dock at twenty. No one seemed to like Snaley much because his youth made the rest of the fishermen feel inferior. But Conrad hit it off with him, largely because he was new too.

"Some guys aren't hittin' their quotas," Brosnan said.

"If we had known about this, we would have saved the drinks for your birthday tonight," Snaley told Conrad.

"Snaley," Conrad said, "you're not old enough to drink."

Snaley's eyebrows flexed and he smiled wryly.

"And you won't be," Conrad warned.

Snaley placed his hand on Conrad's shoulder. "You're a good Dad."

"Man, you don't look twenty," Brosnan said, referring

116

to Snaley's mature build and look. Snaley was a good-looking, blonde-haired and blue-eyed guy, and Brosnan and Conrad often joked they were following a celebrity around the way women followed him with their eyes.

The three of them stood on the pier, ready to take their boats out, when red and blue police lights spiraled into the air behind the dock. "What's up with the police car?" Conrad asked. Another police car strolled in right after. "Now two of them."

"Didn't you hear what happened in the Farallon Islands?" Brosnan asked.

"What?"

Brosnan's eyes grew large as he spoke slowly. "Some scientists had a fake seal tied to a boat with a camera strapped to the bottom of it. They were doing a study on great whites. Well, one of the sharks took the seal and the camera to the bottom and rammed into a shark cage down there. Inside the cage they found a young couple inside, drowned thirty years ago." Brosnan shook his head as if it pained him to tell the story. "The police made them search the entirety of the islands' shores, and they found four more cages with the skeletons still in them. They were all foreigners and none of them had wallets or ID on them."

Snaley looked stunned. Conrad turned away. He hated hearing about great white sharks, but living in the Red Triangle forced him to deal with the fact that they were going to be mentioned from time to time.

"What's all that mean?" Snaley asked.

Brosnan gave a clever smile. "Seems a shark fisherman from around here awhile back was luring tourists to his shark cage and —"

"People want to go down there in the cages?" asked Snaley.

"Sure they do. They see it on TV. Not terribly tough. If they can handle an oxygen tank and the fisherman has a large enough cage, it's a pretty simple procedure. I get asked all the time about it. Those sharks don't want to attack people. They could tear those cages apart if they wanted too. Snaley, you said you saw one two weeks ago."

"Size of a whale," Snaley interjected.

"And teeth as long as your hand and sharper than a butcher's knife. I remember seein' an elephant seal out there floating around by the buoys, and it had two of what looked like clear white knives stuck in it. They could belong to only one creature: the great white. They say you could shave yourself clean with one of its teeth. You ever see one, Conrad?" Brosnan asked, and he immediately turned red. "Conrad, that — that was stupid of me. I'm sorry."

"No, it's fine."

Snaley was confused. He had never heard of the Mayday attack. "What?" he asked. "What's wrong?"

Brosnan waved him off, a signal of shut the hell up and I'll tell you later. "Conrad, are you sure you're okay?"

Conrad needed to get over it. "I won't be if you don't finish the story."

Brosnan smiled at him.

"So, what was the shark fisherman doing then?" Snaley asked.

Brosnan looked to Conrad to see if he should continue. Conrad gave him the nod. "Robbing them," Brosnan said directly. "Before the tourists get in the cage, they leave their personal belongings on board: their wallet, purse, so they don't get wet. This guy must have been dropping the wire that holds the cage to the stern. He probably waited until he saw the first fin, and then cut the line. I'll bet he did this on a foggy day. There is usually at least one scientist on the island every day. But
118

if it's foggy, you can't see a thing from the island."

"So he sank their cages and left them?" Snaley asked.

"Let it sink to the bottom four hundred yards out."

"And every cage…"

"Call them caskets now."

"They just stayed in it? They didn't try to swim to shore?" Snaley looked surprised. He had thought of something. "The cage fell on its side, trapping them in. That's why, right?"

"No," Brosnan said. "In fact, the cages landed with the door either open from the side or from the top, inviting them to swim free."

Snaley was in disbelief. "You're tellin' me all these people decided it was better to let their oxygen tanks run out so they would drown rather than take their chances with the sharks."

"You ever hear of rivers in Africa that are so dangerous that some scientists say you actually would have no chance of survival trying to swim across them?"

"Because of Crocodiles?"

"Yea. That's what it's like in the Red Triangle, especially out at a place like the Farallon Islands. There are thousands of seals out there. Great whites just prowl the islands continuously every day. It's like a continuous dinner bell. You don't want to swim in those waters. You try it, and you're not coming back. Those people knew that. They weighed their decision. They probably made the right one."

"I couldn't imagine being eaten alive," Snaley said.

Conrad had had enough. He headed for his boat.

Brosnan took Snaley by the shoulder. "We need to have a town history lesson."

As Conrad proceeded up the pier, he noticed a man standing by his trawler. He slowed his walk until he recognized the broad-shouldered man.

119

It was Bran. He had his hands in his pockets and his shoulders projecting out boldly. His hair was blowing in the wind. "I hoped I'd catch you before you went out."

Conrad couldn't put his finger on it, but Bran didn't seem himself. He looked angrier than usual. In the years Conrad had known him, he was always impressed with how well Bran hid his temper. Conrad had seen it unleashed during tennis matches, and it was scary.

"What brings you here on the weekend?"

"Stopped down to see my father. I figured while I was here, I'd ask to see if you wanted to play again. Say, today after work?"

Conrad didn't want to. He figured he would lose again, and losing ate at him, but he had the intuition that if he declined, Bran would not take it well. Bran might call him out about his knee, or worse, insult him. "Sure."

"Racquetball this time," Bran demanded.

"Racquetball?"

Bran started walking away. "We'll mix it up," he said without turning back.

Then Conrad remembered. "Bran, it's my birthday."

Bran stopped and turned around. His tongue was pressed into his cheek like he was irritated.

"Micker and I were gonna have dinner."

Bran approached him. Conrad observed how imposing he was. Bran didn't seem to understand the problem.

"We'll only be an hour. Less than that if I'm on."

Conrad couldn't believe he was insisting on playing. "Okay," he said, but Bran had already turned and headed down the pier.

Something was wrong. As big a jerk as he thought Bran was, Bran often concealed it for the sake of propriety. He didn't this time.

120

CHAPTER 18: CONRAD'S BIRTHDAY

When Conrad came home to change his clothes, Micker was unusually concerned about him playing Bran in racquetball. She had a birthday cake waiting for him and a bottle of wine. She was about to put some lamb chops on the grill, Conrad's favorite meal.

When he came downstairs in shorts and a t-shirt, Micker started kissing him. "Don't go. It's your birthday," she said.

Conrad didn't kiss back. "I'll only be gone an hour," he said, and made his way past her for the door.

"It's your birthday, ya' know."

He turned and faced her, putting on a navy blue Nike hat. "I'll only be gone an hour."

Micker sensed something was wrong. It was unusual for Bran to visit Conrad at his job and then ask him to give up time on his birthday to play racquetball. She thought of calling Bran to find out what was up, but she didn't. She wanted to keep him at as much a distance as possible.

Bran was never late to things, but when Conrad arrived

at the racquetball courts, Bran wasn't there. For fifteen minutes Conrad sat outside the walls in the back of the gym, listening to the popping sound of shots ricocheting around the walls. Eventually, he decided to warm up.

Conrad didn't really like racquetball. He thought of it as a personalized version of tennis. Instead of outside, you were inside. Instead of across the net, your opponent was next to you. Instead of lines judges, you were the judge. And there weren't any boundaries. You were in a box with your enemy. It was the most primitive of racquet sports.

Conrad didn't enjoy playing Bran at racquetball. Granted he had an advantage over Bran because he was lefty, and his record in racquetball against Bran was better than his record against him in tennis, but Bran had a way of intimidating him almost into submission. When Bran started losing, he became loud and obnoxious. Sometimes he would chastise Conrad, and when he was really losing, he would sometimes try to hit Conrad with the ball. The other thing that Conrad hated was how Bran controlled the center of the court. With other players, Conrad could find ways to dictate from that part of the court, but Bran was too big and too strong. Opponents, no matter how big they were, always capitulated to Bran.

The good news was that if Bran started a tirade or if he started dominating Conrad, Conrad had the excuse to leave early. It was his birthday, after all.

Conrad heard a thud in the hallway outside. Seconds later, Bran peeked his head through the door, his goggles on and his racquet in hand, held like a spear. The match was on.

Things could not have gone more perfectly for Conrad. Up 15-5 and leading 13-9 in the second game, it all seemed to come too easy. It was the best he remembered playing competitively in any sport in a long, long time.

122

In the time off since he last played racquetball, Bran looked shabby and mechanical. His kill shots were popping off the floor and his four attempts to utilize the back wall failed so miserably that Conrad wondered how he lost to him before.

Conrad made sure to keep the points short and sweet. Bran was the type of player who thrived off of long points that conflated his rhythm and timing. He also thrived off of anger, and Conrad, while refusing to give up space in the center of the court despite two collisions into Bran's brawny shoulders, made sure to compliment Bran's winning shots. He also made sure to stay humble when he hit a great shot. "Lucky shot," he'd say demurely.

"Unbelievable!" Bran griped as his backhand return off of Conrad's tricky lefty serve didn't even make the front wall. "I'm playing like a frickin' twelve year old girl!" he whined.

Conrad finally had it. Match point.

He was nervous now. He needed to play aggressively, but his mind was telling him to play it safe. *Bran is self-destructing,* he thought, *so let him self-destruct.* Conrad decided to do what he had done the whole match. He served with a safe margin of error into Bran's weaker backhand side. The serve felt good when it left the front wall. Conrad peeked back and saw it hug the wall, forcing Bran deep into the corner. Conrad expected to be shaking hands soon.

Whap! From an improbable position off his back foot, Bran rocketed a kill shot with a single fluid wrist snap into the corner. Conrad was stunned.

Bran moved confidently for the first time to the service line. "10-14," he announced. He crushed his serve and it died off the wall.

"11-14," he announced energetically, but he was still shaking his head in disappointment that he was even at this stage. It made Conrad fear the inevitable. It was no longer his match to win.

Another powerful serve, this time directed into the opposite corner. Conrad couldn't control it.

12-14, and then it became 13-14 with another service ace.

Conrad just needed to get the return in play. He was terrified now. *Watch the ball,* he thought to himself. Bran set his feet, dropped the ball and then unleashed the hardest serve Conrad had ever seen. It sounded like a gun going off, and it came right for Conrad's stomach. With a single quick reflex, Conrad stuck his racquet out defensively, and the ball bounced off of it and fortuitously landed against the ceiling, forcing Bran to retreat and start a rally. It was just the luck Conrad needed. Now the war could begin.

Bran whipped him all around the court, belting ferocious forehands crosscourt into Conrad's backhand. But Conrad kept his composure, returning each of them high on the ceiling, disallowing Bran a kill position. When Bran mistimed a forehand and it softly left the front wall, Conrad knew his time had come.

He stepped into the court and seized control. Moving Bran side to side like a marionette, he could hear Bran's panting. He was out of shape, and the longer the rally could go, the better chance Conrad had of winning the point. But something came over him this time. He had always played it safe, and where had it taken him? He could hit shots safely like this all day, but he knew it wasn't going to get him the win.

As the two traded positions in the court almost poetically like theater actors, Conrad could see a faint spark in Bran's eyes. He was waiting to come alive. Conrad decided to go for it. He uncharacteristically waited for Bran's return to drop off the back wall. Conrad set his feet, kept his eye on the ball, and waited for it nearly to drop. Then he stepped in and

124

blasted it.

The ball never bounced again on that point. It drew a straight line all the way back to Bran's foot.

Conrad saw the spark retreat entirely. Sweating profusely and struggling to breathe, Bran's eyes were activated by fear. He was tired suddenly, and he knew fatigue was the biggest enemy of the mind. It stopped you from caring about losing. And that's where he was.

Bran picked up the ball at his feet, and when Conrad asked for it, Bran petulantly tossed it at his knees. Conrad couldn't control it and had to run across the court to retrieve it. Bran offered no apology.

Conrad had a surge of confidence now. He knew the match was his. His first serve was one of his better ones. Bran couldn't get to it.

"Short," Bran said.

Conrad looked at him oddly. "Short?"

They both knew the serve was good.

Bran tried to stare him down. "It was short!"

Conrad smiled. He didn't even care at this point. "Match point, second serve," he announced. He decided to direct his serve into Bran's forehand side. If he served it accurately enough and powerfully enough, it would catch Bran off guard. He knew Bran wasn't expecting it.

Why not? Conrad asked himself. Bran knew where it was headed, but his body was leaning the wrong way, and there was no way he could get there in time. He felt helpless. After the second bounce, Conrad pumped his fist.

"Good match," Conrad said, moving toward him to shake hands. But Bran took a step back, like he was going to return serve.

"Let's go again," he demanded.

"Nah, I have to get back. Micker is cooking dinner."

125

"One more game."

Conrad was anxious now. He wanted to get out of there. "We'll play next week."

Conrad took a step forward, and Bran took a step toward the door. Bran was standing in front of it.

Bran smiled. "Come on," he said. "Just one more game."

"I can't."

"Fine, to seven."

"No."

"A game to seven."

Conrad tried to reason with him. "Bran, it's my birthday, man."

Bran didn't react or say anything. He just stared.

"Come on, we're adults here, right?" Conrad said.

"Game to seven."

Conrad was astonished. "No," he said more forcefully and moved toward the door.

"Don't be a woman," Bran said.

Conrad had had enough. He reached for the latch on the door, but Bran stood in front of it. When Conrad attempted to move him gently with his arm, Bran wound up and punched him square in the face with his left fist. They both heard bones breaking.

Conrad caught gushing blood with his hands. He grew dizzy and fell back against the wall. Once Bran saw the blood, his rage grew stronger.

He gave Conrad a roundhouse left in the temple. Conrad's vision went blue. Unable to see where the punches were coming from, Conrad kept his palms shoulder height as Bran kept pounding his face, each roundhouse taking bones to new extremities. Conrad fell to the ground. He was knocked unconscious.

126

Bran stood there, examining him. Conrad didn't even seem to be breathing. Bran grew anxious. He wondered just how badly he had beaten him. He listened for sound in the other courts. There was nothing. He needed to leave and gather his thoughts. It was starting to seep in what he had done.

There was no one in the gym when Conrad limped out an hour later. The blood on his shirt was bright purple. He knew he was badly injured.

He sat in his car, grimacing while trying to close the door. He looked in the rearview mirror reluctantly. His face resembled a rotted white apple. Big blotches of brown and what looked like rubbed black mascara aligned his eyes. His nose was splintered, and a huge dent was visible in his forehead and left cheekbone. Worst of all, he was embarrassed. He didn't even get a swing off. He was clobbered, bullied. He didn't know what to tell Micker, and the last thing he would do was go to the hospital where he would have to admit that he nearly had the life kicked out of him.

He drove slowly out of the parking lot with just his left hand. He was fine for the first hundred yards until his body grabbed hold of nausea. He became lightheaded, his brain very much so turning out the lights. Despite the steering wheel leaning to the right, staying on the road no longer seemed of crucial matter, and with no guardrail, he slowly descended a steep hill.

A huge oak tree stood at the hill's end, and before his car slammed into it, the airbag ejected, becoming a flower and covering his face.

Micker sat at the kitchen table, absorbing the pink walls with her eyes. She blew out the candles she had lit, put the lamb in foil and shoved it in the refrigerator.

127

She had spent hours fixing herself up; she adorned a lime green top and skirt with round gold earrings. In her mind she looked exquisite, and Conrad wasn't here to see it. She was irritated at first when he didn't answer her calls. Now she was just concerned. She wasn't sure if Bran would say something to him about them.

The backdoor thudded closed. Micker froze. She heard barking from the dog next door.

She heard footsteps. Someone was in her house. She hid behind the wall in the kitchen. Someone was searching for her, moving in and out of the rooms. She grabbed a butcher's knife and held it out forcefully in front of her. She looked out the window. No car was in the driveway. She looked down the street. A red Acura hugged the side of the road.

Bran showed in the kitchen light. She gasped.

"What are you doing here!" she screamed, setting the knife down. "Are you out of your mind sneaking in like that!"

Bran didn't budge. He looked battered emotionally, a nervous wreck. "I need to talk to you."

"What's wrong? Where's Conrad?"

"I don't know," he said.

She didn't believe that. "Did you say something to him about us?"

"No, I swear," Bran answered.

"Then where is he?"

Bran held her shoulders. "Leave with me – tonight."

She was frightened by the activity in his eyes. "Where are you going?"

"New York." He watched her expression carefully.

She grew pale.

"I can't live here knowing I can't have you," he said.

"What about Marjorie? Your job?"

"Everything is planned out. Trust me."

128

It was too much. "Just go, Bran," she said. "Just go. I can't – I'm married, I'm going to have a child –"

"My child."

She looked at him fiercely. "It's Conrad's."

"I don't believe you."

She looked into his eyes and saw that he believed it was his. She clenched the top of her raven hair. "This is a nightmare," she said. "What have I done to my life!"

"I'm leaving, tonight!" he shouted. "I have everything packed. Marjorie's already wondering where I am. The only time I'll ever contact her again is with the divorce. I quit my job today."

She was shocked. "You what?"

"It's a clean break. I've done my part."

"This is crazy. Bran, you'll ruin your life if you do this."

His hands were shaking. She'd never seen him this nervous before. "I'll be fine. You know I will. I know it's drastic and a little crazy, but that's why it feels right. Leave with me, tonight, right now."

She dropped her head and tears fell on her lime skirt. "I'm sorry, but no."

She had said it in such a definitive way that he couldn't reply. He closed his eyes and walked toward her. He stood in front of her as she bowed her head. He knew she had made up her mind. He lifted his hands and applied them to her shoulders. He whispered to her: "There will come a time down the road where we will speak again. And I promise you I will have things figured out." She looked up at him. She still loved him. He moved past her and walked out the back door, slamming his hand in frustration against the wall on his way out.

Micker watched him leave, hoping it wasn't for the last time.

She didn't have time to think about it though. Her

129

phone vibrated. It was an unidentified caller.

She answered.

"Mrs. Mayday?"

"Yes?"

"Your husband was in a car accident this evening."

Her hand, still clenching the phone, dropped to her side. The nightmare was only beginning.

CHAPTER 19: REPAIR

Micker visited Conrad at the hospital every day that week. He was projected to stay there for a month depending on how quickly his injuries healed. He had a broken nose, a broken cheekbone, a shattered kneecap, a broken hand, and a concussion. Worst of all, his right lung was punctured and filled with fluid. The doctors said he could have drowned if he wasn't rescued sooner.

"I just lost the car," Conrad told the doctors and police officers when he was conscious. At first they believed him, and he was stunned by their quick reliance. But then some of the doctors began to suggest that the wounds were more consistent with patients suffering from battery. The police questioned him about it, but Conrad stayed steadfast with his story. When one doctor explained that the injuries Conrad sustained could have come from his car accident, the police seemed to close the case. They weren't going to waste their time and energy on making a case for battery when the patient denied it and there were no witnesses.

Micker, however, didn't buy it. She thought Bran had

something to do with it, and her biggest concern was that Bran might have told Conrad about their affair.

She shot up to the hospital one day after work. Conrad's pain medications were wearing off, and it was the most aware she had seen him since the accident.

She sat next to him, waiting for the nurses to leave before engaging him. "You're lucky to be alive, you know that?"

He pulled at the bandages that wrapped his cheek. "What's it look like?"

She smiled. "How can I see?"

"Stupid question."

She smiled again. "It's your lung right now that you need to be worried about. It collapsed, and you're going to need surgery."

He looked away hopelessly. "Scars?" he asked, pointing to his face.

"I don't know." She felt she had her opening. "You must have slammed your face pretty hard in that crash to break your nose and cheekbone."

He didn't answer.

"You've never lost control of a car before. Tell me what happened."

"I already have."

"So you were coming home from racquetball…"

He turned and faced the window.

"I never asked you how racquetball went," she said.

"Fine," he muttered.

"You know, nobody has seen Bran since you last saw him. He served Marjorie divorce papers, quit his job. Everyone's saying he had a meltdown. We know he's in New York somewhere, but that's about it. Did he say anything to you? Give you any clue this was going to happen?"

"No."

132

"You don't know anything? Marjorie's really hurting."

"If anyone would know anything about him, it would be you," he said.

Micker wasn't sure what he meant by that comment. Before she could ask him to clarify, the nurses came to change his sheets. Micker told him she would be back, but Conrad was unresponsive.

Micker never came back. She left the hospital and sat in the car, her fingers servicing her temples. She still hadn't mentioned to him that she was pregnant. She couldn't understand her reluctance to tell him, but she thought it was a sign she shouldn't have this child. It could be illegitimate, and that was something she felt she couldn't live with. If she didn't have it, she would never have to know. She could start all over.

Conrad would never know I was pregnant, she thought. *It would be like it never happened.*

All of the sudden she felt she couldn't catch her breath and began shivering from nervous jitters. *Am I really going to do this?* she kept asking herself. *Is this who I am?*

She began recalling her days at Berkeley. She was the only girl in her women's rights class of sixty-five students that was pro-life. It had been drilled into her at an early age that abortion was murder. Her father always stressed that the child could be put up for adoption. In his eyes the measure of a human being was accorded to how one described the procedure: was it the murder of a child or the termination of a fetus? For Micker, it was irredeemable murder.

Micker could feel the chunks rising in her throat. She opened her car door, threw on a pair of sunglasses to hide her face, and walked quickly back into the hospital. She headed for the bathroom.

Once she entered a stall, she lost all control.

Micker locked the stall door and lay there. Everything in her life was falling apart.

When she regained her strength, she opened the stall door and stood before the mirror above the sink. She looked at herself in the mirror below a dimly lit yellow light. Her sunglasses were stained by the food particles that shot back at her face. She took them off, and suddenly, the bathroom was bright. There were accented pores in her cheeks that weren't there before. She attributed them to stress. Her eyes drooped lifelessly into the sink, down to her belly. She rubbed it. The baby was growing inside of her now.

She began to think of scenarios that could be worse than having an illegitimate child. *I could be paralyzed*, she thought, *or blind, deaf, indigent, or an orph...* but she realized she was an orphan. That had never struck her before. She had no parents.

The decision was finalized as she stared at herself in the mirror. The child was hers and she would have it. It grew inside her and depended upon her. Right there she built the resolution to bear it, whether it was Conrad's or Bran's. And she swore to herself that she would never try to find out.

CHAPTER 20: RETURNING HOME

They didn't speak much in the car. Except for his grimaces and her subsequent apologies when she hit potholes, Conrad and Micker didn't settle on typical conversation when someone comes home after three weeks in a hospital. Both were about to change their environments, to interrupt newly adjusted routines. Time had come for them to face reality.

A two-story yellow house on the hill had its bushes dressed in blue and white Christmas lights. Micker pulled into the driveway. Conrad was stunned to learn it was his until he noticed the Ferris wheel arched over the roof of the house.

Micker drove into the garage. Conrad looked over at her. He realized she had adjusted to life without him and was nervous for his return. Her hair was also different. It looked almost white when the streetlights fell through the windows and shone on it.

"You dyed your hair again?" he asked.

"Platinum blonde this time," she said while running her fingers through it. "Are you okay with your crutches?" she asked.

"I'm fine." His mouth barely opened when he spoke. A single white patch was still applied to his left cheekbone.

She helped him up the narrow stairs in the basement by holding his back from behind. He struggled for the first two steps, trying to remember to put the crutches down on the desired step after stepping.

They made their way into the pink kitchen. It looked smaller than before. He sat himself at the table facing the window where the Ferris wheel's lights soared in the sky and illuminated the clouds. He set down on the table a plastic bag of painkillers and antibiotics, along with his instructions for usage.

Conrad had heard an unusual rumor about Micker, and he wanted to clear it up first thing once they got settled in the house. "What's this I hear you've bought a boat? Tell me this isn't true."

She wasn't expecting that question just yet. "I did."

"Micker?"

"The firm bought it for me. You know how I used to sail with my dad when I was a kid. It is something to remember him by. Besides, I need a hobby."

He was disappointed. "What kind of boat?"

"A small sailboat."

He shook his head disapprovingly. "They're dangerous."

"I'm careful."

"That doesn't always matter."

"I can handle myself on the water. I know where to sail and when to sail." That was true. Micker had about as much experience sailing as anyone Conrad had ever known. It was an odd hobby for her to take up when she was younger, given that she was a girl. But she didn't care. She enjoyed contradicting people.

"What are we gonna do about the hospital bills?" he

136

finally asked.

She readied herself in her chair. "I checked. You are not covered by my insurance."

"So..."

"We're in trouble."

"How much trouble?"

"With the surgery on your cheek and nose, and the water they drained from your lungs. Plus a three week stay...twenty thousand, give or take."

"Twenty thousand! How are we going to pay that?"

She sighed. "I don't know."

"Why did you make them have surgery on my face?"

"Your cheek was falling out of your face! It was your accident, right?"

Conrad grew white. He touched his cheek and felt the scars that were left. "What about work?"

"He wants you back when you heal. You don't have worker's comp. Then there's the car situation."

"It's totaled?"

"It's totaled."

"Don't fix it. I'll do the bus for a while."

"I already sent it to get fixed."

Conrad stroked his face in distress. "This is a nightmare."

"You need to have a car. The bus stop is a mile in town."

"How much for the car to be repaired?"

"I don't know yet."

"What did they estimate?"

"Five thousand, probably more. I'm off for Christmas soon. Hopefully you'll be better by then and we can get you back to work. I can drive you till then."

"How long's your vacation?"

"I'm taking two weeks. Only thing is the student loans. I just paid the mortgage for October. Now we owe November and December's. The neighbor's offered to loan some money when I told them about the hospital bills. Maybe we could pay the November and December mortgage with it before the grace period. We have to get caught up on the mortgages. We're incurring outrageous fees…in the thousands. I've had collectors calling the house every day. Our credit is getting killed."

"How do we catch up from all this?"

"We can do it. We will take it one step at a time. First, we will start with our spending."

"We were already cutting back on our spending."

"There's another thing…" she felt this was the time to say it.

"What?"

She was out with it quicker than she anticipated. "I'm pregnant."

Conrad stared at her long and hard — he could not register what to say. She tried to smile.

"You're kidding."

Creases showed in her forehead. She didn't expect this type of response. "I want a baby."

"Yea, I do too, but not now," he said. "Micker, listen to me, not now."

"I'm already halfway through the first trimester."

"How can we raise a child in this environment?"

"We can do it," she said in her convincing nature. "I am ready to be a mother." Her blonde hair radiated under the ceiling lamp.

He could already see a fight he could not win.

CHAPTER 21: TENSION

Conrad tried to sleep that night on the couch in the living room, but it wouldn't take. His biggest problem was that he had to sleep on his back because of his cheek and his nose splint, and he was used to sleeping on his stomach. Furthermore, he couldn't even rest on his side or else he would do further damage to his face. He tossed and turned all night, trying his best to feel comfortable, but nothing worked.

Eventually Conrad gave up trying to sleep altogether. He turned on a lamp and sat up, letting his mind wander. He couldn't believe he was going to have a child. He didn't feel ready to be a father. What was bothering him more was the thought of Bran. He was still trying to figure out why Bran beat him up at the racquetball courts. It wasn't just because of a loss. It had to be something more.

His knee started to throb, but he didn't want to take the painkillers. They made him drowsy, and he needed to keep thinking clearly. He took the pain.

Donny Locks' comment started whirling around his brain. *You're wife is Bran Hall's.* What did Locks perceive that

Conrad didn't? Why were there always those pesky rumors about Bran and Micker that never died? Before the hospital, he was starting to suspect something might be going on between the two of them. Maybe Bran couldn't stand the thought that Conrad was with Micker and not him and lost it. There had to be a reason for it.

But what if they were having an affair? And then he finally happened upon a thought that struck his core: What if it weren't his child?

He got up, using his crutches carelessly, and walked quickly to the sink. He felt immediate revulsion. He needed to vomit. Moving too quickly past the kitchen table, he caught his right crutch on one of the chairs and lost control. The crutches both went flying across the floor. He fell face first, blocking his broken hand from further damage by stopping the fall with his shoulder. The thud was sickening and it travelled throughout the house.

He looked around the kitchen helplessly at his situation. He started crying.

Micker heard the thud and descended the stairs slowly. He tried to halt the tears. He didn't want her to see him like this.

"Conrad? Are you okay?" She saw him lying there. "Oh my God, what happened?"

He didn't even know where to begin. She knelt beside him and checked his face and his knee. Her white, silk sleeping gown let off the smell of lilacs.

"It doesn't look like you injured anything." She began collecting his crutches. "What were you trying to do?"

"Getting a drink of water."

Conrad sat up and slid his body to the counter and lay against it.

"I told you to call up to me or text me. My phone's

140

on."

She poured a glass of water.

He couldn't hold on any longer. "Is it mine?" he asked. She turned and gauchely dropped the glass. The water spread out over the floor like a cloud, soaking Conrad's feet. The glass, however, won the battle with the floor. As flimsy as it looked, it came away with only a crack. Micker retrieved it and stared at it in amazement.

"Please tell me the truth."

"Of course it's yours," she replied, but she didn't look him in the eyes.

"I never ask you these things," he began, taking a soft breath, "I never challenge you on them. But I have always wanted to. I think I was scared to know the truth, so I just ignored it. I've always ignored things."

"What, Conrad? What is it?" she asked, trying to take charge of the situation. "What have you ignored?"

His voice trembled. "Did you have an affair with Bran?"

The comment didn't affect her at all. She stood over him, looking down with striking certitude. "Never," she delivered with stinging power.

Her mind was working magically now. There was no way anyone could discern fact from fiction. She sat down at the kitchen table so her eyes were more level with his. "Conrad, for the past year, Bran has been thinking of leaving Marjorie. I'm the only person he has discussed this with. We've met a few times after work because he had decided to leave her and he needed someone to talk to. That is all that has happened. I kept our meetings secret from you because I thought you would be jealous. But nothing ever happened. That I promise you."

"Why did he leave for New York? Why did he quit his job and leave his life behind?"

141

"I don't know."

"Because he couldn't stand to live in this town knowing you were with me and not him?"

She looked at the ceiling. "I think you might be right. I think he did have feelings for me. But I've never had feelings like that for him since we were married."

Conrad pinched the corners of his eyes. "I don't know what to believe anymore."

"You have to trust me. I love you, and I have always been faithful to you."

"It's my child?"

"It's your child."

He gave a weak smile. Then she asked him something. "Tell me, was it really a car accident, or was it Bran that did this to you?"

He didn't look at her. "I've already said what happened."

"Was it Bran?"

"No."

She didn't say anything more. There was no need to. Conrad wouldn't look her in the eyes. She knew it was Bran that beat him up, and it disgusted her. None of this was Conrad's fault, and she had brought him into harm's way.

She stared out the window at the Ferris wheel in the night sky. A powerful gust of winter wind blew along the house, pushing the smell of fallen leaves and dead grass through the cracks in the door. "I don't know how you've survived so long, Conrad," she said. "It's just the two of us now. There's no one left in our lives. I think we need to have this child and see if it makes our lives better. I've known couples that are only together because of their children. When they grew apart, their kids brought them together, and it was like a pearl that smoothed out the rough edges. A child can change everything.

142

We can put our trust in God or fate or whatever have you, lock hands, and see where it takes us."

"It sounds good." He broke with a smile.

She walked over and sat beside him. She clenched his hand. "It does, doesn't it?"

Something drew them together. Conrad slowly wrapped his arms around her neck and began kissing her. Micker was unhesitant. For the first time in years she felt a strong connection to him again. *Things would work out*, she thought, *if he were a father.*

CHAPTER 22: THE DECISION

When Conrad returned to Walker's the following week, he did so having said goodbye to his bandages and crutches. It was the first time he had been at the harbor in nearly a month, and he felt great getting back to work. It would take years, but he and Micker knew they needed to take it one step at a time to pay off their debt.

He spoke with Brosnan the previous week about coming back, and Brosnan was delighted. He missed his friend. But Brosnan had to check with Gilbert Hall to see which duties Conrad could perform before he came back. Brosnan was supposed to call Conrad that morning after he had spoken to Hall. That call never came.

When Conrad arrived at the docks, the sky was gray and a host of snowflakes fluttered in the thin sea air. The water was ripping onto the shore, unusually feisty, even in the Pacific's winter.

Conrad couldn't find Brosnan's trawler anywhere on the dock. He walked up the pier, and saw the trawlers five hundred meters from shore, all sailing toward the pale wafer of a sun that

144

was beating its way through the sky.

A hand tapped him on the left shoulder very gently from behind. He heard footsteps shuffle behind him and Brosnan's deep tone like a news anchor: "Conrad."

Conrad saw his aged friend slouching forlornly on the pier. His beard and hair had just been trimmed and his face was wind-burned brown. His solemn comportment made Conrad greet him with a question: "Are you okay, Broz?"

"I have to tell you something," Brosnan said despondently.

Conrad's eyes grew alarmingly shallow. "Oh, no."

"He's fired you," Brosnan said, barely capable of uttering the syllables.

"What? Why?"

"Well, laid off is how he wanted me to put it. I'm so sorry."

"Where is he? Maybe I can speak with him. My monthly records are good, Broz. He's gotta see that."

"He's in Mexico. Nice way to avoid confrontation."

Conrad's hands clenched. "I can't lose this job, Broz. I can't lose this job. I've got medical bills, a mortgage...."

"It was Bran that did it."

"What?"

"He drove up here the night you," Broz cleared his throat, "had your car accident. He was mad as hell about something." Brosnan stared inquisitively. "You know what I'm talking about?"

"No, I don't."

Brosnan pulled Conrad strongly to his shoulder with his long hand almost the size of a baseball glove. "Look, I know he's responsible for your injuries –"

"No – "

"I understand you're embarrassed, Con, but you've got
145

to tell the police what he did to you. You can't let him get away with this. Hell, I'd even be willing to say I saw him do it to ya' to make your case stronger."

Conrad turned sour. "Nothing happened."

Brosnan exhaled slowly and shook his head. "Have it your way."

Conrad stumbled through the doorway of his house. His legs were light and pain dropped into his temples, making him squint to keep his eyes open.

Micker was sitting at the far end of the kitchen table. She had just got home from work and was waiting, for the first time in years, to watch him enter the house. "How did it go?" she asked him pleasantly, her platinum blonde hair perched up like a headrest behind her.

Conrad had to break her more devastating news, just when things were going so well between them. "He fired me."

"What?"

"He fired me. He said he had to lay off a few people because sales were down."

Her mouth receded in her face as she blurted out, "That snake!" He assumed she was referring to Gilbert, but for a second, he wondered if she meant Bran. Maybe she knew it was the kind of thing Bran would be behind. She walked to the porch door, her tongue massaging the left crevice in her mouth. The kitchen floor was creaking with each step. "Why is this happening to us?"

"How far are you in the pregnancy?"

"Don't even think –"

"Micker, you have to."

"You don't tell me what to do."

"This isn't a joke; you can't have it."

"That's not up for discussion."

146

"Micker, we can't survive if we have this child. The doctor's visits, the pregnancy – how are we going to pay for it – how are we going to buy it clothes and food?"

"My insurance will cover the delivery."

Conrad slammed his fist on the table. "It's not a joke, Micker! This is my life! We're going to lose this house! I'm going to have to get on welfare! We have no money!"

"I'm making money."

"You can't support everything yourself! We are thousands in debt, and we were behind thousands before that. Student loans – we can't pay for anything!"

"We'll make it work."

"How? The only practical thing we can do is borrow money from someone. So who's it gonna be? You and I have no family. We have no parents, no siblings, nothing."

She stood thinking for a few seconds. "My uncle Barrett in D.C."

"Maybe -- I, we can't do this. It's just too much. A baby on top of it all is too much."

"Well, you know my stance," she said. "I will not have an abortion."

"I read somewhere that the average baby costs a family $20,000 before it turns two."

Micker's eyes grew a bright, searing green. "Then I guess you should stop reading," she replied before walking upstairs to their bedroom and slamming the door.

Conrad let her cool off before he went after her. When he reached the stairs, he realized the door she slammed was not their bedroom door. It was her father's. She had left all of Joe's things as they were before he died.

She was curled up in his old bed. She rubbed her face with her hands once she knew Conrad was standing in the doorway. "Why are we so unhappy?" she asked slowly.

147

"I didn't know you were unhappy?"

"We have nobody. I woke up one day and I had no friends, no parents, no family." There was genuine sadness in her eyes, grief.

"You have me."

She smiled solemnly. "We have to keep this child. We have to make it work."

He knew he couldn't fight her on this one. "I know," he said.

"We'll just take it day by day. You'll have to get another job, and then we'll just slowly pay it all off."

"I'm with you and I'll do whatever you need me to do," Conrad said. "I've loved you my entire life."

"You're a good person, Conrad. You'd be a good father. Don't ever forget that." She turned and faced him. He noticed she was much less certain than he ever remembered her, and much sadder. "I want this child to have a loving family," she said, talking like she wasn't going to be around for the child. "Above all, though, I want this child to have a loving father." She hesitated. "I didn't have that growing up."

"I didn't either."

They saw each other's pain – pain only they shared.

They drifted in silence for a while until an idea sprung in his head. "We could just leave."

"What?"

Conrad kept his voice soft, almost dreamy. "We could disappear. Go to Mexico. Who would care? Who would know?" She wished the same thing too but was never courageous enough to voice it. "We could pretend we went out on a boat ride, down to the Farallones, and never came back. We could leave tatters of our shirts out at sea. Make it look like we drowned; or worse, like a shark got us. We could transfer your money into a different account down there...take off in the

148

night. No one would know. No one would care."

She broke her concentration with a smile. "A part of me wishes I could share your dream."

"We could always do it, if worst came to worst."

She breathed long and soothingly before tucking her head into her shoulder. "Maybe," she said, and soon closed her eyes. Conrad lay next to her in the bed, wrapped his arms around her, and closed his eyes too.

They both knew they were staying put. Reality always trumped fairytales.

They lay like that, both of them fast asleep, until Micker's phone, which she placed under her pillow, began to vibrate. The pillow's pulsations woke her up immediately.

Her phone flashed a number she didn't recognize. It had area code 212. She silenced it and turned toward Conrad. He was still asleep.

The number kept staying there and staying there, imploring her to answer.

Finally she ignored it. No voicemail came. She figured it was another collection call.

She sat up in bed, tossing Conrad's arm off of her. She rubbed her stomach.

"Eight months," she whispered. "Just eight months."

CHAPTER 23: ONE ENTERS, ONE LEAVES

Those eight months before the pregnancy were nothing that Conrad and Micker had ever expected. As Micker's stomach grew, so grew her distance from Conrad. He got a job as a gas station attendant earning minimum wage. It wasn't much, but it helped them slowly pay off bills and save their house. The problem was Conrad worked the night shift most of the time, and she sometimes went days without speaking to him.

Without the proper support, Micker grew depressed. She gained too much weight, didn't like her appearance, and became obsessed with hot red slashes in her skin around her abdomen. Even the doctor said she had some of the worst stretch marks he had ever seen. She started staying home and missing work, sometimes never leaving her bed for a day.

The doctors told Conrad to expect mood swings and bouts of depression from his wife. When they came he tried to comfort her, and when she resisted his help, he gave her the space he thought she needed.

When Micker was finally ready to give birth, Conrad thought it a blessing. He hoped Micker would return to her normal self.

150

She didn't. If anything, she was worse.

Micker never spoke after the pregnancy. She rarely ate, let her hair grow near her waist, and didn't visit the outside world. A month went by and she hadn't held their baby girl. Conrad took care of her, but he was growing more and more alarmed by Micker's resistance. After awhile, he guessed Micker was suffering from postpartum depression.

The baby remained nameless. Conrad had settled on Evelyn, naming the child after his mom, but he stayed undecided until Micker woke from her stupor. From time to time he would carry the crying baby to Micker, and each time she would push it away.

Mirrors were where he could find her, rubbing, sliding her fingers along the purple scar that had once divided her stomach. Her pregnancy had been difficult, and despite her pleading, the doctor determined a C-Section was the safest procedure for the baby to enter the world. The wounds were deep though, and Conrad could tell they would never fade back into that previously perfect skin.

Conrad imagined the world would pay its respects once he had a child, but if anything, it seemed to become more hostile. Collectors for their delinquent medical bills called and called, the house a constant vibration of rings. Then they started coming to the door two times a day, forcing him to try to calm down his crying baby. But it never stopped. There was an unhealthy fear growing in that house. An unraveling was occurring, like a contest had begun to see who would break first.

He held on though, onto the sturdiness of his promise to be the father he never had. And he kept to it, hoping that Micker would finally wake and be the mother he expected her to be.

But the law was chaos, and more of it came one morning in the form of three knocks.

151

"Mr. Mayday," a hardened voice asked. Conrad ran to the window to see if it was another collector. He was still disoriented from the sleeping pill he took the night before. There was a police car.

He opened the door and knew it was bad news. Two cops, the one taking charge an African American man with duty and honor in his appearance. The cop said, "Mr. Mayday, is your wife home?"

Conrad hadn't seen Micker all morning. Her car was missing too. It was the first time she had left the house in a month.

"I think she may have gone to the store."

"When was the last time you saw her?"

He was embarrassed to say it. "Yesterday…afternoon."

"Mr. Mayday, does your wife own a sailboat?"

"Yes, she does." Conrad was panicking. "But she hasn't sailed it in months. See, she just gave birth a month ago."

"What's the name of that boat?" the cop asked while searching a notepad he pulled from his pocket.

Conrad thought about the name. "Something stupid, um, *Cursum Perficio*."

"Mr. Mayday, we found your wife's boat drifting near the Farallon islands. She was not aboard." Conrad had trouble looking at the man now, as he dropped bombs of tragic news. "We believe she fell overboard."

"What? Then she's out there? She could have swum to shore."

The cop shook his head gravely. "I'm sorry. We found parts of a woman's shirt a few hundred yards from the boat. It was chewed up." The cop looked at the officer behind him as if asking for help in delivering the next bit of news. "We believe a shark may have attacked her."

"A shark?"

152

The cops let him breathe.

"You think she's dead?"

The cop exhaled, hoping this would be the last thing he would say. "There are no remains."

CHAPTER 24: HOPE

When Conrad returned home that night from the police station, he did so with his sleeping newborn in his arms. He was exhausted and confused from the day's events, but he took notice when he saw an old friend at his door.

It was Brosnan.

"I'm so sorry, Conrad," Brosnan said. "How can I help you?"

Conrad stood facing him on the steps. He noticed a white media van parked a little way down the street. The story was already out. Conrad opened the door and sighed exhaustingly. "Come on in."

Conrad tried to clean up the house while Brosnan was there. Brosnan walked into the kitchen from the baby's room where Conrad was picking up dishes from the table. "She's a beautiful girl," he said.

Conrad didn't answer.

"I heard what happened." Brosnan said awkwardly. "I wanted to offer you support."

"Little late for that."

Brosnan swiped his black cap from his graying curly hair and held it in both fists. He felt unwelcomed. "I understand if you hate me for not coming sooner and for not fighting for you."

"Forget it," Conrad said, and he finally sat. "We all do what we gotta do. Sit."

Brosnan sat quickly. "Have you found work?"

"Gas station up the road."

Brosnan peered around the house. "I'm not gonna beat around the bush. I came to ask you if you want your job back."

Conrad was surprised. "What about Hall?"

"Gilbert Hall has cancer. He stepped down last Saturday so he could begin his treatments. His brother's in charge now, James Hall, but he's not like the other Halls. He was cut from a cleaner cloth. He's a reasonable guy – a good guy. I always looked forward to working for him one day. Anyways, I asked him if I could bring you back on board. He didn't think much of it and said yes."

"What kind of cancer is it?"

"Stomach cancer."

"Did they catch it early?"

"It doesn't look like it. Besides, stomach cancer has one of the worst cure rates. I don't think he'll be around much longer."

"I don't know," Conrad said.

"You'd be working for me again. Same rate, same boat."

Conrad stood up and walked to the kitchen window. "I've got a child now," he said.

"Which makes it all the more important you get some solid income now. Put her in daycare."

Conrad turned around quickly. Something else was on

155

his mind. "Did the neighbor's come out when you walked up to the door?" he asked.

Brosnan nodded.

"I think they suspect I was involved in her death somehow."

"Why would they think that?"

"You know how people are. Then this neighbor," he said pointing in the direction across the street. The neighbor was Diane Soto, the town's gossip queen. "She's saying she saw me getting into Micker's car with Micker late that night. Micker hadn't left the house in a month! She wouldn't even speak to me let alone get in a car with me in the middle of the night!"

"What do the police say?"

"They think she's a quack. Apparently she had conflicting answers as to why she was up at two in the morning. Then I guess her times changed."

"What do they think?"

"They think she doesn't like me and is trying to stir the pot." Conrad sat thinking. "She never did like me. She always liked Micker. She thought I didn't belong with her. I wasn't good enough."

"So, who cares what this crazy neighbor says. My question is what was Micker doing sailing in the Farallones anyways?"

"She started sailing again about nine months ago. She said it was a hobby she wanted to resume."

"No human being should be sailing in the Farallones! That's like playing Russian roulette, except the chances you take the bullet are much greater – all those white sharks out there. The seals – if she fell in, they'd have no sense she was human. And at night!"

"I can't get it out of my head."

"They're sure it's her? They never found her body."

156

"There was blood on her shirt – or what was left of it. A scientist said that from analyzing the bites in the shirt, he could determine that it was a great white that got her. Like my mother. That's why you've got the media van out there now. They figure, what are the chances his mom and wife die from a shark attack? That species has not been friendly to me." He smiled in desperation.

"What kind of boat was it?"

"Small – cat-rigged dingy. The *Cursum Perficio*," he said oddly.

Brosnan couldn't let the frustration flow out of him. "A white shark could rip a dingy in pieces if it wanted to!" He was baffled a woman of her intelligence would dare venture such waters. "What a tragic accident. Such a beautiful woman." Brosnan steadied himself. He was not here to depress his friend even more. "You'll get through this. I promise you."

"It's not just that; it's the debt," Conrad said solemnly. "I can't find my way out of this hole."

"I don't want to sound callous, but what about life insurance?"

"I'll get some as long as I don't mention that it was suicide."

"Suicide? Conrad, it was ruled an accidental death."

"She killed herself, Broz. She went out there to die." *And I gave her the idea*, Conrad thought. *I told her we could fake our deaths out there, leaving behind tattered clothes.*

"Don't beat yourself up like this, Conrad. It was a tragic accident."

"I know what she did. She couldn't take this – this family. This debt. She couldn't take me."

"No."

"But I have to play along."

Brosnan no longer felt his presence was helping matters.

157

He stood, told Conrad he would be out of his way, and tipped his hat. "You can start Monday, if you're up for it." He opened the door, and then held it open before leaving. "By the way, what's cursum pers – pers –"

Conrad corrected him. "*Cursum perficio.*"

"What's it mean?"

Conrad lifted his coffee cup to his mouth. "It means 'my journey is over,'" he said and sipped his coffee.

Brosnan looked away like he understood something, and then he was out the door.

Conrad went back into the baby's room. He looked into the carriage, the baby sleeping upright. Small, helpless, and without a name. He lifted her, and the crying began again.

He pressed her tight to his shoulder, caressing her gold locks of hair, hoping it would stop the crying. And then, it did. She stopped crying. She went back to sleep.

He rocked her, nervously waiting for her to cry again. After fifteen minutes she was fast asleep. He cradled her in his arms.

He stared at her, concentrating on the small dimensions of her face. *How helpless.* Then unexpectedly, her eyes opened and looked at him. Green eyes. Conrad looked into them. She had green eyes just like Micker. Then the eyes closed and the head tilted to the side and she went back to sleep.

Conrad smiled for the first time in a month. He remembered his mother's middle name, and it stuck. "Belle," he said, the name seeming natural.

PART 2

CHAPTER 25: BELLE'S TESTS

Seven years later

Hilland Elementary School in San Sangre had not changed since Conrad was a child. The walls were still crusty orange and the carpeted hallways a faded blue. From Katherine Grey's door window he could see the locker he had in the first grade. He could still see himself as a kid opening it and hiding behind it from the other kids.

He sat in one of the student desks waiting for Katherine Grey, Belle's first grade teacher. He had never met Katherine Grey, which is why he was surprised when he first saw her sprawl through the door. She was a beautiful blonde woman of twenty-seven years. She had a curved body like a swimsuit model and thick, brown eyelashes that circumscribed her hazel eyes.

She walked swiftly to him and held out her hand. "Mr. Mayday," she said warmly. "Thank you for coming."

He rose to shake her hand. "Not a problem, Ms. Grey"

"Please have a seat, and call me Katherine," she said,

fixing a manila folder on the left side of her desk. "I usually conduct parent meetings over the phone because of work schedules, but I thought this called for a personal meeting." Conrad stayed silent. He rubbed the right side of his face with the palm of his right hand. He was watching her closely with heavy eyes. Katherine knew he was ready to fight whatever infraction his daughter committed. "I have had some trouble with your daughter, Belle, this year. I'm afraid she has not been meeting 1st grade standards in reading or mathematics. Does this come as a surprise to you?"

"Yes," Conrad replied with a touch of sarcasm, drawing out the vowel in his affirmation. "She seems very smart to me. She did well in kindergarten. She reads all the time at home."

Katherine squinted incredulously. "What does she read?"

"Some children's books. I've even caught her reading my newspaper at times."

"The newspaper?"

"Yes. Is that normal for a seven year old?"

"It depends. Do you know if she's comprehending it?"

"I don't ask her. I just assume she's trying to impress me."

She got right down to it. "Mr. Mayday – your daughter received a zero percent on both her standardized tests in reading and mathematics," she said in an exculpatory way to dismiss any wrongdoing and get right to the anomaly. "Now, normally we would place a student with such scores with our learning support team to develop these rudimentary skill sets – many of which were frankly learned in preschool. But I think there's something more here." She closed the manila folder and set it aside. "I think there may be a chance that your daughter is…" Katherine rolled her tongue around her upper lip, "is faking."

"Why would you conclude that?"

161

She pulled from her desk a copy of Belle's test scores. "There are one hundred and twenty questions between the reading and mathematics tests." She handed him the copy gently. "Multiple choice: A, B, C, and D. The test is administered over two school days. If your daughter were to have taken these tests seriously, the chances she would have missed every question on a multiple-choice test, where randomness adheres twenty-five percent correctness, is one out of a thousand. To have done it on both tests – well, that's nearly impossible."

Conrad's head jerked up from reading the test. "You think she deliberately picked the wrong answers to every question."

"It's not just that," Katherine said. "She finished the test, having answered every question, almost an hour before every other student."

"Why would she do that?"

"That is what I brought you to answer."

"With my job I haven't –" Conrad stopped. He suddenly thought about how lucky he was, as awful as it seemed, that Gilbert Hall died of stomach cancer all those years earlier. If he hadn't died, Conrad wondered where he'd be. "The daycare knows more about her than I do at this point. I've been a fisherman the last eight years, and the hours were tough when she was growing up. My wife passed away when Belle was born, so it's just me and her. I haven't spent enough time with her."

"I see," Katherine said, but she didn't seem to be learning anything new from his statements. Micker Mayday's death was one of the most talked about occurrences in San Sangre history.

"So what would you like me to do?" Conrad asked, hoping to settle this and get back to the docks.

She folded her hands and perched over her desk. "Belle

162

doesn't cooperate in my class. She has a very domineering personality. She intimidates the other students, even bullies some of them. I've had to send her out into the hall a number of times. Getting her to pay attention is nearly impossible. At times I feel the work is a joke to her. Every question I ask of her she deliberately answers incorrectly. I would like you to sit in during today's class. We will be reviewing subtraction. Maybe she will behave in your presence."

Conrad was shocked to hear such reports about his daughter. "I'll stay."

"I think it will do some good."

Conrad sat in one of the students' chairs in the back corner of the classroom. When the students returned from recess, they confused him for a principal and immediately stopped talking. When Belle saw him in the corner, she had a look of betrayal in her emerald eyes. She sat in the front of the class, presumably moved there for bad behavior, and never turned to look back at him.

Sitting tensely as class began, Conrad caught the excited eyes of Katherine, a signal, he thought, that she was about to test Belle. Katherine asked, "Who knows what we do when we have a question like sixteen minus nine?" Katherine proceeded to write the problem in exquisite handwriting and big firm numbers just six inches above the chalk stand.

A number of little anxious hands flew up in the air, their fingers spiriting in front of Conrad's face, eating half of Katherine's body. "Oh me oh me me me," the chorus whispered frantically. After five seconds every hand was up but Belle's and the little spectacled boy in the back corner who picked nervously at his wrist.

"Belle," Katherine said sweetly. "We haven't heard from you this week. You want to try this problem?"

"I don't know it," Belle answered.

"Iz seven!" a small boy with blonde, swervy hair exclaimed. His feet were tucked under his butt and he had been leaning over the desk as if he were peering over a railing at the zoo trying to see an animal that had traveled beyond his periphery.

"Bobby, what did I tell you? Don't answer questions out loud unless I call on you," she snapped.

"But you neva call an me," he said perplexed.

"Ya there's a rea–" Katherine looked back at Conrad, regained her posture, then continued. "I would call on you if you wouldn't shout out all the time. Okay?"

"Okay," Bobby said defeated.

"Now Belle –"

"It's eight, Bobby. Not seven," said Belle with convincing, adult vernacular.

Conrad watched Katherine's face turn nonplussed. She stroked the belly of her chin with her entire palm as if gearing up for a tantrum. "Belle…why do you think it's eight?" she asked tentatively, knowing that the question needed to be asked even though she was playing right into Belle's hands.

Suddenly, Belle shot a mean glance back at Conrad, her baby-soft face and perfectly curved nose squinched up for him. Then she responded, not to Katherine, but to Bobby by searing her green eyes into his: "It's eight, Bobby," she said tauntingly. "Try again."

"Seven," whispered voices behind her, but there was an apparent showdown between Belle and Katherine without the two of them ever locking eyes.

Bobby looked back to the board after letting his eyes follow the swarming whispers for confirmation. "Iz seven. Siksteen minus nine is seven. An da –"

"It's eight, Bobby," Belle said. Her eyes grew big and

mean as she cuffed her hands into tiny, soft creampuffs in front of her face. In sequence, tiny little digits, starting with her right pinky, shot up: "Sixteen, fifteen, fourteen, thirteen, twelve, eleven, ten, and nine." Eight fingers were extended in front of her face before she lowered them like a stack of cards. "There's eight."

Her explanation seemed so persuasive that even Conrad had to revisit the problem a second time. *Count the numbers in between. Fifteen, fourteen, thirteen, twelve, eleven, and ten. Six.* He knew he was wrong. He wanted to count on his fingers but was too embarrassed to do so. *Count the sixteen then go down nine. Sixteen, fifteen, fourteen, thirteen, twelve, eleven, ten, nine, and eight. Seven left. Seven is right.*

Something had come over Bobby that Conrad witnessed. His face had turned red like someone was squeezing his neck and his knees slunk slowly out from under his butt, dropping him a half foot. "buh-buh, you dohn cuhnt da nine."

Belle looked shocked. "If you don't count the nine, Bobby, then you don't count the sixteen either. It's eight."

Katherine was zoned in on Conrad. He had his knees playing coasters to his elbows, locked in a stiffened gaze upon his daughter.

Bobby continued to flounder. He blinked a hundred times a minute, and Belle had locked him in her searing green stare. He replied again, "Iz gotta be seven."

"So you're counting the sixteen and not the nine?" Belle said.

"No," he said breathily. He looked at Belle and began to turn a bright candy apple.

Conrad was tickled by her power. He looked around – every single kid had his and her mouths open in confusion. Even the little spectacled boy sat up. *This was exactly the way Micker was in elementary school,* he thought. This is why kids

165

avoided her on the playground – she had an eerie way of forcing you to believe a lie you knew was a lie. Immediately, he sought to wonder what exactly Belle had done on the playground to make every student believe her. What intelligence did she bring to those outside courts to make them so afraid of her?

"Then it would be six if we follow your rules," Belle said. "We either don't count the nine and the sixteen, or we count the nine and the sixteen." Then she imitated Bobby's Midwestern accent. "sikuhsteen oh nan?"

The students, including Conrad, turned with their mouths open to Katherine. "Okay, so we have some different answers here," Katherine said, stroking her blonde, shoulder-length hair behind her ears. "Class, anyone have any other suggestions?"

The class sat still.

"Okay, who thinks it's seven?" Katherine asked.

One hand shot up, waived, then slowly wilted like a dead plant when it learned no other hands breathed such air.

Katherine swallowed hard. "Eight?" she asked dreadfully. The entire class slowly raised their hands like dominos. Even Bobby, still hypnotized by Belle's stare, elevated a defeated arm. "Okay, Belle, come up to the board and show us what led you to eight."

Belle pranced to the board. Katherine handed her the chalk very slowly with a secret scowl. Belle held the chalk in her hand and felt it in her fingers: chalk fragments powdered into them. She held the white utensil like an extension of her pointer finger and slowly turned to Conrad. The stare frightened him. It had excitingly depressing qualities to it, like she was about to blow open a huge secret to her dullard of a father: *this is who I am. Nice to meet you.*

Belle took the chalk and added in a squiggly handwriting a three to the sixteen and a forty-nine to the seven so it now
166

read: 163 - 497.

"Belle, why are you adding numbers to the problem?" Katherine asked with a detectably tense tone. She bent over to grab the only eraser on the chalkboard stand, but Belle grabbed it and moved it behind her back. "Hand me the eraser, Belle."

"Can you answer that?"

"Give me the eraser."

"Why can't you answer that?"

Conrad was confused as to what to do. Should he stand up and ask Belle to accompany him out in the hall? Should he yell at her, or should he let his daughter go on embarrassing the teacher?

"Okay, that's it," Katherine warned. "You're in timeout. Go sit in the corner."

"Fine by me, just answer my question."

Katherine looked around. The kids looked anxious. She turned to the board in a frustrated pose and examined the new problem Belle had set. *She's just seven years old*, she thought. *This is easy.* She grabbed for the chalk before Belle screamed, "Do it in your head."

Suddenly Katherine saw the numbers jumping together, the nine with the six and the seven with the four. She wanted to reverse the numbers to make it easier for her to subtract, but there was something wrong, something, in her mind, illegal in cheating it. She saw a thirty-four but then had to start over. Then she saw -334. *I can always just say I'm not going to answer this and move on*, she thought. *I could even send her to the principal's office if necessary. I've more than earned that right from her insolence.*

But -334 looked good enough. She turned back to Belle, and before she could respond, something in her throat stopped her: She really wasn't sure if -334 was the answer, and what would it say to Mr. Mayday if she couldn't even subtract hundreds?

167

She found her answer: "Belle, the other students in here are trying to learn, and maybe their learning level is not on par with yours. If that is the case, we can stay after class and I can give you an assignment with harder problems for you to solve." She looked hard at Belle whose big green eyes looked like thick emerald stones were smoothed out in ball shapes and stuck in a white mound.

"I didn't know the answer anyways," Belle said, and sat. "It's too big for me."

Katherine, however, didn't believe that for a minute.

CHAPTER 26: BELLE EXPLAINS HERSELF

When they met again after class, Katherine suggested to Conrad that they fix a test for Belle later that day. The idea was to give Belle a fourth grader's test while all the other students received tests appropriate for 1st grade. If Belle were truly a genius, her score would indicate so.

Katherine was supposed to call Conrad at 2:30, fifteen minutes after school let out and enough time to allow her to send Belle's test through the scantron. It was 2:47. Belle would be bursting through the door any minute.

Conrad picked at the skin hanging around his nails from scrubbing the boat. It was dried and purple. He watched the pieces as they dropped to the floor, all the while thinking about the possible results he would hear. He had weighted his options singly. At worst Belle was slow for her age. At best, she was a genius. The unhappy medium: Belle was smart for her age but nothing spectacular – nothing demanding the world's fascination.

Conrad only thought the worst because he was superstitious. He was convinced that if he thought the worst, the best would happen. He waited for the phone call. It came on queue. He answered it slowly, allowing it to ring twice so he didn't appear anxious: "Hello?"

"Mr. Mayday?"

"Yes. Is this Ms. Grey?"

"Please, call me Katherine." There was something unusual in her tone. It was with agog.

"Okay. Call me Conrad." Conrad was weary to bring up the test scores. "So how was your day?"

"Fine. "I –" she stopped herself. "How was yours?"

"It's been good."

"Well, I have Belle's test results," she said evenly. Then she asked, with a warm tone like she was delivering a surprise gift: "Are you sitting down?"

Conrad's mouth broke open and air pulled loose from his knotted stomach. "Yes."

"Well, she did it again. She answered every single question wrong."

Conrad gasped. Normally that would be bad news.

"How many were there?"

"A hundred."

"Now there's no possibility she could just be missing *all* these questions?"

"Not a chance."

"You're sure of this?"

"Yes."

Conrad held the voice box over the phone and gasped again. "So where do we go from here?"

"Well, we can't jump too far ahead. In my estimation, her results suggest superior intelligence. But it would seem to me that any little girl who can answer every question wrong – in this case, deliberately wrong – on a test four years beyond her expected intelligence is a genius, pure and simple. The question is – can she answer all of those questions right? That will be the

170

real challenge. If not, then we may just have a bright but extremely bellicose child. We will have to test her again, but she needs to take the test seriously."

"I'll talk to her today. When can I test her again?"

Katherine stalled in answering. She could sense an unhealthy fervor in Conrad's new question. "Well, we can test her next week."

"I understand. I would like to have her tested again as soon as possible. I will talk with her today and try to talk some sense into her."

"That would do some good I think."

"Well, thank you for the phone call and have a good day, Katherine."

"Wait. Conrad?" she asked to make sure he was still there. She sounded nervous. "I know this is highly irregular and I never do this, but I was wondering if you might want to grab coffee with me sometime. Perhaps today after work?"

The last thing Conrad wanted was a first date, but having someone interested in him for the first time in a long time was hard to resist. "Sure. Um, what time do you get off work?"

"I have to finish grading some tests and then I have to prepare for tomorrow's lesson. Would seven work, or is that too late?

"No, that's perfect."

"Good. There's a Starbucks a few blocks from the school, on Ralle Boulevard. Are you familiar with it?"

"I am. I'll drop Belle off for swim practice and shoot over."

"Great. I'll meet you then."

"See you then." He hung up the phone and slid it underneath his chin. He felt giddy and excited, but a little surprised. He thought Katherine was way too good for him.

171

But he didn't have time to think about Katherine. Belle had just gotten off the school bus.

Conrad watched her from the window. He stood to the side of the window so she couldn't see him, but Belle had already seen the pink drape to the living room window oscillate.

He watched her with awe: she was tall for seven – about four-foot-four, and gangly with long legs that gave way at times like a newborn deer. She had a face beyond her years – a spitting image of Micker: a soft, perfectly sized and shaped nose, white skin, and soothing dark auburn hair. It was wrapped back in a pony tail and held together in a red ribbon.

She hooked her fingers around the strings to her pink book bag and walked through the yard with her head high and arrogant. As Conrad moved away from the window, he caught Belle smirking as though she had seen him the entire time.

He opened the door before she could enter and said, "Belle, go sit down at the kitchen table."

She stared as though affronted by her father's doorman role and replied, "Can I at least put my book bag down?"

"Yes, then meet me in there," he said sternly. He waited for her in the kitchen, which was turned into a heated pink because of the afternoon sun.

He sat at the far end of the table, his fingers rubbing together in anticipation. He had yet to concoct a plan to have her release her genius on record. He was nervous too. She had a way of talking that made adults feel like they were talking with one of their own.

When she entered the kitchen, she rode her fingers through her hair, gently untying her ponytail and holding it in her hand. "What?" she asked askance.

"Sit down." She descended slowly in the chair and stared out the window, protruding her lips and sulking. "Why

172

the pout?" he asked her.

She rolled her eyes. "What did I do?"

"Nothing. Why do you think it's something bad?"

"Always is."

"No, it's not. Well, I'm extremely unhappy with your behavior in school today –"

"Why were you even there?"

"We'll get to that. But if you ever act like that again in the classroom, I'm pulling you out of swimming lessons. Understood?"

"Fine."

He sat back, pleasantly surprised at how obeisant she was.

"Is there a good part?" she asked.

"Well – let me start by asking you some questions, okay? I see you reading a lot of the times…," he began picking his index finger with his thumb. "What are you reading?" His forehead had tightened now and creased. Her face remained impassive. "I mean I know you read *The Boxcar Children* and stuff, but, what else? Anything?"

"Why?"

"Because – just answer it."

"I read Mom's books."

"Which ones? Like Stephen King, Tim O'Brien?"

She looked at her bright red shoes hanging dead beneath the table. "I try to read them."

"What about Nancy Drew or something your age?"

"I've already read them."

"I have books too, ya' know?"

"History…"

"What's wrong with history?"

"I read the comics in the newspaper every morning."

"Yea but if you don't read up on history, how will you

know how we got where we got?"

"Don't need to. It will all happen again."

Conrad smiled. The first question he was always asked in history class was why study history? The answer was always to learn from our mistakes. He investigated her, and then answered quite deliberately, "touché."

Then Belle's mouth did something unusual that sucked the blood from Conrad's face. Her lips, still stuck to one another, imitated a frown for a half second and her bottom lip broke from the upper and bulged above it the way someone would if told something impressive. But Belle had not only understood the meaning of the word (a word Conrad didn't own until his second year of high school), her gesture was intended for Conrad's correct use of the word. He was frightened and had a sudden look of unhealthiness. His daughter had assumed him a moron.

His head ducked and his fingers twittered together. "How did you do on your test today?"

"Ms. Grey, that idiot."

"Why do you say that about her?"

Belle wouldn't answer.

Conrad skipped ahead. "Why are you doing this?"

Belle rose from the table in anger. "Why try!"

Conrad turned to face her. "So you deliberately fail them? Deliberately miss every question?"

"Let them figure it out!"

"And now that's what they've done!"

"Huh?" she asked tremulously as if she had missed something. Sites of computers and doctors and test screens and gadgets stuck to her head came into frame. "How?"

"By screwing around on these tests, you've just bought yourself a whole new load of them."

"But I missed them all...so they send me back?"

174

"Send you back where?"

"Daycare. Anywhere but with those stupid kids and stupid teachers."

"You're too old for daycare, Belle."

"I want to go back. At least they cared about me." Tears began forming in her eyes.

"Why do you say that? You're saying I don't care about you."

"You didn't even know I read your newspaper."

Conrad looked around for it stupidly. "So you've started reading it."

"I've read it for years."

"All of it?" Conrad asked. "Who reads all of it?" he said to himself.

Belle began to fume like some angry gambler and grabbed the newspaper sitting on the kitchen sink and threw it across the kitchen: "Just the front page!" She ran into the living room and threw herself over the couch.

Conrad held his temples, trying to make sense of her outburst.

He proceeded into the living room and sat by Belle on the sofa next to her. A few years ago he would have picked her up so she could sit on his lap, but now she was like talking to a young adult, and Conrad was thinking about this and kicking himself for not noticing the change earlier.

"Do you want to talk to me, Belle?"

"I just want my books."

His daughter was turning into a puzzle.

"They're upstairs in your room."

"They're all that will get me through this."

"You can't talk to me?"

"Not for this."

"Oh quit the dramatic crap, will ya'!" he exclaimed. "I

175

get a call from your teacher who says you deliberately answer every question wrong on a fourth grade test and..."

Belle looked up betrayed. "fourth grade?"

"Yea, fourth grade!"

"Why was I taking a fourth grade test!"

"Because –"

"Why?"

"Because you might be a genius!"

"When were you going to tell me!"

Conrad's eyes bulged. He placed his hands up as if pushing someone away. "This is becoming the weirdest conversation I have ever had." He fell back against the sofa and stroked his hair stressfully.

Belle gathered herself. "I'm a genius?"

"When you take those tests," he asked her slowly, "like the one you took today, do you know the right answers to each question and then choose the wrong one?"

"I – I was mad."

"Mad at what?"

"Being there. I get lonely. All the other kids have a mom who picks them up and I don't."

"I'm sorry, baby. I know what you're going through. Believe me I do. I also didn't have a mother like the other kids did. I didn't have a father either." He wanted to add that you never get through it, that the pain seeps deep inside you and never leaves. That the sight of your best friends hugging their parents will send daggers to your gut. *But things will be different for Belle*, he thought. *She will never be orphaned and never feel that pain as she grows older.* "The pain will go away one of these days. I promise you."

She looked at Conrad, her glassy, green eyes pulling him into her in a way he would never forget: "I know I'm smart."

Conrad hung on the edge of the sofa cushion. "Pretty

176

smart?"

She nodded.

"Did you know all the answers to the test you took today?"

"Uhuh."

"You're sure?"

"They were easy."

He sat back against the sofa. "How do you know them, though? Do they just appear to you?" It was a question he had always wanted to ask someone of high intelligence but never did, not even Micker.

"Kind of," she said, her voice growing stronger from its quaver before. "I just know them, like I've just got done learning them."

"Belle," he said carefully, "I am going to need you to take another test, only this time I want you to answer each question correctly. Can you do that for me? Maybe we can get you to a place that has special attention, where you're challenged. Can you do that for me? I need your agreement, babe."

"Yes," she said. He smiled brightly, walked over to her and wrapped his arms around her and kissed her.

CHAPTER 27: CONRAD AND KATHERINE

The conversation between Conrad and Katherine was remarkably easy that evening. Once they settled down with their coffee in the back corner of Starbucks, they talked for nearly an hour about balancing family and a career, the disrespect and misunderstanding teachers face, and the difference between the public and private sector. Conrad found her smart, interesting, and most important, lacking some of the egotism that often defines people in their twenties. The conversation was between him and her; it was not her talking and then pretending to listen and sound involved. She truly cared about what he had to say, and always let him talk just as much as she did. She was like a clock in that way: she seemed to know when to step in and ask a question and when to change the conversation.

No one paid attention to them as they talked like longtime friends. They were naturals, so much so that Conrad was ready to ask her a personal question.

"All right, I have to ask: How old are you?"

"I thought it was coming," she said smiling.

"I'm sorry."

"No, it's okay. I'm twenty-seven."

Conrad grimaced. "You know I've got you by seven years next Halloween."

"You were born on Halloween?"

"Yea. Just my luck."

"Oh wow," she said, folding her blonde hair back behind her ears. "Ya know, I can see how you would react to that, but I think I'd kind of like to be born on a holiday. It makes you unique."

He took a long drink of his espresso before saying, "I'm unique all right."

"So did you talk to Belle?"

Conrad smiled to himself. He was thinking how Katherine had done it again. They were talking about her age and now they were on to Belle. She was a master at it – smooth and subtle.

"I did…"

"Not good?"

"No, no. She admitted to answering every question wrong on purpose. Bottom line, she needs to know that I know about it and that no one is going to play her games anymore."

"Why do you think she did it?" Katherine asked honestly.

"Ya' know, when my wife died, it wasn't easy on me as a parent. I can't say I've been there for her like I should. I had to put her in daycare until she went to preschool. I don't feel like I've ever developed the relationship with her that I should have. I always treated her like an adult in many respects."

Katherine's hazel eyes grew wide. "She is like talking to an adult," she admitted. "In all my years of teaching, I've never met a seven year old who spoke as well and articulately as her."

"She gets it from her mother," Conrad said.

"Did you ever think of getting remarried?"

Conrad laughed. "No chance." Then he asked, "Have

179

you been married?"

"God, no. I've only been out of college a few years."

"Where did you go?"

"Berkeley. How about you?"

Conrad hesitated a moment. "UC-Santa Cruz."

"Oh, my brother went there. He swam for them. He said he loved it."

"Yea, it was a great four years," he said, but he wanted to get back to marriage. He had a point about it that he wanted to make to someone who would listen. "But remember what I tell you about marriage: it is just you and your spouse *all* the time. I think that's why people have kids, so they don't have to deal with their spouses anymore."

"Little skeptical, don't you think."

"I'm telling you. Married couples have kids because it saves them. Finally, they have someone else to talk to."

"Well, I don't know about that, but I certainly know my share of unhappy marriages."

"These last seven years have gone by so fast. It's like a blur, honestly." Conrad was looking down at his coffee, drifting into deep thought. Katherine stared at him. She was admiring his openness. "Well, I better go pick up Belle from swim practice."

"Yea, I better get back too." She picked up her coat from the chair and folded it over her right arm. They continued their conversation smoothly as they threw away their coffee cups and prepared to leave. "I'm wondering how much longer Belle is going to be with me this year."

"Oh, yea? I'd think it'd still be awhile. They'll have to run more tests you said."

"Yea, but they might want to test her for an advanced class by next week."

"That soon?"

180

"That soon."

They hugged outside the Starbucks, a short, professional hug, and thanked each other for their company. As he was opening his car door, she asked him if he wanted to do dinner next Tuesday after school. He gave the safe response: he would check Belle's schedule with swim practice. Then they traded phone numbers and were off in the night, both feeling as though they had found, at the very least, a new friend.

There were few nights when Conrad couldn't sleep, but that night was one of them. He had awoken randomly in the middle of the night after having taken two bright blue sleeping pills. He awoke conscious and was sure he had not been dreaming in those five hours of sleep. He felt cold and lonely and he could sense a panic attack was in its premature stages.

He tried to go back to sleep by holding his eyes shut, but his mind was wide-awake and wanted to wander. It took him through the house without his moving, to the kitchen where Micker sometimes sat to ponder, to the doorway where the police told him that Micker had died, to Belle's bedroom where Micker's father once slept. He thought, in particular, of the struggle the old man must have had the day he died, envisioning his courageous battle up the stairs, blood gushing and flowing unremorsefully from his body.

There was only a wind chill outside in the moonless night. The world around him seemed so distant. He was beginning to spin. Time was moving at an alarming rate. One day he would wake up an old man with no family. Belle would be off to college or married and he would still be in that house dining with the ghosts of those he felt he had helped put in the grave. It was a real experience for him. He was in a time warp, and he could see himself waking thirty years from now with this same mentality and feeling. He would walk to the kitchen one day and Belle, the last person attached to him by blood, would be gone.

He massaged his forehead and began to wince, expecting tears that never came. "Please, God, get me through this. Please get me through this," he whispered around the lonely pink bedroom. He sat up and finished off a bottled water that only seemed to foster his angst with more energy.

The panic attacks he faced after Micker's death were coming again. He could hear their footsteps coming to rob his mind. He was spinning, and he knew if things kept getting worse he would start pacing around in circles in the kitchen like he did after she died. He tried to take deep breaths, but reality was on him now. What if he lost his job again? What was he going to do when Belle went off on her own? He was slipping down the hole very fast. Twenty-four hours seemed like a single second in his mind. It was coming. He would be sixty or seventy in no time. Then he searched out the ticking of the clocks in his bedroom, loud knocks that shook the room.

He needed light. He turned on the bedroom lights, made his way downstairs into the kitchen and turned on the bright ceiling light. He sat at the table silently, picking at his lip. He kept thinking of his foster parents. He had been passed through five families before he was eighteen. He kept imagining the life he might have had had his parents never died. Then, as he expected, came the images of his mother taken down in the water and that steel-black triangle treading through the blood-soaked blue. He remembered seeing an airplane in the water – that was it. Had he told his dad sooner, or screamed for his mom, she would have been all right. She would have made it out alive – there was no question. *The shark must have been circling her*, he thought, but maybe his memory was bad. Maybe he didn't see the shark's fin at all. Maybe it was just God playing
182

tricks on him. Why on earth would God let a child live with such an image?

Conrad remembered his father walking like a zombie into the sea. He was standing on the sand at the high end of the beach looking down as his father made his way out there in the blue water. His father had turned to look back at him right before he went under. *Why did he do that? Why did he want me to see that? Was he trying to come back? Maybe the rocks were too heavy and he was trying to come back to me. I would have been all right had he made it back. I would have had a normal life.*

Conrad paced the house, finally ascending the steps and entering Belle's bedroom. It was warm in there and Conrad made his way gently into her bed. She woke when he curled up beside her. She turned around, opened her wide green eyes, and turned toward him out of the moonlight. She didn't hug him like she wanted to but instead curled her head and laid it atop his and closed her eyes. He watched her silently, and soon the panic was escaping like a door had opened to let it ooze out. It moved out of him slowly, eventually seeping out till it was gone. He shut his eyes and soon was dreaming.

CHAPTER 28: A SECOND DATE

When Tuesday came along, Conrad decided to call Katherine and plan a second date. They agreed to have dinner at an Italian restaurant called Mancini's. It lay in the heart of San Sangre. They sat on the deck of the restaurant overlooking the beachfront. They had good Italian pasta and shared a bottle of champagne. Discussion was never dry or lacking flexibility as they talked about the town and different parts of the country they had been to.

Conrad was eager to talk about something else though. Belle had retaken the fourth grade test, and Katherine said she expected to have the results that afternoon. After they finished their meals and their bottle of champagne, he finally asked the question: "Well, I've avoided it all night. How did she do?"

Katherine smiled and padded the tablecloth. "I was saving it."

Conrad felt positive vibes. "What is it?"

"She got a hundred."

Conrad was amazed. He clenched his fist.

"They are thinking of advancing her three years, to fourth grade," Katherine explained. "I think you're going to receive a lot of attention around here pretty soon once word gets out."

"Why?"

"No kid has ever advanced that many years in our school system. The local media might run with a story like that."

"Is she a genius?"

"We'll need to do some more tests, but I'd say yes. I've never seen anyone like her."

The waiter took away their plates and glasses. Conrad sat back and studied the people on the deck of the restaurant. He smiled.

"What is it?" she asked.

"My kid, a genius," he said. "Who would have thought with my genes."

She looked at him curiously. "I take it you don't give yourself a lot of credit?"

He answered with a quick smile.

On their way to their cars, Katherine asked Conrad to come back to her apartment and watch a movie. Conrad explained that Belle was at a friend's house until nine and that he would have to be home when she was dropped off. She acknowledged his parental duties and accepted them easily.

What Conrad did next surprised him.

He invited her back to his place, and she accepted. He knew it might create a problem with Belle when she came back, but he didn't care. *It will make for an exciting evening*, he thought, *hiding her from Belle*. He wanted that type of excitement in the house. He needed it in his life.

They rested on the couch after watching *Chinatown*, both tired and nearly falling asleep. It turned out Belle ended up staying over her friend's house. Conrad liked spending time with

185

Katherine. She was different from Micker in every way. While Micker was dominant and incorrigible, Katherine was passive and adaptive. With Micker he always felt like her student; with Katherine he felt like her peer. He could never have shared a silence with Micker. Never.

He put his arm around her. She lay on his chest, breathing slowly, but not calmly. Something was on her mind.

"I have to tell you something," she said. "I don't think it's a big deal, but I think I need to tell you anyways just so I don't reveal it later down the road and it's awkward."

"What is it?" he asked.

"Your wife," she began hesitantly, "I used to work for her."

Conrad moved away from her gently and sat up on the couch. He raised his legs into mountains and wrapped his arms around them. "You did?"

"Yes."

"When?"

"About ten years ago I think," she said trying to remember. "Should I not have said anything?"

Conrad sat there silently thinking.

"No, I'm sorry. It's just – I don't have many people I can talk to who knew her anymore," he said.

"Well, I only knew her as a boss," she said.

"Which means you knew a machine," he replied. They both laughed, breaking up some of the tension. "I guess we knew the same person."

"Yea, she really was a machine. Best boss I ever had though."

Conrad smiled and shook his head.

"What?" she asked, confused by his reaction.

"Everyone who worked with her or for her says something like that about her," Conrad said.

186

Katherine smiled, her eyes intense. "Don't get me wrong; I was terrified of her. I was just an intern then. It was a big deal to be her intern that summer."

Conrad had lain back on the bed next to her. "What made her so good?" he asked curiously.

"Everything," Katherine said, already reminiscing. "It was everything about her. She was a genius. I worked so hard for her."

"Why?"

"Because she demanded perfection in the realest sense of the word. She was never late, she was always organized, she never misspoke, she knew everything, she had the best advice. I could go on and on. She had such a presence about her. Such a dominant presence. I can't imagine how good she must have been in the courtroom when she was a prosecutor. Back then I was thinking about law school, and she was my idol. One of my biggest regrets was never getting to see her work a case. When she was at Walker's, I only got to see her in meetings."

"As a person, did you like her?" Conrad asked.

She thought about the question. "I did," she answered. Then she said, "I have to be honest, and please don't take this the wrong way, but I never understood how someone could be married to her. She was so critical – in the right way for a lawyer but the wrong way for a wife. I imagine she must have been impossible for you sometimes."

"So why did you like her?"

"I caught her crying once," she said instantly. Conrad sat up and looked at her inquisitively. "It must have been during one of her breaks. I left my folder in her office. I looked in and saw that she wasn't at her desk and the lights were off. So I opened the door and saw her sitting on a ledge by the window in the back of her office. She wasn't sobbing, but there were tears in her eyes and she was holding a tissue in her hand like she had

187

been crying harder before I came. I apologized and quickly shot out of there. But then I remember her catching my arm the next day, and she told me she was sorry that I saw her that way. It was the only time I remember her opening up like that. I felt bad for her. It made me like her more. She was real."

Conrad held his knuckles over his mouth. "Did you know Bran Hall?"

"Yea. He was our instructor during our induction."

"Did you like him?"

"Yea. I delivered documents to him from time to time. He was always nice to me, but he could be..."

"What?"

"I don't know how to explain it. He was never mean to me personally, but he had a mean streak in him that I didn't really like. He could also be really arrogant. But again, he was always fine around me."

"Did you ever feel that there was something between him and Micker?"

"Your wife?" she asked.

"Yea. Like a thing?"

"No. Not that I remember. Why do you ask?"

"One of those rumors. Obviously it doesn't matter anymore; they're both gone."

"Where did he go?"

"New York, the last I heard."

Katherine stretched her arms, deciding on how to ask the next question. "How did you get over her death? Everybody knew about it. Everybody was shocked. I didn't think she could die."

Conrad surveyed the living room. "It was hard at first. I thought I would die. But then something happened."

He looked into the kitchen. His intensity made her do likewise.

188

"You see the window in there?"

"Yes."

"One night I was on the couch right here. This was shortly after her death, maybe a year, and I had taken something strong to help me sleep. And I was in a deep dream, honestly the deepest dream of my life to the point where I thought it was real. I must have heard something on my porch because I woke suddenly. And when I woke, I looked across the living room into the kitchen and saw the face of some man staring back at me through the window. His eyes were bugged out, like he was on something, and he had this huge smile, from ear to ear." Conrad stared at her. "I knew that smile. It was Donny Locks."

"Who got you fired?"

"Same one."

"I used to live close to him," Katherine said. "I knew his mom well. I couldn't believe how he turned out. He went on that rampage –"

"This was the same night."

She sat up tall. She didn't know what to expect next. "You think he came to kill you?"

Conrad didn't answer her yet. He continued, "I couldn't remember if I had locked the door, and – my heart. And then he disappeared. Nothing happened. I sat there, confused and drowsy from the pills, and I did nothing. I thought I was still dreaming. I fell back asleep.

"When I woke, it was early in the morning – still dawn. I immediately remembered Locks' face in the window. I ran upstairs to check Belle, but she was okay. Then I checked the house to see if anything had been stolen. Finally, I walked out on the porch. I was now convinced it was a dream, but there, directly below the window, was a small pool of blood and a series of bloody footprints. When I opened the door to go inside, my hand slid off, covered in blood. The blood had yet to

189

dry. He must have been out there quite awhile trying to get in.

"I called the police to report it, but they acted strange. They told me they would send a cop over, but in the meantime they asked me to turn on the news. I did, and saw Locks had gone on a shooting rampage that night, killing four people. He had hit a grocery store and then the restaurant on Tieta Drive. My house was his last stop before he drove down to the Golden Gate and ended it. It was horrifying."

"I remember that night," Katherine said. "It was shocking."

Conrad was speaking in a daze now. "You know what's ironic about that rampage? It vindicated me. I became the guy who saw it coming, who knew Locks was a bad guy. People started to lay off of me. For years they suspected I might have something to do with Micker's death. There was no proof, I was never charged with anything, but still some of them couldn't stop from sensationalizing it. But with Locks' fate, I felt I was finally vindicated."

Katherine waited awhile before she spoke. She wanted to absorb the story before speaking. "You're a good man, Conrad," she said, rubbing his shoulders, caressing with them the impact of his story.

He held her tight, and as they fell asleep, he began to realize he was developing legitimate affection for her. It was a feeling he hadn't had in a long, long time.

CHAPTER 29: HAPPENING FAST

Over the course of the next few months, things happened very fast in the Mayday household. Once word spread that Belle had skipped three years of her education, she became a local celebrity in San Sangre. She not only skipped from first grade to fourth (an advancement that garnered a spot on the local news and a profile in the San Sangre and San Francisco Almanac), but she was, after the completion of an I.Q. test, inducted into Mensa International, a "high-I.Q." society selective of only those who score in the 98th percentile. In the annual *Mensa Bulletin*, Conrad observed Belle finding her place on a list that included Isaac Asimov, Albert Einstein, and Jodie Foster.

At school Belle found her stardom had made her life, oddly enough, easier. While there were certainly some fourth graders who called her a freak and a nerd, she seemed to find her place among the students. She was tall for her age, which allowed her to blend in with the fourth grade class, and she was brilliant, earning her respect particularly from the students at the top of her class. Most important at that age, she was pretty and had a mature look about her. Though only seven, she appeared like she was nine or ten, which engendered a respect and admiration from many of the students.

Fourth grade was just that age where the boys no longer told parents they hated girls and began asking them out for petty week-long relationships, and where strong cliques began to form – cliques that in some cases would last until high school. While Belle didn't find a clique instantly, she always found a welcoming seat with the geeks at the lunch table. There she saw her interests piqued: talks of the school's administration, literature, social studies, the dumb answers of the day, and future ambitions.

At home Belle and Conrad had grown closer than ever before. For the first time, Conrad was paying close attention to Belle and catering to her needs. Belle, on the other hand, was opening up to him and treating him not just as a caring father but also as her best friend.

As Conrad frequented town, he saw more eyes upon him than ever before. Belle had, frankly, made him once again an important person, only this time he was no longer in the shadows as he was with Micker. While married to Micker, he could always assume jealous eyes from men wandering how he ever landed such a beautiful woman. His presence with her made him eligible, privileged, important, but only important by the accident of luck. With Belle, there was this sense that he had something to do with her genius – that he was responsible for cultivating her natural gifts. When he took her shopping for school clothes in town, walked her to the school bus, or watched her during swim lessons, there were always haunting eyes of jealousy upon him that secretly wished they could trade places if given the chance.

To the residents of San Sangre, particularly those that were white, Conrad Mayday was sitting on a lottery ticket. While they were worried their sons or daughters would be passed over

192

come college admissions and later job hunts for the Hispanics and Latinos that dominated the town, they saw Belle with the potential to stand above them. Her genius alone would likely propel her to seek admission to any Ivy League school she wanted. Better yet, her genius offered limitless opportunity and, if the cards were played right, money. Her gifts, as far as the town was concerned, were just waiting to be exploited.

And to bring things close to perfect, Conrad had allowed Katherine to enter their lives. It was broken to Belle that he was seeing Katherine, and though Belle's reaction was harsh at first, she slowly warmed to her dad's new woman. While Katherine was welcomed to his world, he kept her at a distance, a distance Katherine was happy to obey. They were careful not to rush into things, and usually only saw each other on the weekends.

It didn't take long before a day someone never forgets came. Conrad received a call from a man named Grear Wolfowitz:

"Is this the father of Belle Mayday?" a slated and clever voice said into the transmitter.

"Yes, this is he," Conrad affirmed. "Who is this?"

"Mr. Mayday, my name is Grear Wolfowitz, producer at the Evory Broadcast Company, EBC."

"EBC – as in the television channel?" Conrad asked.

"Yes," Wolfowitz said. "I have been following your daughter's story here in the San Francisco Almanac, and I think she would be the perfect candidate for a new television show I'm hoping to produce."

Conrad lost his breath for a few seconds. "That's great," he said. "What kind of show?"

"Well I'm working under the title, *Wonder Minds,* but I'm sure the title will transform a few times if it is picked up. But the

193

show will be run something like Jeopardy or the quiz shows of the fifties where two contestants will compete in a quiz game of sorts for money," Wolfowitz said. His voice then trailed off as he began thinking out loud. "I can't think of anything more exhilarating than the prospect of watching children winning thousands of dollars."

Conrad didn't want to sound overly excited. "Well, what would Belle have to do? I mean, what's in it for her?"

"If you sign off, we will fly you and your daughter out here to Los Angeles free of charge, and we will ask Belle to compete in a couple of test trials with the format we will hopefully be using for the show. I will have some judges during the trial-runs help decide along with me which child stays and which child goes. From that batch of candidates we will probably select about ten to compete on the show during the first season."

Conrad felt goosey. He leaned up against the wall in the entry way and slowly slid down it like his legs were jelly until his butt hit. He asked, "What are the chances Belle would be selected? I mean, how big is the candidate pool?"

"About four hundred kids."

"So her chances are slim?"

"Her chances on paper are slim, but there is a lot that goes into the judging. Let's just say it's not strictly about performance."

"What else goes into the judging, if you don't mind my asking?"

Wolfowitz hesitated for a second. "Well, the looks of the children, their demeanor, their life story, their families' story, that kind of stuff." Conrad smiled instantly. He knew why Wolfowitz had called him: Belle's picture had been in the Almanac and on the Internet, and Belle looked particularly striking in her picture. "I can tell you this, Mr. Mayday, without
194

saying too much. I would like your daughter's chances. She possesses many of the qualities that I look for in contestants that would make her candidacy very, very strong."

"Well, I would be interested in taking her out there to try-out. When is the date?"

"I was actually wondering if you could come the weekend after Easter, the seventeenth and eighteenth?" Wolfowitz said hesitatingly, realizing the inconvenience. "I know it's spring break, but we figured this was the best time considering most kids are out of school."

"No, that date should work."

"That's good to hear. I will have my secretary get a hold of you later today or tomorrow, and she will go over the trial procedures, your flight plan, the date and time of Belle's test-run, and your demographics. Sound good?"

"Sounds great! Thank you sir."

"Then have a good day, and I hope to see you after Easter."

After the phone call, Conrad looked up Grear Wolfowitz's name on the Internet to discover that Wolfowitz was the television producer famous for having spearheaded #1 shows like *Double Down* and *Working for the Stars*. All of the websites that housed his biography, though, also included his notorious negotiation skills. Wolfowitz was known as being seductive and implacable.

Why would this man call me personally? He assumed Wolfowitz had a bevy of subordinates capable of making preliminary calls. Then the statistics began rolling around in his head. Ten out of four hundred. Some parents won't put their children through such an ordeal, so narrow it to three hundred fifty. At least a hundred of those kids are not going to look the part, so ten of two hundred fifty. About fifty will screw up their audition…about ten of two hundred. In Conrad's mind, Belle had a five percent chance of making it through. He could go no higher or no lower in his estimates. But something abstract, like a premonition but more aligned with emotional whim, gave him a safe feeling inside like a warm blanket that Belle would have no problem making the final cut.

CHAPTER 30: THE TRIAL

The trip to Los Angeles was much easier than Conrad expected. Like Wolfowitz had said, everything was done for them. The flight was taken care of, a taxi picked them up and took them to the EBC studio, and from there they always had someone walking alongside giving precise directions on where to go and what to do.

The only thing Conrad didn't like about the trip was that it was without Katherine. She stayed with her parents for Easter somewhere north of Sacramento. Katherine didn't seem warm to the idea of a seven year old being on a quiz show, but she didn't say why. She politely declined to go with them.

Once inside the EBC studio, Belle was taken from Conrad by a few women with personalities and suits marked by gravitas. He didn't see her for three hours as she completed her rounds of interviews and tests. When the interviews were said to be nearly finished, Conrad was taken to a conference room in the Marriot Lobby where a semi-spherical table lay in a horseshoe shape before deadening white walls. The carpet was burnt yellow, uneasy on the eyes.

"Please, take a seat," one of the three women in lapis

suits said on the other side of the table, directly across from Conrad. They were all dressed uniformly and had brown hair pinned neatly behind their heads. Soon after a woman named Anna DeSilva, a co-producer of the prospective show along with Wolfowitz, entered through a back door and took a seat at the head of the table. She was older than the other women. She wore an ivory suit and her hair color was light brown. Conrad could tell immediately that she was a smart, sophisticated, and a proper woman with miles of authority. No one dared speak until she had spoken first.

"Mr. Mayday, we have called you here to talk about your daughter," DeSilva said. Conrad observed she had a pointed way of talking. It made you want to listen. She was also the biggest of the four women. He sat up in his seat, his darting eyes telling of his nerves. DeSilva took a moment to look at her colleagues sitting on her flanks. "Mr. Mayday, how would you characterize success?"

Conrad asked confusedly, "How would I characterize success?"

"I promise this questionnaire has some meaning," DeSilva assured in an arrogant pitch. "Please, indulge me. How would you characterize success?"

"Success is…getting what you want in life."

"And how do you go about achieving that?" she asked, always emphasizing the last syllable in words.

He folded his hands, a signal he had just found an answer. "Through hard work and dedication – and a little bit of luck. Actually a lot of it."

Finally, another person, a man at the end of the table, spoke. "Can success ever be described as nothing but luck?"

Conrad thought about the question for a few seconds. "Yes, I believe it can."

"How so?" the man asked.

198

"I think everything we are in life is marked by luck: who we are born to, how we look, what talents we have. Many of the successes I have had have more or less fallen out of the sky without rhyme or reason."

DeSilva asked coldly, "Could you then say that success, if by luck, improves the harder one works?"

"You could say that, but frankly, I think it depends mostly on luck." Conrad looked over at DeSilva. "Being here today is luck," he said, shocked by the confidence he had in delivering his words.

DeSilva looked down at her half-opened manila file, her eyes waving over the information like a machine. "Mr. Mayday, I wanted our panel to ask you that question because we have found that parents who believe success is earned through hard work tend to put too much pressure on their children. Those that see success as luck tend to take their children's success, or lack there of, more in stride. Pressure from parents to succeed at a young age can have very adverse affects on children. Mr. Mayday," she continued, her mind very much on an intended course, "we've come across a problem with your daughter's candidacy." Conrad's stomach tightened. Those were the words he didn't want to hear.

"What happened?"

"I think it's a good problem," the man at the opposite flank said. "The kind of problem you want to hear, but the kind of problem, twenty years down the road, you might not." The man paused a few seconds to capture his place in the conversation. It was the first time he spoke. "Your daughter, Mr. Mayday, is a genius." The table went silent. Conrad took a few seconds to take in what he had just heard.

At that moment, Grear Wolfowitz, who looked much younger and fresher than Conrad imagined, like an aging model, walked through one of the back doors and stood against the

199

wall, checking his cell phone and sipping his coffee. He had silvery hair and a silvery beard.

The man continued talking: "When I say genius, I am talking about not just the tests we had your daughter take or retake: the I.Q. and Wechsler tests, but her communicative skills, which we have estimated to be about the same as a fourteen year old, someone twice her age. This is a great thing, a superlative thing that is rarely seen in our lifetimes. But this can be, or become, a bad thing. Do you know why I say that?"

Conrad thought about it. "Frankly, I can't."

DeSilva's mouth contorted like a fish. She slightly averted her head before interrupting her colleague. "Mr. Mayday, most people are under the assumption that people, like myself and Mr. Wolfowitz whom you spoke with over the phone, are only interested in success, money, and fame, and that we are willing to exact any measure or exploitation to achieve it. We are prepared and expecting to take a lot of flack for creating a show like this. People are going to say we are taking advantage of children."

She paused quite effectively before continuing. "I can't speak for all of us, but our objective here is in fact for the betterment of the children participating in this exhibition. As you know, quiz shows of this liking can have damaging ramifications on young children because of the pressures of competition at that age and because of the world-altering effects of fame. The unfortunate thing is that children in this case aren't given a chance to make this decision, and in most cases, they aren't able to decide its course. Do you know how many parents we have had over all these years and through all the kid-led talent shows turn our offer down to have their kid on a show? Would you care to guess?"

"Maybe ten percent," Conrad guessed.

DeSilva held up a zero in her palm. "It's never

200

happened."

Conrad's eyes ventured around the room before falling into Grear Wolfowitz's steely eyes. "What are you trying to tell me?" Conrad asked, hoping to arrive at the point.

"We want your daughter to be on this show. We want you to fly back out here in three weeks for the taping of the first episode. We want her to be one of the first two contestants the public sees when our show airs. We think your daughter," she looked to both sides of her table, "given her looks, her manner, and her mind, is going to be a huge star." Conrad's legs began to quiver in unbridled excitement.

Wolfowitz proceeded out of the darkness and stood over DeSilva's shoulder. He took another sip of his coffee and began to speak. "Mr. Mayday, we don't think *you* quite understand how powerful the gifts your daughter possesses are. Our goal is to make sure you make the right decisions for her, and you keep in mind that she is only a child," he said. His voice was indeed seductive.

Conrad nodded his head twice. "I understand. Can I see her?"

DeSilva stared at him speculatively for a moment before asking Wolfowitz if Belle was done with her interviews.

Wolfowitz looked at his watch. "She'll be done with the last audition in ten minutes."

Conrad carried Belle to the gate at Los Angeles International Airport. It was raining outside and the palm trees planted in tiny islands in the sea of pavement were blowing furiously in the storm. Conrad figured they would be awhile.

"I can walk," Belle said. She still sounded exhausted. Conrad had been carrying her since they left the studio.

"Are you sure?"

"Yea," she said.

He put her down, and they took the only empty seats at the crowded gate.

Conrad placed his hands on her shoulder and looked her in the eye. "Belle, if you don't want to do this show, you don't have to."

She yawned and rolled her eyes with her fists. "It's okay, Dad."

"So you want to do it?"

She smiled. "Yea."

He hugged her and lifted her to his lap. "If you ever change your mind, you just tell me," he said.

Sitting across from Conrad was an old woman who put her glasses on to get a better look at Conrad and Belle. When she saw Conrad holding Belle's head against his shoulder, the old woman smiled heartily. Conrad smiled back. He felt like a good parent for the first time in a long time.

CHAPTER 31: AFTER THE GREEN ROOM

When Conrad and Belle returned to the EBC studio for the first taping of the show, now officially titled *Question Ten*, they felt like they had never left.

Conrad waited with Belle before the show's start in what was known as a green room, a type of locker room for the contestants. The carpet, ironically, was not green. It was burgundy with black pyramid designs that dizzied the eye. There were tables of garish food set up around the room: croissants, fruits, dips, hors d'oeuvres, and baskets of candy bars for those who were less suave: Twix, Take Five, Snickers, and Butterfingers. Show producers, assistants, and assistants to the assistants were walking in and out of the green room, their bodies sweating and their expressions in constant duress.

"You ready?" Conrad asked Belle. His left leg was vibrating his left elbow, which shook his fingernails on his teeth. Belle noticed the jitters.

"I'm not nervous," she said.

"You just do the best you can and you don't worry what happens. Okay?"

"I'm having a good time."

Conrad looked across the green room where a chubby, spectacled boy who looked like Jabba the Hutt was sitting with his back straightened like a statue, staring at the wall across from them without blinking. His father, a skinny little man with patches of a beard was watching Conrad with a contemptible scowl.

"You just go out and do your best," Conrad repeated.

Belle widened her eyes. Her father seemed a lot more nervous than she.

The same lady who seated them in the green room opened the door and asked Belle to come back with her in a phony greeting: "Hi Belle! Could you come back here with me?" she asked, transmitting a fake smile. "We're going to get her dressed and in makeup," she told Conrad.

Belle left the room with Conrad's worried eyes on her the whole time. A few minutes later, a young male assistant came for the chubby boy across the room. Conrad and the boys' father were left alone, often looking around the room observantly, awkwardly trying to avoid eye contact. Any sense of comity was quickly erased. They realized they were involved in something people hadn't seen in a long time. It was a competition among children, a show that could make stars and break dreams. One of their children had the potential of becoming famous, but at the other's expense.

Once Conrad was seated in the audience, it didn't take him long to understand why the producers felt Belle was a star. She shimmied onstage in a yellow-sheath dress tightly fit and waived to the crowd. Benjamin, the chubby boy, stood alongside her and waived reservedly. Both children then headed to opened booths that lay twenty feet apart, a slight throwback of the 1950's quiz show, *Twenty-One*.

204

Conrad was shocked when he saw Belle's dress. He was convinced it had padding, almost like football pants, around her hips to make them seem curvy. Pads were almost certainly, but subtly, placed around her chest to give her a womanly figure. Her hair was in the iced champagne style and her lips were a powdery pink. On top of all the manufactured elegance, Belle had myrtle green eye shadow and what seemed like double-laced eyelashes. She looked like a princess, a miniature Grace Kelly.

Conrad found the seating arrangements for the audience to be uniquely structured. There were only about a hundred ascending seats, but each seat was separated far from the other, where one could literally stick his or her legs straight out without touching the seat in front. The seats were also wide and tall. Conrad noticed there really weren't that many people in the audience. Every seat was filled, so probably around a hundred or so, but the spacing made it seem as though two hundred audience members, if not more, were present.

He didn't really understand any of it. It was his first time in a studio audience. There were cameras set up in three different locations around the stage where Belle and Benjamin stood in their booths, but there was never an indication taping had begun until the moderator, a man who from the distance looked a little bit like Tom Hanks, walked confidently on stage with a series of white playing cards. He came from a concealed door in the bright red background that broke apart a fraction of the show's name, *Question Ten*. Bright orange letters flickered above a square board that said, "Applaud." A man holding cue cards then turned around and flexed his hands in the air to approve the crowd's applause.

The moderator stood at a podium about ten yards from Belle and Benjamin and briefly introduced himself as Jack Clark to the crowd and explained the rules of the game. Conrad tried to listen closely, but his mind was running around the studio, soaking in the moment and the reality that such an event was actually happening. Clark explained the directions slowly, but too slowly where Conrad understood the easy stuff but vacationed during stretches of the hard stuff.

When he was paying attention and not staring off into the ceiling's studded white lights, Conrad was under the impression that the contest was about whom could earn ten points the fastest. In order to get to ten points, the contestants had to answer ten multiple choice questions correctly. That was the essence of the contest, but like all quiz shows, there were catches.

What made the contest tricky was the fact that everything depended on the first question. Only the first question required a buzzer, and whoever buzzed in first to answer the first question held the upper hand and put their opponent at their mercy.

Potentially, if one contestant buzzed in first and answered the first question correctly, he or she would earn one point and then be given every question afterward until he or she got one wrong. Thus, if they never missed another question, they could answer nine in a row and win. Their opponent could go the entire contest without speaking.

But the producers had fought off ways to prevent such a scenario from happening often. First, each question had a degree of difficulty, as it was ranked one through five. A question with a ranking of one was considered easy, with nearly ninety percent of contestants answering it correctly in trial runs. A question with a ranking of five, however, was considered difficult, with contestants answering it correctly twenty percent of the time. Ranks of two, three, and four varied in difficulty, respectfully.

Questions from each of these five rankings were randomly created and spit out by a computer, meaning that a

206

contestant could have two five-tiered questions in a row.

The most important aspect of the game, however, was the final question – the question that brought the contestant to ten points. That question had to be answered correctly, or the contestant would lose all points and drop to zero and start over.

That was the part Conrad found the most interesting: the idea of being a foot from the mountain top, but one misstep and you fell to the bottom.

Belle immediately got off on the wrong foot. She missed the buzzer to a multiplication question of the fourth tier, 21X13. Benjamin answered correctly with considerable ease, and quickly went on to amass four points before stumbling on a history question of the fifth tier. Belle then earned two points by answering two questions right, but missed the third, dropping the ball back in Benjamin's corner.

Conrad was amazed at how fast the contest was held. Because the contestants had but three minutes to answer, it rolled by like rapid fire. With a score of 4-2, a commercial break ushered the make-up crew to Belle's face.

The questions seemed impossible to Conrad. They had remarkable variance, from typical pop culture and history categories, to math and even science categories. He didn't remember some of the answers or even some of the questions. They were difficult questions, the ones it seemed a Jeopardy contestant might face: Who was the sixteenth President of the United States? Which former Teamster President disappeared mysteriously in 1975? Anthropology is the study of? They were challenging questions for most adults, which is why the crowd excreted collective sighs when one of them was answered correctly by someone so young.

When the thirty-second commercial was over, Conrad observed Grear Wolfowitz standing off the stage with his entourage. When he caught Conrad gleaming at him, he shot him a slow wink and a brimming smile.

When Jack Clark briefly reintroduced the rules and the standings after the commercial break, Conrad studied Benjamin's physique. He was a fat, moonfaced kid with big, fish lips, which sat out further than his knobby nose. He wore round, black outdated glasses that made him look like Roger Ebert. Conrad stared at his countenance intensely in relationship to Belle: it was the chubby behemoth vs. the beauty queen; the monster vs. the princess. It was such a simple set-up, yet it worked so well. Every time Conrad looked at Belle and then at Benjamin, an unrelenting anger brewed in him that went beyond paternal instinct. He wanted Benjamin to lose. He wanted him to lose badly, and he sensed the audience felt the same way.

Benjamin was the perfect villain. He looked intelligent, and he was horribly unappealing. To make matters worse, his appearance, though bitter to the eye, had a built in pompousness, particularly in the circuitousness of his face. With his tiny eyes glinting under those robustly framed glasses, and his perched lips and ability to spew remarkable facts from them, he was inauspiciously built to be hated. Then there was his voice: loud, grating, high-pitched until the last syllable, and reeking of arrogance. He was the perfect foil to someone like Belle. He was a handpicked villain.

Conrad grew warm and tingly. He was watching Belle now. Her face was tense, and he noticed her score was at eight while Benjamin's was at nine.

"Benjamin, you now have the chance to win this competition if you answer this question correctly," Clark said. "Remember, if you happen to answer it incorrectly, your point total will drop to zero and you will have to start all over. Are you ready?"

"Yes," he said impassively.

The number "five" lit up between Belle and Benjamin's

208

booths. The crowd gasped.

"Here goes. How many moons does the planet Venus have? A. 0. B. 1. C. 7. D. 40. Take your time. You have three minutes. Let me know when you are ready."

It was subtly clear that Benjamin did not know the answer, for his head had dipped timidly. Belle turned and watched him through the open sides of her booth, her lips slightly trembling in an otherwise statuesque pose. After thirty seconds, as Benjamin moved his eyes to the lights without blinking or turning his face, it was apparent he was as unsure as the crowd.

"Thirty seconds," the host said excitedly.

Belle stopped watching Benjamin and looked toward Jack Clark. She seemed to sense her opportunity.

"Twenty seconds."

Benjamin was sweating. He stared at Jack Clark before pressing his head with his fingers, muttering to himself.

"Ten seconds."

His hands flew up effeminately and he looked around in frustration.

"I'm sorry, Benjamin," the host said wonderfully, "but time has expired. I need your answer."

"I don't know," Benjamin said frustratingly.

"What is your guess? A, B, C, or D?"

"I don't know," Benjamin snapped.

Murmurs began in the crowd.

Jack Clark was confused. "You're not going to guess?"

Tears formed in Benjamin's eyes. "I don't know," he repeated.

Jack Clark looked to the crowd for assurance. "I'm sorry, but I will have to accept a wrong answer then. Because this was question ten, your point total drops to zero."

Conrad suddenly felt bad for Benjamin. He was just a

kid, and he let frustration get the better of him. *It will play well with audiences though*, Conrad thought. *They might be screaming at the screen.*

Clark continued: "The question now goes to Belle. Remember, every question is in play until it is answered. Belle, you have three minutes."

Belle did not hesitate: "The answer is A, zero moons," she said with a loving smile. The crowd cheered, and all the tension that she had had was now pushed out of her system.

"Zero moons is correct. That leaves you with nine points and now a chance to win." The crowd moved to their seat's edge in unison. "If you answer this question right, you will have ten points and be crowned the first champion on Question Ten!"

The number "five" lit up again in red. The crowd sighed loudly. Conrad couldn't watch. "Here goes," Jack Clark said as dramatically as possible. "It was your generation's September 11th. On what month, day, and year did the Japanese attack on Pearl Harbor occur?"

There was an interesting reaction in the crowd. Most of the people over sixty seemed to know it, as did most of the men. The majority of the women, on the other hand, shook their heads in confusion. Conrad realized the genius of quiz shows. When you finally did know the answer to a question that the contestants didn't know, you felt a surge of superiority. It was an amazing feeling, no matter how momentary it was.

Conrad had that right then. He knew the answer. It was stitched on his brain: December 7, 1941. He was worried though; Belle didn't seem to know it.

"Two minutes left."

Benjamin did what Belle had done earlier. He turned slightly so he could catch her reactions. Belle looked to the floor. The same numbers kept swirling around in her head: 7,

210

41, 6, 42. She was certain the attack happened before Christmas, and that U.S. involvement in World War II didn't commence until the forties, but which year and which day? She didn't know the answer.

"One minute."

She still had plenty of time. The dates were moving around in her head. She honed in on two possibilities of which she was certain: December 7, 1941, and December 6, 1942. In her head she was convinced 7 and 42 didn't go together, and that 6 and 41 didn't go together either.

"Thirty seconds."

She had made up her mind. She was going with December 6, 1942. She was sure she was right, so she decided to wait for her time to expire before answering. The producer's had told her beforehand that if she knew the answer to a question, she should take her time to make sure she was right. *Remember, it's not about who answers the quickest after the first question, but who answers the most.*

"Belle, the time is up. I need your answer."

She was about to give it when something internally told her to hesitate. An image from one of her mom's books of a crocodile came to her from the recesses of her mind. Suddenly, she was six again and reading about, what was it, oh yes, the Battle of Ramree Island, where Japanese forces were pushed by American troops into the Ramree swamps that were teeming with saltwater crocodiles. Nearly fifteen hundred Japanese were eaten alive by the crocodiles in one night. The name of one of the men who witnessed the account was Bruce Wright. He had been stationed there in Ramree since U.S. involvement: 1942-1945. Now it all made sense to her. If the attack happened in December, it would be unlikely Wright was in Ramree before the New Year. He most likely started in 1942. It was the logical answer with the information she now had. It made sense suddenly. The date, December 7, 1941, was floating in her mind now. The fact that it didn't go away made her sure she was about to answer correctly. More remarkable was that this epiphany came to her in a matter of seconds. That was how quickly her mind culled, collated, and processed information.

"Belle, I must have your answer."

"The answer is," and for her own dramatic purposes she delayed and looked across at Benjamin, "December seventh...nineteen...forty...one."

Crowd members who knew the answers audibly gasped. Jack Clark turned back to hold them in suspense, then he said, "That is...correct!" The crowd erupted. The person they wanted to win had won. She had beaten the arrogant chubby kid who would no doubt go on to bigger and better things. But not today.

"Come on out here, contestants!"

Belle walked out gingerly, too shocked to believe in her achievement. "Let's give our contestants a big round of applause, everyone," Jack Clark said, and the cheering went on and on and on. A huge cardboard check was brought out by two women of very motherly appearance and nature. They never stopped smiling. Conrad looked at the check.

$20,000.

She had made half his salary in an hour.

A hand from behind fell on Conrad's shoulder: "Congratulations," a voice said. Conrad turned and saw that it was Grear Wolfowitz. He was wearing a silver suit, and with his silverish hair he looked like something out of a chic men's catalog. "I have a feeling we're going to see her for a long time to come," he said. And Conrad knew just what he meant. Belle was a natural, a star, a talent maybe no one had ever seen.

The moments after the show were like Christmas.

Conrad and Belle were ushered back to the green room where there was champagne and fresh horsd'oeuvres and loud celebrative commotion. Grear Wolfowitz was there along with Desilva and her suit-posse. From their jubilation, Conrad seemed to think they were sure they struck gold. Wolfowitz said that he had never witnessed a more entertaining show. He was ecstatic that their first show would crown Belle their champion. The win would guarantee that Belle return for another episode, and if she were to win, she would keep coming back and keep coming back. Conrad could sense that Wolfowitz was willing to do anything to ride Belle as long as he could, and Conrad was okay with that. This show was going to make Belle and him a star.

What Conrad overheard in a conversation between Wolfowitz and Desilva, this while he was supposed to be listening to the show's lawyers who were explaining his contract, was that they were hopeful the controversy of staging such child-theater would generate buzz and attract viewership. With Belle as the poster child of the nascent show, they were sure media attention would be prodigious. They seemed to talk confidently about it, always in future tense as though they had an oracle stored away somewhere in their brains. Conrad could tell they wanted the negative reactions from the country; they wanted people to be outraged over what they would certainly call child-exploitation. For them that meant ratings and interest and notoriety. When they put Belle out there in that dress looking like a miniaturized woman, there was sure to be outrage. But they had to control it. The show at its core was simple and fundamentally innocent: showing off child prodigies. There was nothing externally threatening or harmful about it. That, of course, was their secret.

Belle stayed in her dress after the show so they could catch the first plane ride home. She wanted the make-up off of her, though. Everyone in first class was staring at her like she was some type of freak. Conrad gave her some towelettes and she sat in her seat and rubbed the make-up off. She needed five towelettes before she had removed all of her make-up. There was no garbage can on the plane except in the bathroom, and she wasn't about to walk all the way back to coach looking the way she did. So she sat in her seat with her meal tray down in an unusual way: four towelettes were lying on the meal tray in front of her colored in red and pink spreads. Conrad asked the stewardess to throw them away.

Conrad was fighting his tired eyes and could not read Belle's contract on the plane. It was nighttime and they would be in the air another hour. He suddenly had the emerging need to vomit. He hadn't eaten anything, so he likened the ailment to airsickness, but the feeling in his stomach was something different. It seemed to be caused by the built up pressure and expectation of the show. He undid his seatbelt and rushed to the back of the airplane to the bathroom and slammed the door. Those in coach who were sleeping were awakened by the sight of a grown man running down the aisle in desperate need to hold his fire.

After twenty minutes of waiting and being tired of answering the question, "Are you all right?" from the stewardess, Belle headed back in the sea of unfamiliar faces to check on her father. She tapped on the door to the bathroom a couple of times and whispered, "Dad, it's me. Can I come in?"

Conrad was sitting on his butt against the door. He wasn't used to throwing up, even when he had food poisoning or a virus. He didn't want his daughter to see the sight, but he needed company at the moment. He was disoriented and he needed to talk to somebody.

He opened the latch without getting up. She came in

214

and stood next to him and asked him what was wrong.

"I don't know, sweetie," he said. "I think it might be from all the excitement the last few weeks. And then with what happened today. Sometimes I get like this when I'm stressed," he said. But that was a lie. His health was like an iron man's.

"Are you upset about Katherine not coming with us?" she asked innocently.

"No," he answered with a smile. "She couldn't take off work."

She sat down next to him and he held her in his arms. He looked at her carefully. She seemed so much older than her age. He was amazed that he was her father, honored in some way. He thought of her as a gift. At times he was even tickled by her power. *She's smarter than I am. In just seven years, she's learned more than I have.*

CHAPTER 32: DIANE SOTO'S NEIGHBORHOOD PARTY

When Conrad and Belle arrived home, a special invitation was waiting for them. It was an invite to the annual neighborhood block party, an event held each year on the Saturday before Memorial Day. Conrad hadn't been invited since Micker died. He knew who kept him out each year, but this time, ironically, it was the same person who now made sure he was in. The invite was from Diane Soto herself, Conrad's power-hungry neighbor across the street, and it didn't take Conrad long to realize why he was invited.

Diane Soto was a pudgy, forty-two year old woman with curly black hair down to her shoulders and glossy skin that made her look like she had been made from wax. She was known as the gossip queen of the street with strong connections in local government. With four exceptionally athletic boys ranging from five to seventeen, she had built those strong connections right in the stands at her kids' sport outings.

Diane Soto's power came from knowledge. She seemed to know all the rumors and gossip in the town, and people liked to seek her out to find out what she knew. She had a subtle way of making people trust her and confide in her even though they

216

knew she knew everyone and was a parasite of freshly spilled rumors. It was her special gift. As a result, people wanted to stay in her good graces, so they often granted her favors. She had to make an effort of it. She had to be in public often and she never missed social outings.

Conrad watched her carefully work the party. She had a unique method where she would meddle in an isolated conversation very delicately as though she had been there the entire time. And the conversers were always welcoming to her. It was like the popular girl at school greeting the helpless nerds.

While she made her rounds and Conrad made small talk with his neighbors by the grill, he sensed Diane was watching him and working her way up to him. He, of course, was doing the same thing. He asked Katherine if she could keep an eye on Belle, explaining that it might be good if they spent some one-on-one time together. Belle and Katherine had been having their problems, and Belle wasn't very accepting of her. As soon as Katherine left him, he inched his way closer to Diane so they could finally talk. He knew that if Diane Soto liked you, everyone liked you, and it had been her gossip since Micker's death that caused him to become the pariah of the neighborhood. She, of course, was the one who told the police that Conrad was seen entering a car and driving off with Micker the night she died.

But times were changing.

It didn't take long before they met in a welcomed handshake, and after some flurried talk about the party, they got down to business.

"I heard about Belle," Diane said, flapping her hair aside in the breeze. "You must be so excited."

"I am," Conrad said.

"When will the first show air?" she asked.

Before Conrad could answer, he saw Katherine pull

Belle aside from the small soccer game she was playing with the other neighborhood kids. Katherine seemed to suggest that Belle take a timeout. Belle rolled her eyes and ran back into the game. Katherine put her hands on her hips in frustration. She turned to Conrad. He held up the palm of his hand as if it were okay. She shook her head and walked over to get a drink.

Conrad finally answered Diane: "It should be pretty soon. They just taped the first show. Belle will have to fly out again next week."

Soto's eyes perked up. "So she won?"

Conrad needed to be careful. "I can't reveal that," he said politely. "I signed a legal contract to keep my mouth shut about results unless they decide to air future shows live."

"Of course. Are you nervous for her?" she asked with an inquiring smile.

"To be honest, yes."

"What parent wouldn't be? You know exactly what those blood-suckers are after anyway. Must scare the hell out of you," she said, tempting him to side with her often-fierce judgments.

This was Conrad's opportunity to win over her support. He was beginning to realize that Diane Soto was like a grizzly bear when it came to protecting her kids. "It's whatever's best for Belle," he said. "If I sense they're trying to corrupt her in any way, I'll take her right out of it."

"Despite all the money?"

"Absolutely."

"You're a good father," she said flatly, and meant it. Then she sort of sank back in a lawn chair and relaxed her neck and shoulders the way people do when they are about to share something intimate. Conrad sat down in the lawn chair beside her. "Ya know, I need to be honest here; I didn't like you very much. I was one of the people who thought, well, ya' know,

218

with your wife's death and all. But talking with you, I'm almost disgusted I had those thoughts." She looked back to the party, noticing they were trying to watch her conversation with him. "I think we just – you never came out of the house, you seemed aloof, happy in your own company..."

Conrad cut her off: "How can you be any different when some people falsely think you may have had a part in your wife's death?"

"When the neighbor's were saying everything, why didn't you bother to refute it?" she asked. "I figure someone says I might have had something to do with my spouse's death, I'm gonna take his head off. But you...you didn't do that."

"I didn't have the strength to do it," he said. "And it wouldn't have helped Belle. Without her I couldn't have gotten through it."

Conrad and Diane turned to watch Belle play soccer with the other children in the yard. "Have you thought of remarrying?" she asked ploddingly.

"No. I have all the family I need."

She looked puzzled. "I thought you were with a young woman?"

Conrad realized nothing got by Diane Soto. Conrad and Katherine had been very private with their relationship. But Diane Soto saw everything that happened in the neighborhood, even the stuff beyond the naked eye. "I've been seeing her for a couple of months now," he said. "But it's nothing too serious yet. We agreed to take our time so it would be easier on Belle. Anyways, I find it things are always better in the long run if you don't rush into them."

"That's true," Diane confirmed. "That is true." She smiled firmly and reached out to shake his hand. "I'm sorry it took this long to have a real conversation."

"Better late than never," Conrad said, and shook her

hand. She was pleased with him. She felt she could open up to him, and there was something she had always wanted to get off her chest. "I never believed you had anything to do with your wife's death," she said, and Conrad knew that was a lie, "but I always wondered where you were taking her in the middle of the night – the night she died."

Here was his chance. "I never took her anywhere that night."

"But you were with her that night. You got in her car with her, and at the very least, drove with her down this very street and out of this very neighborhood." Her confidence was unsettling.

"Never," he replied sternly.

Right then Conrad saw a side of Diane Soto he had never seen before but always heard of. She turned into a pit-bull, her face sewn together by fury. Even her teeth showed. "Then you're calling me a liar, and you will surely not get away with that! I saw you," she said with her finger, pointing to his yard. "I saw *you*, under that tree, under that street lamp. I got a good look too. You stood under that street lamp and waited until she came out the back porch. Her car was parked on the street. And then you got in her car and drove off with her."

People around them began to take notice.

He traded anger with her. "That person that you saw was never me," he said convincingly.

They studied each other's eyes. Something happened simultaneously. He realized she was telling the truth, and he would have sworn to it. And she realized something.

He was too.

"But I saw you," she said dubiously, now defeated. "I could have sworn to it."

"You saw someone else. Something else," he said bemusedly. He thought maybe she was just a crazy loon, like the
220

cops suggested back then.

She was withering. "He looked just like you then. I saw his face in the street lamp."

"And you're sure you saw my wife get into this car?"

"Yes, now *that* I'm sure of. On my mother, may she rest in peace, I saw your wife get into that car with someone."

Conrad looked at the street lamp Diane had pointed to earlier. A tree was blowing above it. Its light bounced off the green. "Someone who looked like me…"

She wasn't satisfied. "Well, my question is, if it weren't you who drove off with your wife that night, then who was it?"

The soccer game had ended and the kids all came running over. Conrad and Diane couldn't help but end their conversation. Above them an enormous white blimp with a tethered American flag some fifty feet long floated across the sky. Everyone stopped to take notice.

Belle jumped in his lap, struggling to watch where she was running while inspecting the blimp in the sky. Conrad picked her up, bid goodbye to a now rattled Diane Soto, and walked down the street following the blimp.

"I haven't seen a blimp that size since I was a little boy," he said in amazement at the blur of American colors penetrating the blue-night sky. He held out his hand and Belle squeezed it gently. They sat down quietly on their neighbor's hill and watched the blimp disappear over the trees. It was a perfect atmosphere, a perfect moment, until Conrad realized Katherine was not with them. He looked around for her, but she was nowhere to be found.

He left Belle in the yard. He told her to stay where she was and that he would be right back. She didn't ask why. She continued to look for the blimp.

He made his way up the hill to his house. He had a suspicion Katherine was in the house.

As soon as he entered the house, he heard zippers to suitcases. He was sad now. He walked tiredly into the bedroom.

She had already packed two suitcases. They were lying on the bed in a neat order of one behind the other. She was working on number three when she stopped folding clothes and heard his footsteps creak. She looked up at him. Her eyes were red and she had been crying.

She cleared new tears from her face and said, "It's not working," then continued to bend down and pack.

"You just moved in. Give it a chance," he pleaded.

"It's not that," she said lowly.

"It's Belle?" he asked. She didn't object, so he said, "She needs to get used to you. It's awkward enough for her considering it's just been her and me for seven years, let alone the fact that you used to be her teacher. She will treat you better the more she gets to know you."

"That's not it either," she said more firmly.

"Then what?"

"You're so shameless," she said to him. "So shameless."

"Katherine, what are you talking about?"

"You're parading that girl around, putting her on display so people will like you," she said. "It's getting worse each day. You're not looking out for her best interest. You're only looking out for your interest."

"You don't know what you're talking about."

"I don't?" she quipped. "Before today you had never been invited to one of these parties, right? And then suddenly, when these people who have never offered to help you with Belle and have only talked behind your back for years invite you over, you go."

"So what?"

"You're doing it to show off! To show her off! You

222

know everybody knows about the TV show and they think they can get something from you and you're giving into them. I mean, where's your dignity?"

"I don't see what the big deal is in going to the party."

"That's why we're different."

While Katherine was in the throes of making her exit from Conrad's life, Belle had left the party and headed back into the house. She shut the door very carefully, waiting nearly thirty seconds to let the door close. She walked on her toes and sat on the bed in the adjacent room and listened carefully.

"You're really going to take her out to Los Angeles in two months so the suits can suck her dry?"

"Of course I am. Who wouldn't? And don't tell me it's *you?*"

She finished packing her last bag. She zipped it up and turned to him. "I have to go."

"I don't accept this. If it's the age difference, I can understand that. Even if you lost interest in me, I get it. But this excuse won't do."

She picked up her bag. "Then I can't do much for you," she said and began walking toward the door.

Conrad stepped in front of it. "Don't. Please don't go," he said.

"Are you taking her to LA?"

"You never objected to this before?"

"It never changed you before. Are you taking her?"

"Yes."

"Then I can't be with you." And that was it.

She went out the back door.

When Katherine shut the trunk to her car, she saw Belle standing by the passenger side. She had snuck out of the house. Katherine initially thought Conrad had sent her after him. She looked around the neighbor's yards where the party was. He was nowhere. She walked over toward Belle gently.

Belle had tiny tears in her eyes. "It's my fault you're going," she said.

"No, sweetie," Katherine said warmly. "Things just didn't work out with your daddy and me. This is something adults go through."

"Please don't go," Belle said desperately.

Katherine was confused. For months Belle had been her toughest adversary. She wouldn't talk to her. Sometimes she wouldn't acknowledge she existed when she was in the house. "I thought you didn't like me?" Katherine asked.

"I do now. I don't want you to leave."

Katherine walked over to her and hugged her. She bent down to her level and pushed Belle's hair behind her ears. "You take care of yourself, you hear me? If you ever feel uncomfortable in Los Angeles, you tell people that. Don't let them make you do anything you don't want to do? And if you ever need me, you know where to find me. And you come to me." Katherine wiped a tear from her cheek. "Go back to your house now. I'll watch to make sure you get there safely."

Belle put her head down and began walking home. She turned around halfway and saw Katherine was still watching her. Belle walked a few more yards and looked back again. Katherine was smaller now next to her car. Belle kept walking, along the neighbor's fence, sidling along it. She was in her own backyard. Her view to the street was narrower now. She looked back one last time, and Katherine was gone.

CHAPTER 33: A VISIT FROM THE PAST

Between lamenting Katherine's absence, Conrad kept playing his conversation with Diane Soto in his head that night. He journeyed to every corner of the house, thinking, trying to make sense of it. He was glad Belle decided to sleep over at one of the kid's houses. She would never have been able to sleep with his pacing.

He tried to remember back to the night Micker died, but he knew his efforts were futile; he had never been able to remember anything – no sound, no lights flicking on and off in the house, no car engine revving, nothing. Micker had simply disappeared.

He had always taken Soto for a liar, someone who would fabricate anything to make an interesting story for trade at the market. But when he looked into her eyes, he knew she wasn't lying. She had seen someone with Micker, but that someone happened to be him – and that wasn't possible. *Maybe she saw a man and wanted him to look like me*, he thought. *She never did like me much.*

But he knew that was too simple. There was more to it. Who else looked like him? And then it struck him, and he felt himself a fool for not realizing it earlier.

Bran did.

People had mistaken the two for a long time. They indeed looked alike. Conrad hated that fact, but now, he couldn't avoid it. It gave him goose bumps imagining Bran's face was the one that shown in the streetlight.

If it were Bran who drove off with Micker in the middle of the night, where did he take her? He was in New York City at the time, and no one else saw him that day. Actually, no one had set eyes on him in seven years. At least, no one Conrad knew. If someone had seen him that day – on a plane, on the road, in the neighborhood, they would have said something to Conrad. Everyone suspected Bran was the reason for Conrad's steep medical bills anyways. Conrad would have been the first person they talked to.

Unless he killed her. Conrad couldn't believe the thought entered his mind, and yet he couldn't believe he never considered it. Bran always loved Micker, he was certain of that, but would losing her drive Bran to kill? The police said the waters were rough that night, which meant swimming to shore from where the boat was found would have been reserved for Michael Phelps and perhaps a handful of other God-like swimmers. Couple that with prowling great white sharks lurking in the night for prey and the chances of surviving a swim to shore were, in the words of one of the officers, "about the same as fitting into this coffee mug." So if Bran killed her, maybe by pushing her overboard, how would he have gotten to shore? The boat never made it to the beach. Maybe they fell overboard together.

It didn't make sense.

Conrad reverted back to an old theory – suicide. Maybe Bran did come back to San Sangre to see Micker, but whatever happened that night, she was unsatisfied with what he had to

226

offer, and she took her own life. He could assure anyone that Micker was in the most dire of mental states after the pregnancy. Her depression was so severe that he couldn't even speak a word to her and get a reply. Whether she was eaten out there or in the house, Micker was not going to survive.

There was a number on a small sliver of paper that rested in the back of Conrad's desk drawer. He always wanted to throw it away, but he held onto it just in case he ever needed it. He twirled it in his fingers. The blue ink was showing its age.

He had looked this number up right after Micker's death. It had taken him days and some help from Brosnan to know where to look. Eventually, he got it.

He wasn't sure what he was thinking then or even why he wanted the number. It might have been just to have contact, or maybe to ask some questions, now that she was dead. Clarity and closure were important parts of his life. Now he rubbed that number with the intention of opening everything back up again.

212-546-8179.

He wanted to hear his voice. The first time in seven years. And if he got him on the line, would he hang up, or would he have the strength to ask the questions he had always wanted?

It took more strength than he anticipated. He would dial the area code and hang up. Dial and hang up. Each time he seemed to be dialing an extra number until he finally ran from two to nine.

It was ringing. He couldn't believe he was doing it after seven years. His heart was racing.

It continued to ring. He expected some young bachelor he never met to answer the phone. There was no way Bran was still at this apartment.

Click.

He stopped breathing.

He couldn't tell if it went to an answering machine.

"Hello," the voice said. It was a very proper and assertive voice. He nearly dropped the phone. He thought he knew who that was, and it wasn't Bran. He needed it to speak again, and this time he would be sure to identify the voice. He waited and waited, his heart rattling around for freedom. And there it was: "Hello?"

His eyes burned rage. He began panting. The phone clicked off.

He didn't hesitate. He dialed the number again and again. No one would pick up. He kept dialing, and dialing. There was no voicemail.

He wanted to hear that voice again. He was in a state of panic. He was confused and angry.

But he had gotten a good read on that voice.

He knew that voice. He could identify it in a stadium of voices sixty years from now.

For the first time in seven years, he had spoken to his wife.

CHAPTER 34: A TRIP TO THE FARALLONES

The temperature in San Sangre dropped below fifty that night, a record of cold for Memorial Day. It had the effect of adding to Conrad's abrupt depression and confoundedness. Summer didn't feel around the corner anymore.

He had to get out of the house. He drove into town in the hopes of understanding the events in solitude. But the streets were too cold to think and walk on. He just needed a place without the interference of people, so he stopped at a dark park in one of the neighborhoods only to see small little eyes glowing in the moonlight from his window. They were homeless people sleeping in the park.

"Quien es ese?" they said nervously. "los que vienen aquí?"

Conrad rolled up his window and drove out of town.

He was a stranger here.

Something led him to Walker's and told him he would be alone there. The docks were lit, but no one was on the pier. He unleashed his trawler and headed out into the peaceful ocean. He stopped about midway to the red buoys, knowing that once the "Walker's" sign could be covered by his thumb from the sea, he was halfway to the markers. He turned off the engine and realized the current was pulling him closer to the beach. That fact alone made him feel safe. He would not drift out past the buoys.

He lay against the starboard side of the boat and decided to make sense of everything. He looked up into the sky and the stars and moon were glowing white wafers. He turned to look back at the pier and thought that the distance he was from land was figuratively the distance he was to understanding the hardest reality.

She was alive. She was living with Bran. He couldn't get the idea out of his head that she was willing to leave him, to fake her own death. Was he suffocating her in some way? What did he do to make her so unhappy?

The questions tired him, and with the cold wind and the pleasant quietness of his surroundings, his body grew cold and wanting rest. With the ocean's clever drumbeat, he was softly swindled to sleep.

He awoke almost naturally out of fear, as though his body was drifting into a place it didn't want to go – that it feared. He awoke to total darkness. A black scarf had fallen over the water. The sea was nastier than before, and his trawler was bumping against the waves. He rubbed his eyes and looked up into the sky and saw the moon appear through the thickness of a cloud, and he noticed the clouds were thick but starting to dissipate in the sky. Within seconds the moon, in its half-life, broke free of its veil and punctured his eyes. He took the time to adjust, and as his eyes grew stronger he saw the stars – now tiny little perforations in the blackness.

The barking began. Out at sea there was the trembling-induced sound of dogs barking; dogs whose voices had grown

230

coarse and weak from fatigue and strain. They screamed, hundreds of them, and their howls echoed in the wind and bounced among the waves.

Conrad kept still along the starboard side, for he knew that if he stood he would fall overboard. He kept low on the boat so the nape of his neck was firmly against the wall but a foot from the deck like a drunkard. He looked as best he could without losing his balance, and he could not see the lights from Walker's. For the first time it had hit him: he had drifted past the buoys.

The sea turned still all of the sudden. There was no more rocking and hammering. He slowly rose in the boat, first to his knees and then to one foot. He looked out to sea in the opposite direction and saw nothing. The moon shone brightly but not bright enough to cast an impression on the distance.

There was movement in the water now. A small object was peddling directly beside him. It appeared to be going at a leisure pace, almost like an old person swimming laps at a gym pool. Conrad peered over the side and heard insignificant flapping sounds in the water, like a bird was swimming atop it but a bird with a more spherical shape. The flapping sound continued until something burst through the water vertically, creating a gargantuan rush. A baby's cry was heard and then cut severely. The moon disappeared. Then it came back, which meant the object that covered it would land on the water.

A tidal bomb exploded to the side of him and a pool of erupting white water rushed his boat and pulled him relentlessly overboard. The stinging taste of salt and the smell of stale sea water raped his senses. His body was contorting in the rush far under water and he felt the tight pulls of different currents stretching his body to the depths. Force and instinctual procedure thrust him vertically and he soon galloped to the top and ripped through the blackness to meet the moon above.

231

The barking was more fervent than before now and he felt, again instinctually, that the creature that had just covered the moon was below him checking him out. He even pondered that the currents he felt pulling him were more the immediate result of the creature's immensity.

Staying atop the surface was hard enough that it abated the fear of being pulled under and losing his legs. He swam furiously to where the boat had been, but he could not see anything. The moon only provided light to a restricted area of water, which meant the boat must have been pulled closer toward the barking sounds.

Conrad swam front crawl as fast as possible. He hoped his head would hit the boat, but instead he simply ran out of air. Panic soon set in and he was convinced he lost the boat. He looked up into the sky and could hear but not see Storm-petrels swooping above him in a circle. He treaded water now and hoped not to cause too much excitement with his movements. He continued to spin around in the water, hoping his boat's outline would grow apparent in the moonlight.

The eerie feeling that he was being watched below the surface was upon him now, and he figured it only a matter of time until he was lifted from the ocean by some enormous shark with teeth as effective as a scythe. He did one last round and the boat was nowhere to be found. He couldn't believe that this was his oeuvre: to die like his mother. The terrible coldness of the water made him think he might die of hypothermia first, and if he didn't, the bite wouldn't feel so bad with numbed flesh.

He let the current take him now and he backstroked along with it, always staring at the moon and thinking it would be the last thing he would ever witness in his life. *It's not such a bad way to go*, he thought. *Seeing the moon before dying, and not seeing the creature. Never seeing what is below.* He thought of the pain and that queasy feeling of giving blood in the doctor's office. *It won't last long if I'm missing a leg. It will come and go.*

As he closed his eyes, something struck him with maximum force in the head, causing him to bleed immediately. He turned and saw his boat ready to run over him. He treaded frantically to the port side, reaching his arms up as far as possible into the air, hoping to catch the end of the boat's walls. As the boat lulled, he waited for it to teeter to his side where it would be lower and easier to pull up.

If only a helping hand could appear above him. If only a helping hand. But this was not a land of help.

He waited instead, and when that moment came, he reached straight up and caught hold of the top of the wall. It was easier than he thought. At that second a ruthless thought entered his mind: it would charge from the water and take him under just as he thought he had survived.

He hung onto the wall, his feet dangling above the surface. He needed to catch his breath before he tried to heave his shoulders onto the ledge. He waited and waited, his wrists starting to tire. He sensed again that he was being watched, only this time it was right below the surface. He looked below him. Only black. Whatever watched him probably had good eye sight at night. He couldn't wait.

Every muscle in his body was in use. He grunted and groaned, saliva spraying furiously from his mouth, but he made it atop. While every second of the half minute it took him to get aboard felt like an hour, he made it back unharmed. A blanket stored below in the cabin kept him from hypothermia, and within minutes he returned the boat back to its course, its prow ripping through the blackness back to home.

CHAPTER 35: KATHERINE'S HELP

Still wet, Conrad paced the house for three hours straight, mumbling to himself, playing the sound of that voice on a loop like a madman only to be stopped by the replays of his near brush with death. He needed to talk to someone — someone he could trust. A helping hand.

But whose hand would that be?

She put up a fight, even hanging up the first two times. When she ended a relationship, she ended it, but the stress in Conrad's voice alerted her to the direness of a special situation. Paranoid, he wouldn't say anything over the phone. He asked her to meet him on the boardwalk at dawn in one hour.

She found him pacing on it, the sun beaten by the clouds and the only sound the thick rasping of waves. The boardwalk was a spooky place at dawn. Miles of wooden pathway and palm trees and not a runner or walker testing it yet.

He was a nervous pulse.

"This has nothing to do with us, I promise," he said. "Katherine, can I trust you?"

Desperation beamed from his eyes.

"Yes. What is it, Conrad?"

He couldn't hold it anymore. "What if Micker is still alive?"

Immediate: "How much sleep have you gotten?"

"No, don't start this way."

"Yea, I am. You need a dose of reality right now, and I'm going to give it to you."

"She's alive."

"No, she's dead." She looked around to make sure no one could hear them. He could see she was embarrassed by him.

He was embarrassed of himself too. He looked out to sea.

"I have to know. I have to know the truth."

"Well, I've known you long enough to know this isn't just a premonition, and you didn't just wake up with it in a dream." The sun began to peak. "Come on, I know a coffee place around here."

They sat far in the back of the diner like two detectives. The water settled him down a bit. The coffee warmed her up. He didn't waste time. He delved right back into it.

"I didn't tell you this, but during the party, right before you…" he didn't have to finish the thought, "I spoke to Diane Soto."

Katherine wanted to make sure he remembered history: "The gossip queen, the one who spread the rumor that you were with your wife driving to some 'mysterious' place in the middle of the night before she tragically vanished? And then she essentially told the entire town and every newspaper she could find that she thought you were the killer. Sure, I understand why you would be chatting with her."

"Please."

She exhaled. "What did she say?"

"She told me she saw me that night."

"Of course. So, where's this going? Are you a sleep walker, did you kill her?"

"Stop with the sarcasm, all right! She said she saw me, and she believed it."

"But she didn't?" she asked incredulously.

"That's right."

She pressed her forehead. "Conrad, is this some kind of riddle?"

"She saw someone else, okay! Someone who looked like me."

"Someone who looks like you," she repeated, still not getting it. "Who looks like you?"

"Who indeed?"

When her eyes looked away, he knew she got it. "Mr. Hall."

"Bran Hall."

"What does Mr. Hall —"

"Bran Hall! You don't work for him anymore."

"What does Bran Hall have to do with your wife being alive...unless..."

"I think so."

"The rumors were true."

"I don't know."

"You mean you never found out if they were having an affair?"

"No," he said exasperatingly.

"Well, for him to be the man in the night, I'm pretty sure they have to be —"

"I'd bet my life on it."

"Then let me ask you another question, and I want an honest answer. Your scars," she began. He rolled his eyes and
236

turned his face. She studied each scar, now white lines in his cheeks, barely visible unless under a light. "Those scars. Who?"

He nodded, finally admitting to it.

"And you never reported him?"

"I was embarrassed."

"About what? That he beat you up?"

Conrad was uncomfortable, but he knew he needed to get it out. In a sense, this was therapy. "Yea."

She felt sorry for him right there. She didn't respond instantly. In a way, she understood his embarrassment.

Anger then took hold of her. "Who beats the crap out of a man without a motive unless you are one mentally deranged, deeply disturbed, and violent person!"

"He might be a hole in one."

"So, let's say they were having an affair. Maybe he just went there to talk to her. Maybe they had a fight. Maybe…" it pained her to say it, "she loved him." Her words wounded him, but she needed to press on. "It still doesn't mean she's alive. And maybe Diane Soto did what she always does – she lied. Did you ever think she's putting you on a wild goose chase just for the fun of it? When a rattlesnake bites, Conrad, we shouldn't act surprised."

"I heard her voice."

"I'm sorry?"

"I heard her voice on the phone," he finally told her. Now she could really pass judgment if he was crazy – hearing voices from a dead wife. But it was the truth to him. He couldn't hide it. "She's alive," he said.

Katherine squinted. "What?"

"I had Bran's number. I've had it for years. I called it last night, just to hear his voice, and she picked up."

"Mrs. Mayday picked up."

"Micker."

237

"Micker I mean."

"Yes."

"Did she say it was her?"

"No."

"Then how do you know? What did she say?"

"Nothing. Just hello."

"Hello?"

"Yea."

"Goodbye," Katherine said and began to leave. He caught her arm. "Katherine, I'm not making this up!"

She sat back down. "Conrad, I think you need to get some sleep, and after you've done that, I think it will resolve everything. You'll realize how crazy you're sounding, and you'll come to your senses, and I have a feeling you'll be apologizing to me right after. Okay? Get some sleep."

He didn't resist her leaving the second time. She left the diner calmly, saying thank you politely to those who held the door. But when she looked back to see what she was leaving, she saw a broken man – a broken man in dire need of someone's help.

And she was walking away from it.

CHAPTER 36: THE BARRACUDA

Katherine lay in her bed that afternoon, her hands behind her head, watching the ceiling fan twirl its wind. Something was on her mind.

She didn't like being called crazy or taken for a fool. Her dad had done it to her before she moved to San Sangre. He called her a failure in the making when she passed up Stanford's law school to become an elementary school teacher. People would say that they were happy she was following her heart, and that she was doing the right thing because she was true to herself. They were lying. They were laughing at her. She knew it.

She hated nothing more in the world than a fraud. And she had called Conrad a fraud in many respects, and right to his face. What was bothering her more so was that the part of her living beyond logic believed him. He seemed to be telling the truth.

She headed to the computer, where research was done. Her nickname from the staff at her high school newspaper was the barracuda because once she was on to something, she wouldn't let go until she found the truth.

Micker Mayday's death was in a series of searches. She read each article, all of them summarizing the events of her disappearance in the same manner: "*San Sangre lawyer disappears without a trace in Farallon waters; Police find woman's boat and pieces of clothing, but no body; Blood found on clothing; DNA matches the woman's; boat was found in shark-infested waters; scientists estimate between thirty to fifty great white sharks in waters that night; woman is believed to have been eaten; no trace of remains.*"

The article was dated seven years, so pictures of the event were harder to find. But one article, a number of searches deep, yielded the one and only picture detailing the sight. Police were standing on the beach, looking out to sea, and the boat, the *Cursum Perficio*, a red dingy a fourth of the size of a great white shark, sat on the deck of a larger boat with its sail still perfectly stiff. The police looked out to sea, some pointing, but there was one man, one who clearly didn't belong.

He wasn't a cop, and he wasn't a reporter. He was a lighthouse watchman, the name Hargo, Delbert Hargo, and he had been the only one on the island that night.

Lighthouse keeper, Delbert Hargo, seen standing far left, gave evidence that police say conflicted with their findings. Hargo was later detained as a suspect, but no evidence of any wrongdoing or of Hargo's involvement came to fruition.

Katherine printed the article and circled Hargo's head.

"Where are you now, Mr. Hargo?"

240

CHAPTER 37: BELOW THE CRATE

"I need to head back in," said Conrad, his mind never really part of fishing. It had been just a few hours since his talk with Katherine.

Brosnan turned and pulled his fishing gloves from his hands with an icy stare. He was now Conrad's Regional Manager, a position Brosnan was reluctant to take but took. The pay was great but he missed being on the sea. He used any excuse to be out there again. "Ya' know, you could of told me this before we came out here," he grumbled. "I could have inspected Snaley's boat first."

Conrad offered him no reaction.

"I said I could of gone on Snaley's —"

"I heard you," Conrad said relenting. "I heard you."

"So what the hell do you have to go in for?"

"I forgot I have a doctor's appointment. I have to pick Belle up from school before I go." Brosnan didn't seem pleased. "It was the only time I could schedule it. I've been sick a lot lately."

"What's wrong?"

"Throwing up."

"Probably stress, from that quiz show."

"Yea."

"Well, what time is the appointment?"

"Two."

Brosnan erupted, "It's one thirty now! We have to turn it 'round now if you are going to make it in time!" There was a shallow detachment ironed in Conrad's face as he stared back at the harbor. Then it broke suddenly, his face lively again.

"I'll get the crate up now," he said. He stared down into the grayish-blue water where the crates of crabs were bellowing in the water near the stern, the sound of creaking doors. The sea turned cold and tranquil unexpectedly. He grabbed the crate with both hands, his face a foot from the water where ocean spray stung him in the eyes and mouth and he tasted the salt.

His arms went dead. He did not drop the crate, though his mind had ordered his hands to let go. He was caught in a sudden and penetrating body shock at what he witnessed below the crate.

It was like seeing an apparition. Below the crate was a large, white, cylindrical shape oscillating in the water, the top of its shape strangely still as ice. Slowly it took form and a big square mouth showed, as did two black eyes staring up at him. The creature was not moving but for the tail, and its mouth was open as if salivating like a hungry dog.

Conrad backed away from the crate, his heart galloping. "Brosnan," he said tryingly in fear. "Look." Brosnan peered over the edge gently. "Is that what I think it is?"

"It is," Brosnan affirmed with a wicked smile. The creature slowly descended and disappeared into the gray. "They follow the scent of the crates sometimes. I told Ben to wash this crate good. It's not the crabs they're after, it's the smell of the tuna still on the crates from yesterday."

242

The boat was then bumped and Conrad fell to the side of the boat, clutching onto the starboard side. "Did it hit us?"

"Crouch down! Get on all fours if you have to. I've seen fishermen thrown overboard."

"Should I start the engine?"

"No. Let it run its course. It's just curious. We're a big red square that smells like a fish in its playground. It just wanted to take a look."

There was apparent movement in the water, but Conrad could not see it. When the water remained tranquil he grew courage to look out over the water. There was nothing moving in it. "He's taken off," Brosnan said lightly. "Is that the first one you've seen on the water?"

"Yea," Conrad answered.

Brosnan picked up speed to twenty miles per hour. Conrad sat behind him on one of the crates. After a mile, Brosnan slowed down. He turned back to see how Conrad was doing, but his attention was grabbed by a red puddle at the stern. Brosnan followed the tail of the puddle to Conrad's shirt.

"I didn't even notice," Brosnan said staring in amazement.

"What's that?"

Conrad followed his eyes. He felt his nose. Maroon crust broke off in his hand.

"That shark wasn't after the crabs," Brosnan explained. "He was trailing your blood."

"How do you know?" Conrad saw the drying red puddle by the stern for the first time. Droplets were still fresh on the wall.

"You didn't even know it was bleeding?"

"I've been having them a lot lately. Sometimes I don't even know it's happening?"

"How frequently?"

"Two times a day, sometimes more."

Brosnan turned out to the sea. He didn't want Conrad to see worry. He knew chronic nosebleeds were no good.

"Get that checked out too when you see the doctor."

"I will."

Brosnan stared out at sea. The red buoys were yards behind them.

Far in the distance, draped in fog were the peaks of craggy brown mountains in tight formation. They were incongruous and uneven. They had no business in the middle of the sea, but there they were. They looked like the tips of some massive creature's head had breached.

"The devil's teeth," Brosnan said, almost prideful. "That's what some people call them. The Farallon Islands."

That's where Micker was, and I'm too scared to venture down there. He had a feeling, though, that he would see them up close one day. Perhaps soon.

They were eerie in the day, inhumane boulders, laughing at him, laughing as Brosnan reversed course and made them smaller in his view.

Conrad continued to study them until wetness was felt in his hands.

Another nosebleed had started.

CHAPTER 38: A DOCTOR'S VISIT

Conrad signed his name at the secretary's sliding glass window, and as he did that, he noticed the eyes of the waiting room upon Belle. She turned away uncomfortably. They had all seen her before.

Conrad asked the secretary curiously, "Whom will I be seeing today?"

"Dr. McNaughton," she said. "He's one of our best." Conrad had heard that name before, but he didn't know where he last heard it. "He would also like Belle to get her physical while she's here."

"Really?" For whatever reason, Conrad found that presumptuous. Besides, how did he even know if Belle was here?

"Kill two birds with one stone kinda deal," she said.

"Tetanus shot?"

She read the charts. "She's due for one," she said ominously.

Conrad sighed. "Ya' know, I'm not even sure if I should be here. It's just for feeling sick, throwing up occasionally. That's a part of stress, I'm sure," he said. Then he remembered the nosebleeds. He needed to be here.

"It's gotta be," the secretary replied.

"And I've been getting nosebleeds for the last few days," he added.

She looked up a little more concerned this time. "I'm sure it's nothing. Don't worry. I once had a nosebleed every day for a month. You probably just broke a blood vessel up there. It's been unseasonably cold lately, so with the changing temperatures, it's not uncommon for one to burst."

"I see. Thank you," he said.

Now he would have to explain to Belle in the jolliest way possible that a long and thick needle was going to be piercing her arm soon.

Dr. McNaughton walked in, still talking to another doctor in the hallway as doctors always do. When he let the door shut behind him, Conrad saw Belle sitting in a chair in a room across the way. She looked nervous as the door slowly closed on her figure.

"Vomiting, huh?" McNaughton asked.

"Yes, for about a week, ever since I brought my daughter back from Los Angeles."

"Oh yes, everyone in town is looking forward to her appearance on that show. Congratulations."

"Thank you," Conrad said, but he felt McNaughton's words were insincere. The doctor had a funny way of talking. He was condescending and he seemed disinterested in what was said.

"I'm more concerned, actually, with my nosebleeds."

"Nosebleeds?"

"Yes.

"How long have you had them?"

246

"About a week."

"Do the nosebleeds happen around the same time each day, or do they come and go."

"Come and go?"

"How often each day?"

"I'd say three times. One day it was five."

"Anything you're doing in particular when they start?"

"No."

"Have you ever had periods of time in your life when you had frequent nosebleeds?"

"When I was a kid, maybe, but none since then."

"Well, let's do this, something rather painless." McNaughton turned to his medical table and rolled on his latex gloves. He grabbed an instrument that had the shape and texture of a Q-tip, and asked Conrad to open his mouth. McNaughton told him to hold still while he slid the instrument in Conrad's mouth and rubbed the inside of his cheek. He rubbed hard and continuously. It felt a little like rug burn. Within ten seconds, he was done.

The doctor placed the instrument in a tightly sealed bag.

Conrad was confused. "What's that for?"

McNaughton hesitated. "There's a very bad virus going around. It causes nosebleeds."

"Really?"

"I highly doubt if you have it," McNaughton replied as he checked his charts. "But it's better to be sure."

"What's the name of the virus?"

McNaughton had heard him, yet he remained silent.

"Doctor?"

McNaughton actually laughed. It seemed like he laughed at the ridiculousness of himself. "It's..." and he couldn't respond. "It doesn't have a name. It's usually found in the saliva."

The doctor scratched his balding head. The few gold strands he had left up there waffled over to the other side. "I'm going to get an instrument to check up your nose, make sure everything's okay, and you'll be out of here."

Conrad noticed the file folder McNaughton was holding was brand new and it had a curious penmanship: the letter "D" in "Mayday" was done with a complete circle and the stem cutting about ten degrees to the right of the middle. It almost looked like a zodiac sign.

McNaughton was gone in a heartbeat, through the door that he shut safely when he was outside it.

Doctors. He was amazed at how incompetent McNaughton seemed. *And they said he was the best.*

Conrad looked around the room while he waited. So many pictures of diagrams: skeletons, the digestive system, the brain, the heart, the lungs, ailments, diseases, all of it hung up there. Conrad hated seeing what the inside of a human body looked like. The room made him quiver, and he hadn't even looked to see what was behind him?

He turned. Finally something normal: framed pictures of the doctors' staff. There was staff in action photos, new initiatives, even doctors and their families. But one picture immediately stood out way at the top.

There were palmettos in the back. They wore Hawaiian shirts. Four or five men, three doctors, one...who was that? Conrad looked closer.

It had been awhile, but he'd recognize those pale strands and that monstrous forehead anywhere. It was Gilbert Hall. And standing next to McNaughton, at the end of the chain, was Bran. A big smile draped across Bran's tanned face.

They were all holding a check, but Conrad couldn't make it out, but he knew it was something for fundraising.

The Halls are into everything, he thought. They were even

248

invested in this hospital. They must have been family friends. That's what the photo looked like. They weren't accidental acquaintances.

The picture made him uncomfortable the rest of the appointment, even more uncomfortable than the four-inch long instrument McNaughton brought back with him to stick up his nose.

Belle kept holding her cheek on the way out to the parking lot.

"What's wrong?" he asked her.

"My cheek?"

"Did you get a shot in your mouth? I'm pretty sure tetanus is in the arm."

"It was," and she twirled around to show him the Band-Aid that covered where the needle made its incision on her arm.

"Then why are you holding your cheek?"

She threw her pretzel down. "Cuz they stuck that thing in my mouth and rubbed it."

"He did that to you too?"

"Yea. It felt weird."

"Does it hurt you?"

"No."

"Then quit holding it," he said. "It's to make sure you don't have a virus."

He stopped walking when he looked at his car.

"Dad?" she asked.

A newspaper clipping was pinned beneath the wipers. He grabbed it. It nearly blew loose in the wind. It was Katherine's handwriting.

Seek out D. Harlo. He still lives in the lighthouse keeper's cottage.
K.

Conrad's eyes took him to the picture. Red pen circled

the face of a man who looked like he had been stuck on an island too long. His eyes were bugged out and his hair, even though the clipping was black and white, was clearly white and too long.

Below that was the word *conflicted* highlighted by the red pen.

Conflicted? Conrad asked himself. He quickly began reading the news clipping, growing more and more interested the further he read. Once he finished, he was certain he had to find this man. The only problem was that if he were to find the man, he would have to venture down to the Farallon Islands.

250

CHAPTER 39: LANDING

The buoys were well in his distance now, bobbing up and down like forgotten toys. The Farallon Islands were twenty-seven miles from the harbor. He had just a quarter of that measurement to go.

The fog was massively thick out there. He felt he was cutting through it along with the water. A brown object bobbed submissively in the waves.

He slowed down, spotting it over the port side, up nice and close. It was the remains of an elephant seal, its head chewed completely off. The bites in the carcass were large and penetrating. Only one creature in the world could have done such a thing.

The islands shown crookedly in the fog soon after. He slowed, studying the size of them in fascination. They were mountains, hundreds of feet high above sea level. He was on the wrong side of the island. He could see the elephant seals hammering at each other and the Storm-petrels, western gulls, and other species of bird that swooped above them. Those birds let out merciless cries in the sky. Mixed with the cacophony of barking and it sounded like the symphony the devil would listen to.

Landing was where the lighthouse stood. He rode around the island, careful not to hit one of the rocks that occasionally jutted a few feet above the sea.

There were the cottages, grey and bilious green, matching the feeling of this place. It was not meant for people. But people there were, and one stood on the hilltop, waiting for him.

"This cottage was built in the 1870's," said Edward Lansing, the current lighthouse keeper, as he struggled to steam water and fix Conrad a cup of tea. "Unfortunately, the cottages' utilities were too." He was a young man, in his mid-thirties, with a goatee and sly face. He looked like he was up to something at all times, even though his hospitality contradicted that report. "You know, if the police were to know about your arrival, they could send you to prison for up to six months."

"I didn't," Conrad replied. He wasn't scared of him or his threat.

"I take it you are on a very important mission if you've come this far to risk jail." Conrad thought Lansing spoke like he was from the 1870's too.

It was already three o'clock. It would be dark in two hours, and it took him an hour to get there. Conrad was playing with precious time. He pulled out the clipping that Katherine had printed for him and set it on the table. "Do you know this man?"

Lansing steeped the tea bag on his way over. He turned his head oddly around while staring at the picture. "I did."

"He's dead?"

"No."

"He's moved?"

252

"No."

"Then what?"

"He's upstairs."

"Then why did you say..."

"I used to know him. Dementia, you see."

"How do you know him?"

"He's my stepfather."

"Can you take me to him?"

"It's not worth your time, I – "

Conrad didn't equivocate. "Take me to him."

Each step creaked on the spiraled staircase. There were even holes in the steps, large sections of wood rotted away.

"You guys live like this up here?"

"Yes. This lighthouse has been in the family name since _"

"1870?"

Lansing turned to him on the step and smiled. "It's good money. We also own the cottages to the north. That's where the scientists come to stay. But they're not here today, lucky for you." At the foot of the landing was a small hallway with two doors on its sides. One was open.

"Come in," a creaky voice said.

Lansing looked at him with an acerbic smile on his face. "Shall we?"

The old man was sitting in a rocking chair, using it to its full capacity. All he had in that room was a small bed, that rocking chair, and a chest to keep his clothes.

"Do you have my toys?" the old man asked. His white hair was still in tack from the picture. "The china figurines. I asked for them."

"I'm sorry, Dad," Lansing said rolling his eyes. "I do not."

253

"Mr. Hargo?" Conrad asked him.

"Yeeees," the old man answered. Conrad moved toward him confidently.

"I have come here to ask you some questions."

"Is that you, Peter?"

Conrad stopped moving. Lansing stood in the doorway, his arms crossed like I told you so. He was going to get a kick out of Conrad's interview. "No, this is, my name is Conrad Mayday."

"Mayday. The first of May. The worker's day."

"It is. But my name is..."

"Mayday," the old man groaned.

Conrad looked to Lansing for help. Lansing obliged. "Dad, this man has come all the way from San Sangre to ask you about – a missing person I take it?"

"My wife."

"His wife, who went missing – how long ago was it?"

"Seven years."

"Seven years ago."

"I know her," the old man said. But already Conrad didn't trust it. "She was a queen. A nice queen who sat on a very big throne."

Lansing smiled.

Conrad tried one more time. "My wife disappeared seven years ago from these shores. She was on a boat, it was called the *Cursum Perficio*, and she vanished from it. Do you know what happened to her?"

The old man had heard what he asked. He stopped rocking. "She died."

"That's right."

"She fell overboard."

"Yes, that's what they say. Is that what you told the police?"
254

The old man looked away from him coldly. "She's dead because they don't follow the moon."

Conrad dropped his shoulders frustratingly.

Lansing turned Hargo's rocking chair so it faced the sea. "I imagine he'll be on Jeopardy soon."

"They don't follow the moon," Hargo hummed.

Conrad turned to leave. "I won't take up any more of your time."

Lansing felt the slightest bit of sensitivity. "I can tell you something."

"What is it?"

He moved toward him. "I wasn't on this island seven years ago. My attempt at a PhD. But I was up here soon after to offer my support for him. His mind was much more sober then, but still they took him for an idiot, and so they avoided his mentioning of one thing that struck me."

"What?"

"The boat he saw had a light."

"A light?"

"Yes. A great big spotlight on it."

"Thank you," Conrad said, but it was still just nonsense. Micker's boat was a sailboat. It had no light. He understood why the police dismissed him.

"Follow the moon," Hargo said again, now twirling around in the rocking chair to give Conrad his sage advice.

When Conrad got back to San Sangre, Katherine agreed to meet him at the back of the same diner. She was curious of his findings this time, though she tried to hide it.

"So?" she asked him after he shared the details of his visit with Hargo.

"I don't know what to make of it," he said. He was

255

running on adrenaline now. He had barely slept in two days.

"Why?"

"The man had dementia."

"Hargo did?"

He nodded. "It was awful. He had no idea what he was saying. At the end he kept saying 'they don't follow the moon,' whatever that means. It's useless." He sat and looked around the empty diner. He was frustrated.

She repeated. "They don't follow the moon?"

"I rode all the way out there, risked my job, for what?"

"Well, do you feel better now?"

He bit his lower lip. "No."

She could tell there was more. "Say it."

"His son told me that his stepfather —"

"Hargo?"

"Yes…told the police that he saw a boat, but it had a light on it." She showed her palms for him to reveal the significance. "Micker's boat didn't have a light."

Katherine was intrigued. "Then it was another boat."

"No."

"Why not?"

"Because the one thing I remember the police telling me was that the wind was close to forty knots the night Micker fell overboard."

"Meaning?"

"Forty knots means large waves. Spray. It's when telephone wires move and tree branches fly off. She would have to have been one hell of a sailor to get as far out as she did in a dingy. Only a big, powerful boat could have made it out there."

Katherine's big hazel eyes searched the ceiling for answers. "But she could have?"

"She could have."

"But highly unlikely."

256

"Exactly."

"Maybe she fell overboard much sooner, and the boat ended up where it did on its own. Maybe she drowned. It happens all the time. The bodies don't turn up."

"Her clothes," Conrad reminded.

"I forgot."

"They were found by the boat. Blood was in them. Scientists confirmed a shark took a huge chunk out of her clothes."

She asked, "Maybe 'follow the moon' has some relevance?"

"Oh get off it. The man was crazy. He had no memory!"

She squinted in the distance of her thoughts. "The moon then. Something with the moon?"

"Yea, he probably thinks he lived on it."

She rubbed her eyes. They were hot under the yellow lamp. "Did you try the number again, where you thought you spoke to her?"

Conrad looked at her cynically. He still sensed she doubted him. "Thousand times. It's now disconnected." He poked his cheek with his tongue.

"Why do you keep doing that?" she asked.

"What?"

She mimicked it for him, pushing her tongue into the side of her mouth. "Oh, I had to go to the doctor's for these damn nosebleeds I've been having. He said a virus has been going around that causes them. He needed a swab of my saliva to test it."

"A virus from saliva, causing nosebleeds?"

"I thought it was weird too. He was a weird doctor."

"I haven't heard of any virus going around like that. Don't you think we would have heard?"

"The more you ask about it, yea," he said, growing concerned.

"The only time I've heard of saliva being used is for DNA tests. You watch CSI?"

"Yea, I don't know." He held his forehead. He was ready to give up.

"Well, anyways, I want to go to the library later."

"For what?"

"I don't know. I always think better there. Besides, something isn't right."

"Like what? Look, just let it go," he said to her.

"Let it go!" she exclaimed. "Before you were begging me to get involved!"

"I know. It's my problem. I've got other things going on."

"Like what?"

He didn't want to mention it.

"LA?" she guessed.

"Yea," he admitted reluctantly. "Her show's going to be on TV pretty soon."

She shook her head disapprovingly. "How'd she do?"

"They shot the first show. They will call her back to compete pretty soon in the second one."

"So she won. She's their star?"

"It looks like it."

"Well, congratulations." She got up shortly after that, pushing her blonde hair behind her ears. Before she left she said, "I'm still going to look into this, whether you want me to or not." She marched off. Conrad watched her with a hidden smile on his face.

CHAPTER 40: THE LIBRARY

Katherine sat under a standard green reading lamp in the San Sangre public library. There were lots of law students grouped together there on the floor with her, each of them studying cases that would only add to their arsenal when they made it to the courtroom. *That could have been me,* she thought. All the investigating she had been doing reminded her of why she thought of law school in the first place: finding the truth had the noblest of rings.

Many of the men watched her, taken by her good looks. She looked away. The lamp was hot and bright. It even illuminated her skin. Someone came into view on her left by the doorway. Another guy gawking, she suspected. He wouldn't move. She gave it a few seconds.

Finally she turned and screamed, "What!"

Heads shot up across the library.

It was Conrad. He stood in the doorway watching her. She puffed hair that fell over her eyes and smiled embarrassingly over at him. He looked so handsome to her there. She walked over. "Sorry," she said.

"Never had a greeting like that in a library."

"Shut up," she said. "I thought you were someone staring at me."

"I was." He surveyed the openness of the library. It had that damp feel and smelled like the inside of a book. "So...this is your place?"

"Yea."

"What do you do here?"

She was embarrassed again. "I think."

He made a face.

"It works," she said defensively. "Trust me. I don't know why."

He continued to stare at her dubiously.

"Come on," she said taking his hand. "Let's sit."

Two dark green chairs faced each other in the corner of the library behind stacks of books. They took them. Conrad massaged his temples. Katherine looked up at the ceiling skylights. Across from her she saw a desk with a green reading lamp still on. The light flickered.

The thoughts finally started tumbling in. "What if Donny Locks had something to do with this?"

Conrad didn't like hearing his name. "He's dead."

"I know, but —"

"Katherine, you're going over the top here."

She stood up. She thought better sometimes when she paced. "I just remembered this, and the thought won't leave my head."

"What?"

"I remember seeing Mr. Hall —"

"Bran!"

She put her hands up defensively. "Bran. He was talking with him once, in the hallway. This was when I worked for Micker. I had just delivered Bran some forms to fill out."

260

"Talking with whom? Locks?"

"Yea."

Conrad took notice. "What about?"

"I don't know. It was in the hallway, but it was a private conversation. I don't think they thought anyone else was there. But I remember Bran was smiling. He was the Regional Manager then. And he patted Donny on the back." She squinted. "No one ever treated Donny that way. Never. Everybody despised him. And Donny looked up at him very particularly, like you would if you were talking to someone –"

"You were scared of," Conrad said, finishing her thought.

"Actually, yea. Donny looked a little scared."

Conrad bit his finger. "Donny Locks wasn't scared of anyone."

"That's why it always bothered me." She started pacing again. "I have to go somewhere," she said, her mind onto something else.

"What? Where?"

She looked back at the open desk with the green reading lamp turned on. The flickering light was driving her crazy. She walked over furiously and turned it off.

"Was that where you had to go?" he said sarcastically.

She grabbed her purse. "I might not be back," she said and started rushing out of there.

Conrad stood up. He thought she was acting crazy. "What should I do then?"

"I'll call you," she shouted back.

"She does think well when she's here," he muttered.

He looked at the string to the lamp Katherine pulled oscillate. An idea came to him too.

The moon, he thought. There was something about Hargo's mentioning of the moon that wouldn't leave him. Then

261

a thought sparked and collided with another. He always thought of the moon as a person: sometimes it was vibrant and sometimes it lacked energy and other times it just wanted to stay in and hide. And when it did hide, it affected everyone, particularly seafarers.

Seafarers. Without the moon they had no light.

Light. He kept looking at that lamp, the string still oscillating, like it wanted him to take notice of it.

A question came to him, strong enough that he had to seek its answer: What kind of moon was there when Micker died?

Katherine thought it was a long shot, but she decided to drive by the old Locks residence in the hopes Mrs. Locks still lived there, that's if Mrs. Locks was even still alive. She parked her car in the parking lot of an abandoned playground. Across the street was the Locks residence just the way she remembered it, a tiny ranch, the brick moss-covered, fitting no more than three rooms and a bath. There was no garage – just a small, cracked and potholed driveway. The yard, with what little grass remained, was burnt, and in some sections, dead. It all resembled the Locks' lives.

Katherine had grown up a few blocks from there but on a more affluent street. She rode the same bus as Locks since kindergarten. *He was always a troubled child,* she thought, *but he always left me alone.* He wasn't like that with the other girls. He seemed to have a respect for her. Maybe it was because she was always nice to him. Maybe it was because of his mom.

Mrs. Locks always liked Katherine. She used to sell Girl Scout cookies to Mrs. Locks, and from the get-go, Mrs. Locks found her charming. As Katherine grew, Mrs. Locks would always ask Katherine to date Donny to "get him in line," half-jokingly, half-seriously. She wanted Katherine's influence on

262

him. She would sometimes stop Katherine on the street and talk to her about Donny's misdemeanors or his dropping grades. Mrs. Locks cared about Donny; that's what people never realized. She just couldn't get him straight. She was a single mother. It was too hard a job, and Donny never knew his father.

Katherine approached the house very carefully, not fully sure of what she would say if she saw Mrs. Locks. She noticed some of the windows were broken, probably kids throwing rocks through them. They were never fixed.

Waiting for Katherine in the doorway was a tiny blonde woman, now freckled and with haggard hair. It took Katherine awhile to figure it was Mrs. Locks. Katherine remembered Mrs. Locks to be a beautiful woman in her heyday. This woman was all but beautiful.

"Hello, Katherine," Mrs. Locks said.

Katherine couldn't believe Mrs. Locks remembered her. "Welcome back."

They sat in the living room where house spiders hid in webs in the ceiling's corners and centipedes crawled the walls. Flies whizzed in and out of the rooms, seemingly amazed by their freedom.

Mrs. Locks sat across from Katherine. She didn't even offer a drink. She seemed to let life stop since Donny went on his murder spree. Pictures of Donny when he was a kid were covered in dust on the table. She was with him in some, a vibrant blonde, all smiles.

Now Mrs. Locks was a frail, helpless woman.

"Mrs. Locks, I know it sounds crazy, but I was wondering if you knew – " Katherine didn't know how to ask it. They had barely made small talk, but she felt time was of the essence. "If you knew who Donny's father was?"

Mrs. Locks suddenly came to life. Her tired eyes moved uncomfortably. She held her freckled and wrinkle-stained arms. "Donny didn't."

"But you did."

"I saw a lot of men before Donny was born. There was one man, though. He didn't hide his infidelity."

"He was married?"

"Yes. And he was the one. He became Donny's father."

"With all due respect, how do you know it was him if you say you —"

"Because I fell in love with him. I didn't see any men after that. But he never felt the same way."

"Who was it?" Katherine asked boldly.

Mrs. Locks wanted to tell someone, but still, after all these years, she was scared. "He's dead now. Who would care?" she asked, trying to convince herself that it was okay to talk about him. "He was a wealthy man. He started buying out property all around town. He really scored when he opened a prominent fishing company."

Katherine closed her eyes and said, "Gilbert Hall."

Mrs. Locks didn't refute it. "You always were a smart girl."

"So Gilbert Hall was Donny's father? He was married though."

"He was. Gilbert must have thought himself too old to have another child when he saw me."

"So Donny was illegitimate?"

"Yes."

"Did Gilbert know he was Donny's father?"

"Yes, and I wish to this day I had never said anything."

"He threatened you?"

Mrs. Locks sighed. "I lived in fear all these years. Even

though he's gone, I still worry. Arrangements were made, you see. I was never to speak about it. If I kept quiet, I was given payments monthly, kept my job waiting tables. He could have ruined me if he wanted. I had heard stories about the Halls. Stories they were mixed up in organized crime. Bottom line was I knew that they could make me disappear if they wanted to. So I kept my mouth shut. It didn't turn out to be such a bad deal," she said emotionally, "until the son started coming around here."

Katherine was dismayed. "Bran?"

"See, Gilbert had his idea of propriety. He had screwed up with me, but he paid for his mistakes. But the son."

"Bran took advantage of the situation?"

Mrs. Locks' mouth grew dry. "Somehow, he found out about our arrangement."

"What did he…"

A tear ran down her left eye. "He made me do unspeakable things, corrupt things to propel his career and settle old scores. And then, when he realized he always had to put up a fight with me, he started *educating* Donny. "

"Why would Bran risk that?"

"He had no remorse. He saw us as a free meal. I was powerless. He liked to prey on the weak."

Katherine took a moment to understand. "But Bran was Donny's half-brother?"

"Donny became who he was because of Bran Hall. And I had to sit by and watch it."

Katherine rubbed her forehead. "Did Donny know that Bran was his brother?"

"I don't know," she answered honestly. "I never told him, but I think he guessed. I know Donny was afraid of him, and Donny wasn't afraid of anyone."

"Do you know why?"

"I think Donny knew that they could get rid of me at

any time. He cared for me. People don't know that. The monster cared." Tears plummeted down her face. She tried to gather herself. "I remember Donny being frightened of being sent to jail. I'm not sure, but I think Bran had threatened him with it; he had something on Donny. But Donny hinted that if he did something for Bran at Walker's, everything would be okay. We would be safe."

"You don't know what it was?"

"No. But it was something. Donny, for all the horrible things he did, never got sent away, and we were never bothered again."

Katherine thought about it for a while. The pieces were coming together – the pieces in a broken woman's house. Katherine felt the urge to leave. Mrs. Locks could sense it.

"Go ahead," she said. "Can't stop a girl with a face like that."

Katherine smiled. "Thank you," she said. She walked by Mrs. Locks and then stopped. Mrs. Locks continued to stare straight ahead at a television that was fifteen years old and probably didn't work. She just stared, pictures of her lost son above the TV.

Katherine turned and kissed her on the head before leaving. Mrs. Locks closed her eyes and wept after her screen door shut.

CHAPTER 41: LUNAR CYCLES

Once Conrad found the book on lunar cycles in the library, he didn't waste time.

He found a desk and quickly flipped through it. "August 13 she died," he whispered as he whipped through a rather childish picture book. Simply titled, *Moon Phases*, it illustrated all essential stages of the moon. What he wanted, though, he couldn't find…until the last page.

"Of course it would be all the way back here," he said when he happened upon a collection of calendars dating back fifty years. He flipped through them, tiny little charts, getting to the year Micker died.

He got scared and closed his eyes. Did he really want to see it? Maybe life was better if he didn't know the truth.

He knew he had to look. He got it over with. He saw the month of August. He closed his eyes again. He bent his head, took a deep breath, and opened them.

A black circle was in the box. It was a new moon.

He closed the book, his hands shaking, and ran out of there.

Conrad was driving as fast as the cars around him would allow. He pulled out his cell phone and called Katherine.

"I checked the lunar cycles," he hollered into the phone so she could hear him.

"And?" She tried to keep it down.

"There wasn't one. It was pitch black. When Hargo said, 'they don't follow the moon,' he meant the police. He told them there wasn't a moon, and they did nothing about it."

Katherine stood at her car across from the Locks house. She held her pointer finger in her ear. "Wh—what does that mean?"

"No moon, no light," he said. "It means no boat without a light in that kind of storm is going to make it anywhere without the moon."

"Then how did the boat get there?" she asked.

"A larger boat took it."

"A larger boat?"

"Yea. A boat like Bran's."

She was confused. "I didn't know Bran had a boat."

"His dad owned the biggest fishing empire in Northern California. Gifts for Christmas were boats, luxury boats. He and Micker drove out there together on one of them and dumped the dingy with her tattered clothes."

"Where are you headed now?"

"The doctor's. I want to learn more about this mystery virus, and why the good doctor thinks I might suffer from it?"

"I googled it; there is –"

"I know. There is no such virus. I already looked it up. Can you tell I'm starting to believe everyone's out to get me?"

"They just might be," she said cynically.

"Where are you?" he shouted, losing reception.

She had to tell him. "At Donny Locks' old house."

"Donny Locks' house?" he asked. He had just pulled into the hospital parking lot.

"Yea, I'll call you later. I found something, but it's too

268

hard to explain it over the phone," she said. "Be careful," she added, but Conrad didn't hear her.

He didn't hear her because he was staring at a ghost.

After seven years, Bran Hall had returned to San Sangre.

Conrad watched in a stupor. Bran ran across his rearview mirror from the hospital side entrance and held a file folder under his arm. He fended off the downpour with a jacket thrown over his head and entered a black Santa Fe. He threw the file carefully in the passenger seat.

Conrad sat as still as death. The phone he still clutched to his ear lost reception.

Bran started the car, turned the engine off, and then quickly thrust the door open to look frantically for something in the parking lot along his car. He held his wrist while searching. He was soaked now and looked hard for an object that might already have been lost in the nearby drain. He seemed to have lost his watch. He soon headed for the entrance to the hospital, still clutching his wrist where a watch would be fastened. The Santa Fe was left unlocked.

Conrad didn't have time to think. He had to react, and react fast. There was something in that file, and he had the sincerest feeling it had something to do with him.

He ran toward Bran's car as fast as he could. He headed right for the passenger door, saw the file sitting on the seat, and even through the heavy rain falling on his eyes and the car window, he noticed the unusual oval "D" with the line down the middle on the tab: "Belle Mayday." He was shocked.

He opened the door and quickly grabbed the file, pulling it from underneath a jacket. He shut the door, his momentum already taking him on his course across the parking lot, when he realized he didn't shut the door fully. He thought of going back to shut it, but momentum and fright won the battle. He was on his way.

If Bran had run into the hospital to find his watch, his stay would depend on his success. If he were to find the watch instantly, Conrad had at most one minute to get back in his car before Bran returned. If Bran didn't find it instantly, Conrad had several minutes or more.

As he was walking as inconspicuously as he could, he heard footsteps behind him. He hid the file under his shirt and continued to walk fast without looking back. He entered his car and immediately turned back to look in the rearview mirror. Bran was there.

Take off, Conrad thought. But if he left, he would need to pull out of the parking space and expose his face when he turned. Instead, he decided that the minute Bran left he would switch parking spaces then wait a few minutes to leave. The last thing he wanted was to look across the highway and see Bran staring back at him.

The rear lights to Bran's Santa Fe flicked on, and Conrad exhaled. Then they turned back off, and just as they did, the rain slowed to a drizzle.

The Santa Fe rested there. No movement. No sign of anyone in it. Now Bran could see clear across the lot without the downpour.

The door was thrust open again and two muscular stubby legs let themselves onto the pavement. Bran got out of the Santa Fe, closed the door, and stared directly at Conrad. Conrad sat motionless, hiding everything but his eyes from behind the seat. Bran took two steps forward, still staring at Conrad, the drizzle not affecting his view. A car drove by, forcing Bran to get out of the way, but then he continued on his course. If he were to continue walking straight, he would walk right into Conrad's car.

Something happened. He stopped, and did an abrupt about-face and walked to the passenger side of the car. Maybe

270

he didn't see Conrad after all. He opened the car door, noticing that it had not been fully shut. Conrad saw his reaction and grimaced.

Like an arena bull, Bran charged out into the parking lot ready for a fight. He was looking at all corners of the lot. He looked big and mean, his chest tight against his blue and white-striped dress shirt. He got down on all fours and looked under his Santa Fe. There was a feeling, though void of any accuracy and based totally on sensory logic, that Bran already knew Conrad had stolen the file. *But what was in the file? What was in it that made Bran act like that?*

Bran turned his head toward Conrad's car again, slowly, very slowly, and slowly bringing his body with it. There was clear air again but Conrad knew Bran could not see him through the tinted windows. Then the rains came. Bran looked at the sky, took another look around the parking lot, and returned to his Santa Fe. The brake lights flickered on and he was on the highway.

Conrad stared at the file for about a minute. He had no idea what to expect, and for that reason, he was scared to open it. As he was deliberating, he had a terrifying vision that he would look out his side window and Bran would be standing there facing him.

He had to open it. Despite seeing Bran get on the highway, he knew Bran was a sly enough guy to pretend to get on the highway just to create a false sense of calm. For that reason, Conrad drove into a McDonald's parking lot a few miles down the highway and opened the file.

The contents of the file were medical records: Belle's vital statistics along with her health statuses from previous visits. On the inside cover was a green post-it note in McNaughton's handwriting:

Bran,

On vac until the 4th.

Talk when I get back.

M

It was the last page where something seemed amiss. There was another green post-it note stuck in the middle of a form that concerned Belle's saliva test from the week before. A group of numbers was circled in red pen, and the post-it note read, "She's yours!"

It was signed by Dr. McNaughton.

Conrad read it again, and again, and again, understanding it each time. He knew exactly what it meant. Belle wasn't his child.

He felt the blood crawl out of his face.

She was Bran's all along.

Conrad drove like a zombie to Belle's swim practice that evening. He was lucky he didn't crash considering he wasn't even conscious he was driving. He felt deprived of all energy and all purpose. He turned his phone off when he pulled into the gym parking lot. He didn't even care to know what Katherine's five missed calls were about.

He sat high in the bleachers by himself, unaware of the commotion around him, never noticing that the girl in the fourth lane who always seemed to be beating everyone else by a few seconds was Belle. He kept the file on the inside of his jacket. He was unable to look at it again, but unable to separate himself from it. Its contents had shaken him to the core.

She was never mine, he kept thinking. All this time I've been raising a daughter that was someone else's. And of all those people, it was Bran's. Of course it had to be Bran's. He almost felt cursed.

Feeling so alone up there, a fool, a cheated fool, he descended the bleachers with a single purpose now becoming

272

very clear. He was going to leave San Sangre behind. He was going to get in his car and drive east for as long as it took. He needed to get away from all the tragedy. Nothing good had ever happened for him here.

As he walked past, Belle swam by him. They both were headed in different directions from now on. *Let Bran have her*, he thought. *She's probably better off without me.*

He was at the exit, and the faintest calling of "Daddy" made him turn back. Belle never called him that. He pivoted slowly. She was resting at the end of her lane. She had been waiting for the other girls to finish the race when she saw him leaving. She called out to him again, and when he didn't seem to give an expression, she got out of the pool and ran toward him.

"Did you see my races?" she asked excitedly.

He didn't have the heart to look her in the eyes. "You did a great job out there."

She looked him up and down. "You're not leaving, are you?"

Before he could answer, Mr. Lopez, her swimming instructor, said, "Belle, back in the pool. Five minutes treading water and then we're done for the day."

The exit was Conrad's now. It beamed under the light. Belle, among girls two and three years older, didn't take her eyes off of him once back in the pool. She treaded furiously, her long legs tired but running on adrenaline.

Conrad looked back at her, marveling at how far she had come. He gave her a faint smile and turned for the door.

"Your daughter is the best swimmer I have ever seen at this age," Mr. Lopez said, stopping him before he could go any further.

Conrad looked down at him with wide but unsurprised eyes.

"You don't seem – did you hear what I told you, Mr.

Mayday?" Mr. Lopez said with an Americanized Spanish accent. "Your daughter is…"

"The best at everything, it seems," Conrad said.

He was depressed, almost bewildered. Anyone could see it.

"You're not happy?" Mr. Lopez asked.

Conrad didn't care about the glory anymore. "How is she the best swimmer?"

Mr. Lopez shielded his back to the girls so they couldn't read his lips. "How is she…she's just better, faster than all the other girls. She's two ages ahead of her competition. If I were you, I would showcase this talent immediately. Get her into some competitions. See how she does when the pressure's on. I could coach her, if you'd like?"

"How can she be two ages ahead?" Conrad asked exasperatedly. He was tired of hearing how much better she was than everyone else. "It doesn't make sense. How can somebody be that much better than everyone else? How can some people be that much better at something than everybody else?"

Mr. Lopez could tell he caught Conrad in the midst of what must have been a very bad day. "She just is," he said effortlessly, and that ended the argument. He blew his whistle, ending the five-minute treading session.

Belle came over to them soon after, wrapped in her pink towel. Her swim cap was still on and Conrad studied her face and suddenly felt he saw a resemblance to Bran. It was in the face. It was slightly pudgy like Bran's, and her eyes were like his – bright and narrow. She had a bit of a boxer's face too, now that he looked harder at it, a characteristic of Bran's that Conrad had always been bothered by. He just didn't understand why he had only noticed it now.

"Are you okay, Dad?" she asked, but Conrad stood motionless, studying her face like a painter studies a view.

274

Mr. Lopez, uncomfortable with Conrad's silence, said, "Belle, your dad and I were talking, and we discussed the possibility of you getting into swimming races."

"If she's so fast, why don't we just put her in the ocean," Conrad snapped.

"Actually, I tend to take my best swimmers out to sea. Makes them experienced swimming against a current like that."

"Then the sea is her sepal*ch*er," Conrad replied. Mr. Lopez's eyes wobbled a bit like he was caught in an embarrassing situation.

Belle, without hesitation, said, "It's pronounced sep-uhl-ker, Dad." Conrad stared at her with contempt. It was an odd position to be in; he was trying to sound smart by using such a word. Moreover, he was baffled she knew the word. *In what book or poem had she learned such a word?*

"She's not swimming in the ocean. It's too dangerous," Conrad said.

"Most great swimmers start there, Mr. Mayday. I assure you that where some of my trainers take them, it is not dangerous at all. It's very shallow water. That's the best way to build endurance."

Belle was excited by the idea. Her eyes pleaded with him.

"As long as it's safe," Conrad said, not really caring anymore.

Mr. Lopez said, "I'll call you later with some details. Actually, I believe there is a beginners session tomorrow of about forty kids Belle's age."

Conrad shook his hand listlessly. "I'll talk to you then."

Conrad didn't hold Belle's hand when they left. Belle was wary of him. That had never happened to her before.

She kept her distance, until she told him that she loved him and watched a few unwelcoming tears fall down his side.

His mind was onto something else. He was thinking about Bran and the racquetball court that day. What happened to him right after he left me lying there, my face and body maimed?

CHAPTER 42: BRAN HALL

Those seven years living in New York City went by slowly for Bran Hall. But nothing was as slow as that first week. When he told his dad that he had beaten Conrad Mayday so badly that he may have disfigured or even killed him, Gilbert Hall had him on a plane to New York where he would stay with a cousin of his who owed Gilbert a favor. He was told to stay low until Gilbert talked to their family attorney and figured out the right course of action. It was eventually settled that Bran was going to do, at the very least, some jail time.

But that never came because Conrad did the unthinkable: he lied and said his injuries were the result of a car crash. Gilbert Hall expected Conrad to eventually come to his senses, but he didn't. Pride had gotten the best of him.

Bran couldn't return to San Sangre though. He had ruined his reputation, quitting his job unexpectedly, divorcing his wife with no notice, and creating the soft rumors that treaded around town that he might have been behind Conrad's injuries. His sudden departure seemed too convenient. It also didn't help that Gilbert gave him a job as Regional Manager at the New York branch. His coworkers despised him because of the nepotism, so finding friends became impossible.

To make matters worse, Bran hated New York City. All

he could do was compare it to San Sangre. It was fast and frenzied, nobody knew anyone, prices were double, space was limited, trees and grass didn't exist. The city was purely concrete too: long, long lines and rows and columns of huge concrete buildings. The occasional blur of yellow and green cabs was all that offset it.

He hated the people of New York even more. He thought them rude and privileged. He didn't like that they moved underground to travel. To him they were uglier, meaner, angrier, and too ambitious, even for his taste.

The Big Apple was a place unto itself. It never stopped. Bran thought that if a nuclear holocaust did occur, New York wouldn't stop for it. Not for a second. No, the entire human population could be destroyed, and New York City would still be going, night after night, day after day; a world of people who didn't know each other and were too busy to stop and try.

The months went by, some girls went by, but Bran still couldn't shake his desires for Micker. He missed her dearly. Around the months he knew she would be expecting, he began to drink heavily. He knew his behaviors were chipping away at his health, but it was hard to care about those things in times of depression.

In what would have been Micker's ninth month, he met a beautiful woman in Queens. She reminded him of Micker: she was blonde, she had soft features, and she carried a unique air about her. The only difference was she was bigger than Micker and a little rougher in appearance. Her name was Rosaline, and Bran didn't waste time getting to know her.

He was taken aback by how small her apartment was, but then he remembered all New York apartments were tiny. This one was just one room and a bath with a kitchen the size of a closet. He looked around the room and noticed there were no pictures. Usually the women had pictures of themselves or their
278

husband or their family on the bedside table.

Her suitcases lined the room, unpacked. "You're not planning on staying in this city long," he said.

She reached for a bottle of water from her refrigerator. "No, just flew in for a few months to do a story." She shut the refrigerator and opened the cap to her water and chugged it. "Then I'll fly right back." She offered the water. "Do you want one?"

"No, I'm fine."

Bran leaned against a wooden chair by her desk. She had no other furniture.

"Sorry about the furniture situation. The last tenant left me that wobbly chair there and that desk for a hundred bucks. Again, I'm not staying long, so."

"Are you a reporter?"

"Yea."

"What do you report?"

"Purely sensationalism," she said chuckling. "Gossip stories. That sort of thing. Yea, doesn't make the family proud, but it does pay the rent."

"So, what are you here for?"

"The Mayor's money-laundering scandal. You probably heard about it."

"Yea."

"Do you like it here – in the city?" she asked.

"Hate it," he said. "I'd leave tomorrow, but I'm in a sticky situation, so I'm stuck here for awhile."

"Where are you originally from?"

"California."

She smiled. "Me too!"

Bran seemed to slow down when she said that. "You're from California too?"

"Yea," she smiled. "Western girl."

"Born there, or…"

"No, that's where I work. My newspaper's there; that's why I'm here. I'm doing the story for them."

Bran went quiet. He didn't like where this was going.

"Where are you from in California?" Rosaline asked. "Maybe we know some of the same people."

"You first," he said.

"San Sangre. You?"

He couldn't believe it. He smiled astonishingly. "I'm from Sacramento."

She knew he was lying, and he knew she knew. He hesitated too long.

"Well, that's a little too far north of me. So Bran, what's your last name again?"

Bran walked toward the door. He answered her unequivocally. "Hall. Bran Hall."

She knew the name instantly, and she knew she had heard it involved in some type of shame, but she couldn't name it. There was a violent gleam in his eyes now that unsettled her.

"Well, Bran, what do – what do you do here in New York?"

"I told you already. I'm a businessman."

"I see. And what…"

"You ask too many questions." He fastened the security chain to her door and stood in front of it.

She realized the deep, burly size of him. She tried to move by him. "I forgot to check my neighbor's…"

He moved in front of her. Only then did she realize her mortal danger. He smiled at her sympathetically and said, "It's a shame you had to be from San Sangre." His palms came up, a redness in his face and eyes from another world, and pulled her to the ground. She tried to fight his hands from her neck in the first few seconds, but she realized it was useless. His strength

280

was unreasonable and cruel, and he didn't stop until he heard a sickening explosion.

Her lungs had popped. He saw the body bloat instantly and the eyes' meaning recede.

Now she would never get the chance to talk about him.

Bran never felt the guilt or remorse after the murder. There was no pain in sleeping. Like was common in the City of Skyscrapers, the police never came knocking. He had thrown her body under her tiny bed, covered it with her suitcases, and wiped the place down. It happened that she had paid her three month stay, so it wasn't until the landlord came knocking with collections for a fourth month that he noticed the tenant was missing without her suitcases, and a bad smell emanated from the room. It made headlines since she was from California and a news reporter, but soon it fell into the annals of unsolved murders. Within weeks Bran had pushed the crime from his mind.

Still, he couldn't resist thinking about Micker, the idea of not having her, the thought that Conrad had beaten him. When he learned she had given birth, he decided to call her again. He had been calling and calling and hanging up before voicemail. She would never answer.

One night, in front of a bottle of Jack Daniels, he called again, and for the first time, he heard a voice.

Micker had finally picked up.

He had a proposition for her, something he had been thinking about for months, and she listened, never resisting like she would have in the past. In fact, she seemed to share in his desperation. She even liked what she heard.

They came away with a plan – a plan that involved his brief return to San Sangre.

CHAPTER 43: A GHOST'S RETURN

The night Conrad learned of Bran Hall's return to San Sangre, Will Brosnan had attempted to call Conrad to reschedule an inspection. But Brosnan didn't have his number. It had been that long since they talked over the phone. That fact alone nearly brought Brosnan to tears.

He thought moving into upper management would be a positive thing for him, but it wasn't. His coworkers who he had always been friends with started to resent him, and though the pay was better, he badly missed being on the sea. What he missed most, however, was Conrad. They drifted apart, and he felt they hadn't had a real conversation in six months.

He arrived at his office at Walker's at 4:00 am, the only one in the building. He came to search his files for Conrad's number.

An envelope without a return address was laid on his desk by his secretary right after he left the day before. From the perfect cursive, he knew who sent the letter.

He opened it and a small note flew out. He held the note above a candle he lit. The words drifted in and out of the shadows and the flame spears.

Speak to Melissa Sanders. Follow the trail.

-M

Another anonymous letter. This was the eighth. He read it again and again. He imagined Melissa Sanders was another witness from New York, and he knew that if he called this Melissa Sanders, he would get closer and closer to a truth he didn't quite want to unravel. He was tired of this chase. It had been going on for two years now. Some stories were meant to go to the grave.

But he had honor. M, the mystery person sending him this now eighth anonymous letter, certainly knew that.

M was someone he knew. It had to be.

He thought of burning it. Less evidence. If M was helping him solve a murder, then there must be a murderer. Brosnan didn't want that man to come and find him one day.

But he saved it, like all the other letters. He put it in a file folder with the rest of the anonymous letters and clippings that had been sent.

Before he shoved the note in the back of the file cabinet, he took out one of the clippings of a woman's face. A beautiful blonde woman, mid-twenties. Her life in front of her.

Her name was Rosaline Jeffreys. He wouldn't forget that name for as long as he lived. M had led him to many destinations of Rosaline Jeffrey's the day she died. She was a reporter for the *San Sangre Star* who traveled to New York to cover the Mayor's scandal. He even learned of the apartment she was staying in the day she died and the bar she had her last drink in. He had a feeling that once he tracked down Melissa Sanders, whomever she was, he would have a better idea of her killer.

He noticed something on his desk that took his attention away from the note. His candle, a Yankee candle of pine scent, had been turned to a different position. He couldn't see the picture of the pine trees on it any longer. Most people would assume they had moved it themselves, but he was meticulous. He was unorganized in the sense that his files were everywhere, but he knew exactly where they were, in what position, and how and when they got there. That candle had never moved in years. Here, it lay in a different position.

Someone had been in here, snooping, and it wasn't the secretary. It was coming to him. The papers on his desk seemed an inch from where they were yesterday. His chair was pushed in when he never pushed it in.

Chills stabbed him in clustered waves. Rosaline's picture was turned upright in the file. He had always turned it around. He didn't like to see her face.

He heard a thud downstairs. A door closing softly. Someone else was in the office with him.

He shoved the file folder at the back of his cabinet and listened. Someone had come in the backdoor. This person tried to walk softly down the long corridor to the stairwell. Brosnan could hear him.

His door was closed, but it wasn't locked. He sat down at his desk slowly. In all his years, no one had come in this early.

Someone was ascending the stairs to his office.

Now he was panicking. Each step paralyzed him. He stared at the latch on the door. He thought of running over to lock it, but he couldn't move. He was terrified.

The steps got louder. He waited in anticipation. The feet made dark symbols beneath the doorway. The person listened at the door.

Brosnan looked around for a weapon, anything, but there was nothing. He sat still, like a coward he felt, barely moving a muscle.

The person knocked. Brosnan exhaled. No one who

wanted to do him harm would knock first. "Who is it?"

"I'm sorry, Mr. Brosnan. It's Evan Hackery. I didn't mean to startle you."

"You scared the crap out of me. What is it?"

Hackery opened the door and closed it. He seemed startled himself. He slowly took his red cap off and pressed it to his chest. His curly brown hair rose to the ceiling and he ran his fingers through it nervously. "I need to tell you something, but I need to tell you it confidentially. That's why I came in early."

The docks would be filled shortly.

Evan Hackery was known for being a rat. Nicknamed "the Hack," he was responsible for the firing of two previous employees at Walker's for their secret indiscretions, and Brosnan shared the disdain most had for him. But Hackery had been more discreet in recent years, and Brosnan had to give it to him: Nobody knew more that went on at Walker's, and that included him.

And here it comes. *A third firing*, he thought. But he had to hear him. If he didn't, he knew Hackery would report him, and then he'd be called before the suits. "What is it?"

"Confidential?"

Nothing was confidential with Evan Hackery. Brosnan wanted to laugh out loud. "Of course," he said.

"It's Conrad Mayday," he began hesitantly. "He's gone over the boundary lines."

Brosnan didn't say anything at first. He looked inquisitively at the wall in his office where a picture of him and Conrad hung. He was confused. "Why would he be going beyond the boundary lines?"

"I don't know."

Brosnan was deeply bothered. "You're sure?"

"Yes, sir."

"You've seen him do it?"

"Many times."

"Many times?" Brosnan repeated bemusedly. "How many times?"

"About five."

"Where is he going?"

"I don't know. He's gone for very long spans each time. I think he might be going to the Farallon Islands."

Brosnan felt his white beard and shook his head. There was a rough history that Conrad shared with that place, so Brosnan expected that Hackery was telling the truth. Regardless, he tried to cover for his friend. "Well, it can't be that. Conrad's scared to death of sharks. I'm surprised he even fishes in the waters around our dock, let alone the Farallones. No, he's probably trying to capture some Dungeness a little farther out. It's been a tough month. I'm sure he's trying to compensate for a weak month." Hackery stood there motionless. It so unsettled Brosnan that he asked his subordinate, "Don't you agree?"

"He's gone for a while. Well after dusk. I'm the only one that sees him do it. I'm sure he doesn't notice me, but I am positive he goes there."

"You said dusk?"

"Yes."

"When does he leave?"

"Right before dawn."

Brosnan leapt from his desk and pulled back the blinds. The sun had already spiraled out. The water was rough and it shook the dock. He looked for Conrad's trawler. It was gone.

"Where is he now?"

Hackery's eyes were piercing now, matching Brosnan's intensity. "He already left."

Brosnan looked at Hackery with a disturbed expression on his face. He grabbed his slicker and stormed by him. He stopped at the doorway. Hackery was not following him. His eyes were on Brosnan's desk. They were peculiar.

"Miss something?" Brosnan asked.

Hackery was startled. "I'm sorry, sir," Hackery said and made his way past him down the steps.

Brosnan looked back at his desk.

He made sure to lock the door.

Brosnan marched the path down to the loading dock. He was headed toward a trawler but saw that the center console boat he took out just last week to treat Walker executives was just a shoelace's length from jutting him quickly out to sea. The trawler, dissimilarly, would take him ten minutes to start, check, and untie. While the center console was very small – about eighteen feet long and narrow – it was built to move fast over open ocean. What made him hesitate was the thought that never left his mind: Conrad might be headed for the Farallones.

When Brosnan was a kid, his father had told him a story while they were on the open ocean that never left him. It concerned a group of seafarers who happened into the Red Triangle without knowing. While watching a seal walk its tightrope to shore, a great white breached the water, and with seal in mouth, landed in their boat, knocking two passengers into the ocean and paralyzing the wife of the driver who didn't even want to ride on the ocean in the first place because she was scared of sharks. Within minutes the seafarers' boat sank, thanks to the thrashing the great white did at the stern. Without the luck of some scientists studying the area nearby, the passengers would have been treading in water teeming with hungry great whites.

That story was tattooed on Brosnan's mind. Yet something propelled him, be it the meek arbitrariness of the possibility, to take the more convenient center console.

Once land disappeared, the ocean became a scary place. It turned colors while Brosnan was out there: a murky brownish-blue to gray as a raccoon. The sky was no different. The sun was out then overtaken by whiteness. As Brosnan came near the buoys, he looked behind him to see the white rope his boat made from the shore. It slowly disappeared the farther he traveled.

Conrad's trawler seemed to be sitting out there right next to the buoys. If it were moving, Brosnan couldn't tell. It didn't seem to be moving, almost like it was waiting for him. When Brosnan came into view, Conrad's trawler undeniably began to accelerate past the buoys.

The fog came next like God had dropped a white blanket on the sea. The buoys disappeared, and so did Conrad's trawler. Brosnan was scared now. He could hear Conrad's engine hissing and cutting through the water, and he was uncertain whether to follow him out to sea or not. He kept pace with him like that, miles and miles at his stern. By the time he decided it was too dangerous to ride out in the center console, it was too late. He was already in Farallon waters, staring into white fog and trailing just the sound of an engine.

Conrad's engine stopped. Brosnan slowed, fearing he would ram right into the trawler with the fog. As his engine slowed, he could hear the barking of seals from one of the islands. He could also see craggy rock formations showing like phantoms in the fog. When his boat slowed to just five miles an hour, he felt an unearthly sickness in his stomach as he foresaw a force coming up from below his boat in a way he could not describe to any rational mind. But he felt it was coming – and when it hit, he realized that people do have a sixth sense. People can sense things, and Brosnan sensed, as his center console was pushed vertically and as he still held onto the steering wheel like a kid holds onto the handle bars on a ride at an amusement park,

288

that he would not make it out of this one – that his life, in a split second, had reached its finality.

He plunged head first, his center console quickly sinking and surrounded in huge white bubbles. Saltwater filled his lungs in the dark coldness he had entered. He made the top of the sea, his eyes burning from the saltwater. He stared out at only open ocean. Either he crashed into an unseen rock or a shark hit him. The way his boat was lifted vertically, he assumed it was the latter.

"Conrad!" he screamed into the fog behind him. He still couldn't hear Conrad's engine, but he sensed he was just beyond the fog. "Conrad, I need help! I need help!" His screams echoed. They were reaching Conrad out there, but why wasn't he reacting?

The tip of a fin cut six inches above the water, and Brosnan knew it was a matter of time before it started investigating him. But because the current was so strong, pulling and yanking his body in different directions like a giant whirlpool, his concentration was on staying atop the waves, and after just a few minutes of treading, he was physically exhausted. To make matters worse, he saw red floating in the water beside him. His jaw was gushing blood from the impact of the crash.

"Conrad! I need help! There's a shark! Conrad!" He saw Conrad's boat make its first appearance in the fog. "Conrad, please help me!" Conrad's trawler floated forward, slowly, intently.

Brosnan could feel energy all around him. He was in water at least forty feet deep. What was below him, God only knew. *Don't look in the water*, he thought, *whatever you do. It's better not to know.* But just like telling someone not to look down from a skyscraper, he had to look. *He had to look.*

He dropped his head, held open his burning eyes, and saw a huge gray figure the size of a school bus drifting through the ocean beside him, its pectorals moving with the current like a bird.

This shark was longer than his center-console, its mouth wider than his engine. Never before in his life had he felt so helpless. The shark was as big as an airplane, floating through the water, undaunted, knowing Brosnan was there but not going anywhere unless it took him. Its bulk prodigious, it created its own current while it circled and circled, getting closer with each ring.

Underwater, the shark's features were amplified. It had a black eye the size of a tennis ball that protruded from its head in an unnatural way. With its mouth half open, its teeth came like disorganized white knives stuck in raw meat. And there was something in its mouth, something it was gnawing on. Brosnan peered closer under water. Fragments of brown flesh breathed from its mouth. The shark had just swallowed a seal.

The center console was about to sink stern side up. Brosnan thought of making an effort to swim to it and hold onto it until it went under, but the current was so strong he knew he would need to conserve all his energy just to stay atop the sea for a few minutes. The boat made an eerie creaking sound as it went under. That's when Brosnan noticed something tied to one of his stern cleats that wasn't there by his doing.

A rope had been tied in a knot around the cleat with what looked like part of a seal's flipper tied in the rope. The flipper was all that was left. The body had been chewed off, its flesh recent. Brosnan knew instantly what it meant. He turned back toward the island to be sure.

The seal was on Brosnan's boat all along. He had been lured into the devil's den. The shark, hunting the seal tied to his boat, breached, and in breaching, capsized the bow of the console and submerged his boat. It was brilliant.

290

Conrad's trawler had now made an imprint in the fog. Brosnan could see Conrad in silhouette, and instinctually shouted: "Conrad. It's me, Brosnan! Help me!" He felt it weird he would need to spell out his disaster.

As the boat came drifting toward him, however, he realized it was not Conrad.

Like seeing a ghost. All shock and nightmare in his face.

Bran Hall stood at the helm looking down at him, smiling.

"Long time," he said, looking very comfortable above the waves.

Brosnan couldn't help but break a faint smile. He appreciated cunningness, even if he was the brunt of the skill.

"This is for your victim," Brosnan guessed, "in New York."

"You should know not to snoop. But that was never your skill," Bran said, the smirk never leaving his face. "Now look where it's taken you."

"Hackery?"

"Of course. Why would you trust him? He's been my little rat for years." Storm–petrels circled Brosnan in the sky. The fin had gone under. "Uh oh," Bran taunted. "I don't think it's going to be much longer." He pointed up at the death birds. "Good thing because I have other business to attend to here."

Brosnan's body could no longer stay afloat. It was an awful, helpless, terrifying feeling. He was trying to do something as simple as tread water and no longer could. He was going under...and fast.

"I hope you rot in hell," Brosnan replied through the gulping of sea water.

"A lot of people do."

As he sank, he looked down in the water and saw a

291

white fish with its mouth wide in a circle like it was coming to swallow something at the surface, sprinting through the water directly below him – its tail kicking wickedly behind it, the engine of its being. The fish quickly became a shark, then a great white, and engulfed half his body and breached with him back in the air. Brosnan could not emit a sound. His vision turned into a fallen camera. He saw glimpses of things that appeared abstract: the blue sea, the pale sky, a gray tail, and a huge black eye sliding to white. He didn't breathe again, and felt indescribable pressure and popping around his abdomen. For a second he thought he had been dragged to the sea floor and back. He was moving through the green at an unimaginable pace, seeing the ocean floor for the first time in his life – it looking much like forest ground. He was released from the shark's jaws, and as he floated at the bottom of the sea, slowly ascending the top, he noticed he felt lighter. Instead of legs he saw bright red spirals blooming all around him.

Bran slowly drove his boat where Brosnan's sank. He saw blood in the water but no sharks. The stern side of the console was about to go under. He settled the boat against the current so he was in reaching distance of rope tied to the stern cleat. He pulled out a small fishing knife and sliced the rope, dropping the portion of the seal that was left back into the sea, and threw the rope on board. The console, like it was fighting from being pulled into a drain, finally gave way and disappeared. The blood lost its hue in the sea, and everything in nature's order returned. There was no sign of Brosnan or his boat, and there wouldn't be for a long, long time.

Before taking off into the fog, he turned his engine off. He was waiting for feelings of dread and guilt to inundate him, but they didn't. The adrenaline of the situation was tiring now, and all he was left with were thoughts of Conrad's demise.

CHAPTER 44: REALITY

Katherine met with Conrad again on the boardwalk. They met at ten after she learned Conrad had called off of work, and she explained everything she had discovered about Bran's involvement with Donny Locks. Unusually, Conrad didn't seem to care. She could tell something was wrong with him. He stood, leaning against the railing, almost in a daze.

"What's wrong with you?" she finally asked. "I just dropped a bombshell, and it doesn't seem to mean anything to you."

"I'm fine," he replied listlessly. But he wasn't. He was thinking about what he learned about Belle.

"Are you?"

Conrad tried to refocus as best he could. "What I don't understand is why Bran would risk everything to take advantage of the Locks when they had dirt on him?"

Katherine shook her head. "I don't think he could help himself. He preyed on the weak," she said, alluding to what Mrs. Locks had told her.

Conrad dropped his head. By implication, he was weak

too. Bran had preyed on him; he beat him to a pulp. "Why didn't she burn him then? She could have?"

Katherine answered, "To protect her son. Bran must have threatened to turn Donny into the authorities. She wanted Donny to have the best opportunities possible," Katherine said tittering. Having known Donny's fate, she realized the irony.

Conrad remembered: the burglaries in the San Sangre National Park. He had told Bran about them, and Bran said he would take care of it. Then a suspect was named, and Bran said that Locks was cleared. Conrad was willing to bet his life that it was Donny Locks all along. Maybe Bran had something to do with that suspect suddenly being put into custody. And then the rap sheet – Bran must have been protecting him. But there had to be a catch.

Conrad shared this history with Katherine. She wished she had known sooner. Now it was making sense.

"So Bran selects Donny as an intern at Walker's that spring," she said. "You said Kevin Hall was the one that was supposed to take care of the screening process. Real strong-headed about stuff like that?"

"Yes."

"He trusts Bran's selections, doesn't check the intern's backgrounds. Donny gets in through the front door. Then you do some research. You find out about Locks, that he lied on his application. You tell them of his history and your suspicions of his possible involvement in the park burglaries?"

"Keep going," Conrad said.

"Locks continues to aggravate you. He's trying to get you fired." Then she stopped. "Why?"

Conrad thought about it. "That's the one thing I never understood. Locks had it out for me from day one, like something was driving him."

Katherine tapped her lips. "Maybe he was brought on

294

for that purpose. To get you fired."

"Bran hated me that much?"

"Possibly," she answered, but she felt there was more.

"Back up," Conrad said. "Why would Donny Locks go along with this? Donny Locks and Bran Hall, working together? Why wouldn't Locks use his energy to bring down Bran. Bran's the bad guy. Not me."

The answer had finally come to Katherine. She had been thinking about that too. "He wasn't afraid of you. He was afraid of Bran. Donny was afraid of what Bran would do to his mother."

"Donny cared about his mother that much?"

"It seems she was the only person he truly cared about."

"This whole thing is just crazy." Conrad's mind continued to waver. He looked at his cell phone. He expected to see a missed call or text from Brosnan since he called off work that morning, but Brosnan hadn't communicated to him yet. It was unlike his old friend.

"Conrad, focus!" she hollered.

"I'm sorry," he said.

"Here's what I'm thinking," she said and she turned to the sea, speaking in intervals when joggers passed. "I think Donny Locks was there to set you up by the orders of Bran."

Conrad cringed. "Listen, Donny Locks was a lot of things, but one thing he couldn't do was pull this off."

"He got rid of you," she replied.

It upset him, but he needed to hear that. "Then how does Bran benefit if I'm fired? I agree he didn't care to see me gone, but he didn't benefit. He's too smart to risk that. That gives Locks even more dirt on him."

"But he did benefit," she said.

Conrad was thinking.

"You believed Locks was trying to get you to lose your

295

head, right?"

"Right."

"It didn't work out at first. So he really went to town on you that last day, his last opportunity. He's good with computers. He manipulates your email to make it look like that presentation of yours was pushed back. You show up late, making you look bad. You're furious. You're not in your right mind. Then Locks strikes. I think Bran told him that if he didn't get you to lose your head, he would be sent to jail, and Bran might do something to his mother."

Conrad interrupted, "So he brings up Micker cheating on me with Bran, knows that's the one area I'm weak, and hopes I'll erupt, which I do. But I don't hit him the way he wants me to. He flops backward, takes the fall, makes it look like I pushed him down a staircase in front of everyone."

"Yea," she said rolling her tongue around her lips. "Pretty sinister, eh?"

"Unfortunately, it's not surprising anymore."

"It's gotta be something like this," she said. "Conrad, there's no way Donny Locks could have made it through without Bran's protection. He had failing grades every year. He was suspended for nearly beating a kid blind. Then the burglary suspicion. And did anything come of it?"

"No," Conrad confirmed.

"Conrad, in your experience in the business world, do you know of anybody who got away with more?"

"No," he answered.

"Me neither. He had to be protected."

"But if that's true, I still don't see how Bran benefits?"

She needed to hammer it home. "Bran is Regional Manager at the time, right? He's an ambitious guy. He wants to ascend the ladder, but he's got a problem. He has a brother in the way of that ascension. Kevin Hall was always going to be
296

ahead of him unless something gave.

"You have a problem with Locks. As I recall it, you go to Bran and Kevin about Locks, deliver them the news of their flawed screening process. All responsibility falls on Kevin to act, not Bran. Kevin trusts his brother, never assumes Bran would stab him in the back. He takes Bran's advice to back off and wait until Locks is gone and hopes to cover up any discrepancies. Things are going to plan until boom, you push Locks, you get fired. Gilbert Hall gets heat from the newspapers and the community when they learn this all could have been avoided if Locks had never been hired in the first place or been removed after the many times you requested. Kevin Hall is blamed as the catalyst of a big storm. Where did Kevin Hall go after that year?"

"He was demoted and reassigned – somewhere."

She pulled out a few note cards and checked them. "He was sent up to the Sacramento offices as a regional manager. He made about half of what he used to as Vice President. Who became the new Vice President, and the youngest by far of any company in Northern California?"

"Bran Hall."

"Bran Hall," she repeated.

"But even with Kevin gone, Bran had no idea he'd get that position."

"Kevin came out the bad guy. Bran came out the good guy. The papers said Bran was the one who advised Kevin to get rid of Donny Locks. Bran looked, somehow, more competent after the whole ordeal."

"So my firing had little to do with hatred. It had mostly to do with –"

"Ascension."

"Get Kevin out of the way to take his spot, and you get rid of an older brother in the process, moving you just a few

297

spots from CEO when Daddy dies."

"Precisely."

"Why didn't Locks blow the lid on the arrangement then? He was fired too. His reputation was further damaged."

"I don't think he was there to make money," she said. "If he did what he did, his mother stayed safe and he stayed out of jail. Bran must have had something really good on him."

Conrad looked out to sea, wishing he could replay the past. "Bran's played me from minute one."

Katherine sensed his desolation. She wanted to cheer him up. "I don't know. Who gave that job up? Who ended up moving to New York? Who's going to be making millions of dollars here soon? If you ask me, you won this one, Conrad. You're the winner here."

And then it hit him. He instantly turned white. *Millions of dollars.* With endorsements, if the show went well, Belle could be worth millions of dollars. She asked him what was wrong, but he didn't have an answer.

"I need you to do something for me," he began. "I need you to take Belle with you, back to your house."

"Why? What is it? You're scaring me?"

He had a sick look on his face, and even worse, she knew she couldn't get through to him.

"Please don't ask questions. I will tell you tomorrow morning. Follow her typical schedule. Act like nothing's wrong. She has a swim practice with some instructor tomorrow. They're taking her to swim in the ocean. Belle knows what time and where. Just ask her."

"Conrad, what's wrong?"

"I'll explain everything later. I promise," he said, and she let him kiss her on the forehead. She felt so close to him again, and now he was leaving her.

Belle was sitting in the car the entire time watching their

298

conversation. She got some of it down by reading lips, but too little made much sense.

Conrad sat next to her. He had yet to look at her. "Belle, I need you to stay with Katherine for a day or so. You're going to stay at her house."

"Not until you tell me why," she replied worriedly.

"I can't do that."

"Then I can't go."

"Belle."

She sensed the urgency in his voice.

"I need you to do this for me," he said.

She hugged him. He didn't want to hug back. She was never his kid. He would probably lose her soon. The hug was tight. It was genuine. She sensed his suffering and said, "I love you, Dad."

In that moment, he hugged back. She saw him as her father, and once again, he saw her as his daughter.

Katherine sat in her car to wait for Belle. She studied Conrad's face, and had a hunch of what he was thinking. But the fact that he hugged Belle, that he loved her, made her respect him all the more as a father.

CHAPTER 45: THE RATS

On his way home, Conrad began to suspect why Bran was in San Sangre. *Millions of dollars.* It was a good reason, and Conrad was sure Bran had found out about Belle and decided to take her from him, to cash in on her. *Millions of dollars*, if she was used the right way. *Bran must have felt pretty confidently that Belle was his child the entire time to show his face around here again.*

He hated himself thinking about it this way. He was talking about his daughter like she was a product or a business deal. *Bran was cunning*, he thought. So cunning, that he was capable of anything, and Conrad just wasn't like that. Bran had the paternity test, had it administered by his own doctor friend, McNaughton. The lengths the man would go to. He could take Belle right now if he wanted.

Conrad wanted Belle out of his hands until he figured things out. Bran could be dangerous. He had been an eyewitness to his rage and had the scars to verify it. In the morning he would talk to Brosnan. He was the one man he knew he could trust. He expected him to be prickly, however, as Brosnan could be from time to time when Conrad called off of work. He had taken the day off, and Brosnan had yet to return his voicemail.

The only thing Conrad noticed when he arrived home that was slightly amiss was the temperature of his house. It was a little warmer than usual. He drank a glass of water and sat at the table. That Ferris wheel was still carrying people to joy over there. He watched it a little, and made his eyes around the pink walls, such a ghastly pink. He wondered why he never painted over them in all these years.

As he said that, a free-wielding laugh came from his bedroom. It had the arrogance of a queen on her throne laughing after an unjust sentencing. He had heard that laugh before.

He didn't register much emotion. In a way, he had expected it. He set his water on the table, pushed in his chair, and made his way into the bedroom like a gentleman. The lights to his bedroom were on. How did he not notice? The door was slightly ajar. He touched it softly, letting it flow back to surprise him with what it stored inside.

Two purple high heels on crossed legs, then Micker, her back nice and straight. Her hands folded over each other in a pose awaiting his presence. She was in violet – a violet skirt and a violet blouse. A regal look. A queen's look. Her hair as he had never seen it before – a short crop, almost an elfish shape, and a shade of red south of burgundy. She was statuesque, as he always remembered her.

A smile never left her face. "How are you, Conrad?" she said politely. A pistol gleam was in her eyes.

"You're not alone?" he asked.

She looked over his shoulder. "Of course not," she answered, and felt his blow from where she was sitting. She didn't look when he dropped face first to the floor and two thick, sturdy limbs came out from the closet.

Hours later when Conrad awoke, he found his tongue completely dry because it had been hanging on the side of his mouth. He tried to pull it back in but it was stuck to the crevice on the side of his lips. After some concerted effort, he pulled it apart. When he went to rise from the bed, he rose no more than a centimeter when he was forced back down by a weight across his neck, causing him to gag. He tried to move his legs but a sharp pain darted up them into his spine, causing him to roll his eyes in agony. He gagged and tried to sit up again, but the weight of what seemed like a belt was fastened around him. It felt like a brick had been taped to his neck. He wasn't going anywhere.

Though his body was fastened to the bed by ropes, his head was still elevated slightly by a pillow behind it, allowing him to glimpse down and observe his predicament: ropes were wrapped around him, tying him to the bed and each section of rope was separated by a foot.

He grew more terrified when he was assured he was not dreaming.

He could move his neck freely despite the blow he suffered at the back of his head. The lights were still on, so he could see clearly around his bedroom. Bran sat on a chair against the wall near the foot of his bed. He was still as broad as Conrad remembered, but he had aged considerably. Gray specks had fallen in his hair now. Wrinkles pinched his eyes and drooped his brows. He had a more menacing stare than Conrad remembered. A more serious countenance. He looked to kill.

Bran stared back at him, prideful of his setup thus far, but said nothing. His arms were folded in anticipation.

Micker came in from the kitchen. She stood in the doorway and finished a glass of water. The light from the kitchen illuminated her being.

302

"Do you like it?" she asked, cupping the dark red crops of her hair. "Yea, maybe it's not me." She looked around the room. "You could have at least painted the place, Conrad."

She looked at him, rolled her tongue around her mouth, and then set her water glass on the table. "You weren't surprised to see me," she continued. "Now I'd like to know why."

Conrad wouldn't answer. He tried to move again, but realized how futile it was. Bran's eyes were on him the whole time, a radiant black. Conrad had never seen eyes so intense. In fact, Bran was dressed in black. Even black gloves. *Why did he have on gloves?*

Micker sat down in a chair next to his bed and crossed her legs. "When did you find out?" she asked.

Conrad refused to answer.

"When did you find out?" she repeated, this time harshly.

"Not too long ago," he capitulated.

"It was you on the phone that night, wasn't it?" she scratched her head. "I knew I shouldn't have answered that call. You know, I never had before in seven years. I was that disciplined, but with this fool over here who just lets it ring and ring. And then the one time. That's the price you pay. Interesting what fate throws at you."

"Yes it is," Conrad replied. There was venom in his tongue, but she didn't seem to even notice.

"Or is it destiny? It's destiny, yes. Do you know what the difference is between fate and destiny, Conrad? Destiny is the planned events until your death, and fate is your death. I guess I was talking destiny."

"Enough already," Bran said. He rose and stood next to her. "Where's the file?" he asked Conrad forcefully.

"I don't know what you're talking about."

"Yes you do, now where's the file?" Bran asked again.

303

"I don't know."

"One last time, and then you're going to start to lose parts of yourself. Once I start, you can't have them back. Is it worth it?"

Conrad looked down at his feet. Would he begin by pulling off his toes, or maybe his fingers? How much could he withstand?

Bran smiled. "Okay," he said. He pulled out a large duffel bag. He looked at Micker and said, "I always wished that in the movies they said something like that before they tortured someone. The person always talks, but then it's too late. They walk out of there without a hand."

Micker looked away.

Bran walked to the closet, bent down, and what he picked up was not visible to Conrad. He carried it in his palms like a carrier and came slowly for the bed. He set down what was in his hands on the floor, and it made a nice big thud. Conrad heard a zipper whipped.

Bran emerged from the carpet with a portable oven, absent the front door. He set the open side of the oven, which was about a foot and a half long and eight inches wide, on the bed. He then opened the carrier and removed with his hands two large, sedated rats. They were black as tar and the only white showing was their bottom teeth from their slightly ajar mouths. The teeth were long, about a half-inch and the shape of tusks on a wild boar. Bran placed them on Conrad's stomach, parallel to each other with their faces toward Conrad.

Conrad knew what Bran was going to do. His breathing grew lightning quick and he used all of his force to break free of the ropes. He moaned and tried to scream, but it was useless.

"You still a history buff, Conrad?" Bran asked crookedly, not expecting an answer. "I think you'll like this
304

one." He took a long breath. "In Medieval times," he began, "a creative spin was put on torturing heretics. They strapped the prisoner down so he couldn't move, much like you are right now, and then they placed a metallic container overtop a rat. Then they heated the container with a torch," and as Bran was saying this, he placed the oven over the rats. He plugged it in, and quickly an orange light from the grill illuminated the tiny air holes in the oven. He turned it back off. Conrad felt a moment of warmth on his stomach. "Once the container was heated, the rats, having nowhere to go and feeling the wrath of the fire, chewed their way to freedom." Bran tied a strap around the oven and bed. The oven was tightly positioned over Conrad's chest.

"It's not worth it, Conrad," Micker said. "Give him the file."

In her eyes he saw, for the first time since the last time he saw her, sadness. It was behind those eyes and face, no matter how much she tried to hide it. In the light he got a better picture of her. Despite the makeup, there were bruises on those cheeks, and her lip was swollen. He saw tiny scars in her forehead that weren't there before and didn't seem the hand of old age. She could tell he could notice. She turned away.

"It's at the bottom of the closet, in the safe," he said submissively.

"The safe," she said. "I forgot about that safe." She moved some shoes away and began with the password. It clicked after a few whirls. "Jesus, Conrad. After all this time, it's still the same!" She yanked out the file, looked at it, and passed it to Bran.

It was empty. He had put the copies in the back of Katherine's car, under the seat. Only now did he realize what a terrible mistake that was. He should have destroyed them.

"Where are McNaughton's notes?" Bran asked. "Where

are they!" he screamed.

Conrad wouldn't budge.

Micker looked at him inquisitively. "It's with the woman he's been seeing. Katherine, is it?"

Conrad said, "If you touch her –"

"You're such a cliché," Micker said. "How is she? Is she better than I?"

"Anyone's better than you."

"We can compare later when we meet her," Bran said.

"Why Belle?" Conrad asked.

"Why Belle?" Bran was sincerely shocked. "That girl made news all the way to New York! We had to come out of hiding. We couldn't pass that up. Kid genius and future beauty queen. Millions of dollars, Con. She's worth millions."

"She'll never come to either of you. She can smell a rat anywhere."

Bran looked at his chest. "No better than you." He smirked. Bran decided to let him in on his plans. "Once you're dead, it's harder to get your DNA, especially with the plans we have for your corpse. That file proves you're not the father. You'd be shocked, but in order for me to get custody, I need your DNA to fail first."

The rats were still sleeping.

"So have you figured out how we did it?"

Conrad tried to look Micker in the eye, but she wouldn't look at him.

Bran said confidently, "I called her up one day, right after the pregnancy, only to find her the way I promised her: miserable and wanting a better life. So I offered her freedom. I proposed killing you. She didn't like that. She had a different plan. I've got to hand it to her: it was flawless, until today.

"I remember it like yesterday when she laid it all out. I pick her up in the middle of the night, the key making sure no

306

one sees me. I ride her in her car to an abandoned beach where I have docked one of my dad's largest yachts. We ride out with her stupid little dingy onboard, and drop it off in the Farallon Islands.

"The storm was tricky that night. We almost capsized. But we didn't. We sliced her hand, let the blood soak up her clothes, ripped them off and threw them in the sea with the dinghy. No one knew. No one cared.

"You'd be shocked by how easy it is to hide someone in New York City. No one knows anyone. They don't have time in their schedules to be suspicious. We've lived pretty happily these seven years, until our daughter had to go and become a genius and mess up our plans."

Conrad finally caught Micker's eyes. They were wilted, sad, almost screaming to tell a different story than Bran had of the last seven years. Conrad sensed a hostility between them, something boiling below the surface. He needed to provoke its appearance. His mind was moving quickly now. "Micker, I'm just curious how you plan to defend yourself once I'm dead?" he asked.

"Defend myself?" she scoffed.

"You think he's going to keep you around?"

Bran and Micker looked at each other suspiciously. Conrad was on to something.

He kept going. "You faked your death? I'm pretty sure that comes with a minimal sentence, wouldn't you say? That's before the police want to know why. You think he's going to keep you around for that?"

Bran smiled. "It's all been taken care of. Had you not threatened to kill her so many times, which I will testify to, she would not have wanted to do such a thing. But she had no choice. It was life, or death. She chose life. I think a jury would understand that."

But Conrad could tell Micker had thought about that before, and she didn't quite buy that angle. Hearing Conrad's skepticism made her all the more nervous.

Conrad tried to start in on Bran. "Bran, what are you going to do about Will Brosnan when he comes looking for me?"

Bran smiled. "You should ask the shark that got him this morning."

Conrad trembled. "What?"

"Damn shame, really. A seal was tied to the end of his boat when he decided to venture down to the Farallones. He didn't notice...until he was no better than the seal."

Conrad knew he spoke the truth. He imagined Brosnan's death. He played it over in his head. "Why Will?"

"He knew a secret of mine," he admitted openly. Micker tried to grab his arm to make him stop, but he said, "No, it's fine. He can't do anything. You see, Conrad, unfortunately it was a secret I couldn't risk anyone knowing. This isn't the first time I've killed," Bran continued. "A nosy woman in New York, you see."

"And Brosnan knew about it?"

"Yes. See, when you kill your first time, Conrad, you become more than a man. You find yourself at a base that is closer to either the Devil or God, and it revives a confidence in you – a feeling of narcissism that you only have as a young child – when you're sure you can never die. You look face to face with everything: the dark, and even the light. I guess I settled on the dark."

Conrad felt the tin in the oven shuffle slightly.

"Uh, listen," Bran said pointing in the air. "The rats have woken."

Conrad had to do something. Little tiny feet began moving over his stomach. They were tentative movements, the

308

same movements one makes when waking up in the morning: slow, careful, exploratory. Something popped in his head. It was a risk, but it was the only way he could possibly make it out alive. "It wasn't just Brosnan that knew about it," Conrad said, feigning a smile.

Bran stepped forward, his mouth cleverly ajar. One of the rats hit its head off the tin siding. Conrad knew he was on to something.

"What do you know about it?" Bran asked fiercely.

Conrad looked around for weaknesses in the straps. It helped his mind. He kept going, making up history as he went. "He told me. He told me everything."

"He told you," Bran asked. He hated not knowing. He hated being ratted on and never knowing the rat. "Then who's 'M?'"

Conrad couldn't believe the informant was named 'M.' It was a gift, a gift from destiny. He looked at Micker to imply that it was she. And when he did, her mouth opened slightly. That was the one tell of hers. When she got caught in a lie, her mouth opened slightly. Bran looked at her. He knew her tell too.

I'll be damned, Conrad thought. *She was 'M' after all.*

"You," Bran said forcefully. He walked toward her. She backed away. Clearly Bran had suspected it might be her for a long time.

She was quick with her response. "This is what he wants you to think."

Conrad was shocked. For the first time in her life, she didn't sound convincing.

"You've been trying to set me up. You wanted him to find out. Why?"

Micker was forced to sidle near the door. Bran intercepted her. She was helpless. Conrad couldn't help

309

wanting to defend her, as crazy as it sounded.

"Leave her alone," Conrad said, but Bran didn't hear her. Micker locked eyes with him over Bran's shoulder. *Go along. Once I say it, go along,* he communicated. "Belle isn't yours," Conrad told him.

Bran still hadn't seen that file. He had no knowledge of the DNA results. He just assumed, stubbornly, that Belle was his. He felt like a fool standing there. He needed to hit something, to hurt it.

Micker faced him. She knew he acted irrationally when he was angry. He stopped thinking, the worst thing an angry person can do.

"He's right," she said, her convincing flare returning. "You're not the father. Conrad is." No one in the world would have believed otherwise.

Bran was sold. She didn't back down. He turned and looked at Conrad, sold there as well. *All that money,* he thought.

"You've been setting me up the whole time," Bran reasoned. "You want me to kill him. If he's out of the picture, it's only you. She's your daughter by blood. You get custody of her. You make the money. And I trusted you," he grabbed her shoulders and threw her back against the wall with such remarkable authority that Conrad was shocked she didn't come out the other side.

"Micker!" Conrad screamed.

Her head thumped hard and was instantly bloodied. But that she could survive. What worried Conrad was her mouth. It was wide open, and red was on the tongue.

Her body had landed at a slant. She reached behind her shoulders, and then Conrad knew what had happened. She had been pushed so hard that the doorstop pierced through her back a good four inches.

She separated her back from the doorstop and leaned

310

over to the side. Blood sputtered onto the wall. Bran stood over her, his eyes in glossy shock. Color withdrew from her face and her stomach stopped pumping until each was certain that she had died.

"I will kill you for this," Conrad told him.

"I will die eventually," Bran said with that guiltless, perpetual smirk, "but not from your hand." He switched the knob. The oven turned orange.

"I don't lose, Conrad." Bran sat on the bed with him. "If I can't have the millions, then you won't have them." He began to whisper: "I will be your daughter's swim instructor tomorrow, on the sea." Conrad's eyes enlarged. "Yes, I know about that. The Farallon Islands don't have many inhabitants. The fog alone blocks all view from the sea. And I hear there will be fog tomorrow.

"What a nice beach it is, I'll tell Belle. What safe water. And I'll sit back and watch your little girl get eaten alive. They'll be wondering forever, what ever happened to that beautiful child genius that used to live around these parts?"

Conrad began to feel a slight burning sensation, and that's when the rats, all in one chaotic, confused action, began whaling. It was the sound a cat might make if it were hurt or hungry. They seemed to be jostling for position, looking for openings in their hot orange cave.

"Go strongly into death," Bran said, and duct taped Conrad's mouth shut. He left the house to Conrad's struggles and Micker's corpse. He would be back to clean it all up, once the brutality was over.

The rats' increased alarm made them ram into the sides of the oven, but there was no progress. Within minutes they realized this and began to understand that the ground they were standing on was mushy, was weak, was penetrable. They began taking test bites in the ground, tasted the saltiness of the skin,

311

and began wanting more. The heat was upon them and they could sense, innately, that they too could grow dehydrated and exhausted quickly in such conditions. They did not know what heat was, of course, or what it could do, but their natural, fatalist compass was sharper than a humans. They were designed to sense danger, and millions of years of evolution had prepared them for escaping such situations.

Conrad had little time. They could be through him in less than twenty minutes.

He used his strength, an insane surge out of fear, and two of the straps split. It was not enough though. The rats were beginning to bite.

He looked at the door, hoping someone, anyone, would help him. And that's when he saw the most amazing thing. Micker, still face down, began stumbling to her knees. Palms out, she flexed her weak legs and made it to her feet.

"Hurry," he tried to scream. She controlled her movement. She had lost so much blood that her vision was impaired. If she moved too fast, she would go down for the last time.

Conrad couldn't take the pain anymore. The bites were growing more violent, more successful.

Micker pulled the cord. The orange flares went out instantly, but the rats didn't stop. Conrad was still in pain. The rats squeaked and moaned mercilessly. She thought about the situation, using the last of her power. The strap holding down the oven was under the bed. If she bent down for it, she would not come back up. She was feeling queasy. She had little time.

With all her might, Micker pushed the oven, with the rats in it, loose from the strap. Another push and the oven toppled over on the other side of the bed. The rats, now red-mouthed, scurried across the bedroom and into the hallway.

She undid his top straps and his tape. He did the rest.

312

The wounds on his abdomen were superficial, though pieces of his skin were missing. Micker slinked down the bedpost. Her breathing had dawdled.

"Micker," he said. She had saved his life. "Micker, don't go yet."

She smiled at him. She wanted to say how sorry she was, but sorry just wasn't something she could say in that moment. It wasn't her. It wasn't honest.

In her last moment, she wanted to be honest.

"I wasn't meant for this world," she said softly and desperately, and then a surge hit her that took her out all in one sweep.

She was gone. He couldn't hug her body, but he couldn't leave it either. He saw the vibrant green in her eyes recede and return only a dull hue.

He wanted to stay there, try to revitalize her, try to understand all that happened. But he couldn't, and he knew it.

Every delay would cost Belle a chance at living.

CHAPTER 46: SEPULCHER ON THE SEA

Katherine opened the door to a man asking for Belle. He was wearing sunglasses and a blue hat. He kept his face low when he spoke. She mistook this for shyness. He said his name was Charlie Smith and that he was Belle's swim instructor.

"Oh, I thought I was supposed to take her to the dock."

"Oh, no, I was supposed to pick her up," the man said.

"For her first swim lesson?"

"Yes," he said. His voice seemed inauthentic. "That's what Conrad wanted."

When he mentioned Conrad's name, Katherine let up her guard.

"I'm sorry, come in," she said. "Belle is upstairs. I will let her know. I doubt if she's dressed yet." She ascended the stairs. "It shouldn't be long."

"No problem," he said, looking around the house.

After Katherine prompted Belle to put on her bathing suit, Katherine began to get an itch. She wanted a better look at Charlie. She thought she might have seen him somewhere before.

314

To her surprise, he was standing in her kitchen, not in the entryway, waiting for her.

"Can I fix you a drink?" she asked.

He kept his answers short. "I'm fine."

"Are you sure?"

"Is she almost ready?"

"She'll be down in a minute."

The man wouldn't let her get a look at his face. Something was wrong with him. Even if she wasn't Belle's mom, no one in a right mind would send a child with this man. She tried something.

"Mr. Samuels, which beach do you usually take your swimmers?"

He turned and looked at her. "My last name is Smith."

"Oh yes," she said. "I must have forgot. I'm sorry."

Now it was she who wouldn't let the man look in her face. She couldn't respond. She simply walked into her study to catch her breath. She had seen this man before.

She was sure of it.

Standing in her kitchen was Bran Hall.

She walked for the phone as quickly as she could. As soon as she picked it up, she saw him standing behind her in the mirror.

"Recognize me?" he asked. She turned. He took off his sunglasses to reveal menacing, blood-shot eyes. It had been ten years, but she saw the figure that she used to deliver those important documents to.. "My, you've changed," he said. "Put the phone down."

She did.

"I taught you well," he said cleverly, and then he was upon her.

Bran zipped Belle up in her swimsuit once they docked

315

the boat. It was still Conrad's trawler, the awful smell of fish guts on it. He took the risk Belle had never seen his boat. He had guessed well.

He handed her a swim cap and said, "Hold this for now. When we get out there, you can put it on."

"Where are we going?" she asked tiredly, for it was 6:00 a.m. and she was used to sleeping in on Saturday mornings. New instructors never bothered her, nor did strangers. She had seen her fair share with the shows and the swimming meets.

"It's an island," he told her, careful not to mention the name Farallon because he was sure, being as smart as she was, that she knew of the island and its lure of seals and sharks.

"Are there people there?"

"Tons. It's a very popular island. It's just around the corner here."

Trees blocked her view. She looked out over the beach. *An odd place to dock a boat,* she thought. Trees camouflaged the boat too. There were no piers, no houses, no lights, just a rocky beach.

"We aren't taking a plane?" she asked yawning.

"No. This place can be reached by boat in just a couple of minutes."

"My dad will be there?" she asked, her first sign of worry. Until then, Bran was surprised by how trusting she was. Even when she asked where Katherine was before they left the house, his answers seemed to stick with her.

Belle thought he was good looking, and he had a nice manner about him. He had a natural way with kids. Kids made him relax. He was always bigger and smarter than them, so he had no reason to panic. At first Belle kept him on guard because he knew of her intelligence, but after awhile, he realized she was nothing more than a seven year old kid.

"Ya' know, I used to go to school with your dad?"

316

"You did?"

"Yea. We played tennis together," he said as he pushed the boat out into the water. "We hung out together too. He's a good guy, your dad. But I'm sure you already knew that."

"He can be."

"He can be!" he said smiling.

"He puts a lot of pressure on me."

"Does he now. How so?"

"Well, I don't know if you know this, but I'm a genius." She smiled at her awkwardness. "That's what they say, anyways. I don't really think that."

"Well, you probably are."

"He's making me perform in these television shows." She stopped.

The boat was ready.

"Tell me everything on the way over."

She hesitated. "Charlie?" she asked.

"Yes, Belle."

"I don't want to swim."

"I'll tell ya' what. Why don't we ride over there, and then you can see the island, and if you don't want to swim there, you don't have to at all."

"Really? You won't tell my dad?"

"I won't tell if you don't."

She smiled. Charlie was a good guy after all.

Conrad knew as soon as he entered Katherine's house that Belle was gone. He looked for Katherine everywhere, only to find her lying on her back motionless in the study beside her desk. Fingerprints were bruised into her neck.

"Katherine!" he kept screaming, trying to shake her into consciousness. He checked her pulse. It was faint.

He looked around for her phone. He couldn't find it.

317

He needed a phone, and needed it fast. He wouldn't have reception on the sea. He ran back into the kitchen, into the living room, into the bedrooms. She had no landline.

He didn't have time. "Katherine, where's your phone!"

She didn't answer.

He searched the study frantically, tossing furniture like they were toys in a playpen.

Slowly, her hand extended in the air. She held her cell phone.

He held her head and kissed her. He immediately dialed 9-1-1 and set the phone beside her.

"Go," she whispered. "I'm fine."

The operator was on the line. Conrad looked at Katherine. He said to her, "I need you to send the police to the Farallon Islands. I must go right now. Tell them. Save Belle's life."

"I will," she promised, and he was gone, knocking everything over in his way.

Conrad was very careful when he arrived at Walker's. He didn't want anyone to see him, and he saw his boat was missing.

He didn't have time. He needed a boat, a fast one, one that was twice the speed of a trawler, and he knew exactly where to find one.

He walked the length of the pier where his colleagues were out of his sight. He saw Ken Marlin, one of Walker's' security guards who tended to patrol the buoys. To do that, Marlin used one of the fastest boats in the world – the go-fast, a lightning quick fast boat that had a planing hull, allowing it to exceed speeds of one hundred mph. It was the kind of boat mobsters used back in the day to smuggle in drugs on American shores. The drugs would be dropped off, and then the go-fasts

318

would take off like lightning the second the coast guard spotted them. They were impossible to catch and extremely difficult for helicopters to pick up.

Conrad realized that when you're in a panic, you'll do anything to make it work. The second Marlin stepped out onto the dock to untie the go-fast, Conrad jumped from the console next to it and extended the throttle. The momentum made Marlin fall back first into the water.

Conrad took off zigzagging through the harbor. He put Marlin's hat on him and sunglasses in case someone saw him. His hope was that his coworkers on the trawlers around him would think he was Marlin.

It seemed to work until one of the trawlers set off after him when he passed the buoys.

It was time to see what this boat was made of. In wide-open throttle, the go-fast took off, nearly leaping above the waves. He looked behind him. In a matter of seconds the trawler was a distant memory on the water.

After forty minutes on board, Belle wished she were somewhere else. The white fog gave her sight virtually nothing in the distance, and the brutal winds caused salt spray to slap her face and burn her eyes. She lay on her stomach and grabbed onto handlebars near the stern. The transom of the boat was thick and high enough for her to feel safe if she stayed on the deck of the boat. But she knew that if she stood, she would be a goner. The transom was only three and a half feet high, and even she was tall enough to fall overboard if she lost her balance. The engine was also so loud that it muffled her calls to turn back. There was a determination in her instructor's eyes that was unsettling.

Bran kept turning to check on her. He was also looking left to right frantically like a child who is in the moment of breaking a rule. After twenty more minutes, Belle finally determined that she had had enough of the boat ride. She called to him several times, but he did not answer. She knew he heard her. She attempted to rise from the stern when she felt the engine crank and the speed of the boat improving. This time a wave did not give way to the boat so easily, and she felt her body propelled forward. She was still holding on though, and she felt her left side being jammed. The joints in her shoulder cracked loudly but slightly without pain. She stayed low and no longer called for him.

It was when Bran nearly flew himself overboard that he finally slowed down. Altogether, the waves' height abated and the fog turned to mist. He slowed the engine enough so the ocean's boil could be heard for the first time. He looked around. He hoped he wasn't lost. He was listening for something very particular. He waited for it, and then it came: the sound of faint barking.

He smiled. They had arrived.

At first Belle was convinced she was hearing a pack of dogs barking on shore. But the sounds of the barks themselves were throatier and more powerful than a dog's. They sounded more like an animal that had been choking and were attempting regurgitation.

Thousands of these yowls swirled through the air. In the mist she saw three mountains of rock in triangular formation with boulder-like resemblance. The waves smacked against them furiously. Never before had she seen waves this powerful except in a storm. When they passed the three mountains, Belle could see another rock formation but with a very clear brown beach. The island was shaped like a dome really, and on the beach were green dilapidated houses with no clear inhabitants.

The barking intensified as they entered the surf. They were now three hundred feet or so from shore. Belle looked

320

overboard and knew that these waters were dangerous. She couldn't see anything below them. They were like blue cement. For the first time, she grew mortally terrified: the boat was all that kept her safe. She tightened her arms around the side and shrank along the transom. She needed to do something.

"Charlie, where are all the people?" she asked, trying her best not to act nervous.

Bran stopped the engine. "I guess they all went home," he said without turning to face her.

Now she was scared. She stayed low on the boat so she wouldn't fall over, peeping her head up to look for people on the beach or boats out at sea. There was nothing but fog.

Bran finally turned around. The beach was within a hundred yards. "Are you ready to swim?" he asked.

"Swim where?"

Bran took steps toward her. "Here," he said. "It's not very deep. You can start here and swim into shore. It will be great practice for you to swim against a tide."

"Are there sharks?" she asked. It was her primary concern.

"Here? No. I would never take you to a place with sharks."

"What about the barking?"

"Those are seals, but they are far away from here. Miles away even. The sound travels."

"Miles?"

"Maybe not miles, but they are far away. I promise; the water is safe."

His words were disarming. She didn't like the waters here, but she had seen the videos and the pictures hundreds of times of people swimming vast stretches of open ocean.

Still, she had her worries. He was too anxious. There was one way for her to tell.

"You'll get in with me, right?" she asked enthusiastically.

He stopped in his tracks. He wasn't quite sure what to say. "Maybe," was his careful response.

"You get in first, and I'll get in after you."

"I'm not dressed to swim, Belle. You know that."

"You'd mess up your shirt to make me feel safe, wouldn't you?" she asked.

Now Belle was really scared. This man was agitated, like he had to get something done and only had a few minutes to do it. She was hoping he would say he would get in. If he jumped in, she would know the waters were safe and that all her worrying was for naught. But what was she worried about?

He thought about her question for a moment before answering. "Actually Belle, I would get in but someone needs to stay aboard so we can get back to the boat. I didn't bring an anchor with me today." His response was smart, and she knew it. It made perfect sense for one to stay on the boat.

No one was in sight.

"You said I didn't have to swim. We would just go back."

"Oh, come on. Once you get in, you'll see everything is fine."

She had had it. "I don't want to swim here. I want to go home."

"There is nothing wrong with the water here. You'll love it once you get in and swim around. It is perfectly safe."

"No."

Bran surveyed the sea. It was greased by fog. No one could see them. He was still the only boat within miles. "Ya' know what, I drove you twenty miles to get here. I wasted gas and my morning to do it. Now you want to go back in!" There was uninhibited anger in his voice now.

"I can't swim here!"

322

"There's nothing wrong with the water!" he screamed, moving toward her cunningly like a tiger would a deer.

She kept trying. "Who are those people?"

"What people?" He looked toward the beach. The houses could barely be outlined in the heavy whiteness.

"Those people. They seem worried," she said cautiously.

"How can you tell what their faces look like from here?"

She didn't have a response.

"Because you don't see anyone," he said.

He continued toward her. Belle now knew for sure that something was wrong. She could tell he was coming to throw her overboard. She looked back in the water and grew petrified, like someone who is afraid of spiders and moves back when they see one, their hearts racing in uncontrollable terror.

"You're going in that water no matter what you say."

He grabbed onto her hands and began trying to yank them free. She let out a scream. Bran stopped. "Why are you screaming?" He was still acting like an adult, not a stranger, which kept her off-guard.

"I don't want to go in. Please! I'll do anything, anything, just please stop!"

"Enough already. You're the best swimmer in the town at your age and now you're scared of a couple waves? Let's go." He grabbed her this time by her waist, using his powerful forearms to lift her so only her hands were clasping the clamps on the transom. She was holding on for dear life, showing strength so remarkable that when her hands didn't come loose, laws of inertia nearly brought him plunging into the sea. He looked over the edge. The water was a dastardly gray now. Moments before it was blue.

"What do you think is going to happen!" he screamed.

"I'm right here. I'll be right here the whole time."

Belle could not trust this man. He had become her mortal enemy. This she knew, but how she knew it she did not know.

Bran sensed it too. She had seen a cave of darkness in his eyes. There was no going back.

"All right, we'll go in," he capitulated. He didn't offer a reason. He walked back to the bow and turned the engine. It roared and made the boat slightly vertical. Belle looked behind her out to sea, and as she did that she saw what appeared to be a flap of gray rubber puncture the ocean foam and bend in the air. Curiosity brought her to her feet. At first she thought she was seeing a whale breech, but then she realized the fin was clearly smaller than a whale's but edgier, rougher, more precise.

She had never seen a shark in her life, and from occasional interest had only seen a shark in "save the animal" type books. Here, without a doubt in her mind, was one, and a big one. She thought she would collapse on the deck in fear, but instead she was charmed by its size and insouciant manner. It was free of worry, of concern, of conflict. It even looked playful. With its monstrosity of a face veiled below the waves, the creature appeared to be a large dolphin. It inspected the boat from below, and though she didn't know it, it inspected her as well.

The shark could see Belle from six feet below the surface: a small black figure that moved. It did not know what a human was, or what a boat was. It simply knew that movement invited its curiosity. That was all. It rose to the surface again to gain a better view. It turned on its side and flapped its right pectoral fin just to induce movement in the figure above.

Bran, unaware of what intruded on Belle's sight, planned his next move. He had been watching a wave from one of his mirrors slide in a volatile manner toward his boat. It grew

324

in speed, volume, and density the closer it got. Bran knew that when the wave hit it would cause the bow to rise and anything in the back that was not holding on to plunge overboard. He would need to give the engine a start though. He needed to drive into the wave to achieve maximum elevation. He waited patiently.

Once the white wave approached, he pushed the throttle and the boat sped off before being obstructed by the wave. As planned, the boat ascended the wave and came crashing down on the valley in the water that the wave left. He smacked his head off the window and fell to the deck. His boat rocked left to right violently. He waited to hear a scream, but there was none. Just a thud. He knew without looking that Belle was no longer on board.

Belle never knew what hit her. She did not see the wave coming, and therefore her ability to react, to reach down for the cleats on the transom, was futile. She was thrown head first into white foam. Her hearing quickly changed to a seashell's sound. Freezing water crunched her body and made her feel like she was being sucked into a vacuum. The saltwater went up her nose, causing her eyes to close instantly and her arms and legs to flail and do whatever they could to reach the surface.

When she hit the surface and her tiny head burst through, she realized her predicament. The ocean was so rough and wild that she could barely see the tip of the boat despite it being three yards away. Without a life vest, she found staying afloat nearly impossible. Water was flowing into her mouth, and her eyes were burning. The first thing on her mind was drowning; the last thing on her mind was the huge gray thing she had seen casually swimming next to her boat before she collapsed on the water.

Bran drove softly toward the beach, allowing the tide to move him farther from her once he turned off the boat. He was

325

about forty feet from her, enough distance to watch her be eaten, and enough distance not to see the gory details. A cold guilt moved over his body as he watched this little girl, who he once thought was his daughter, struggle mightily for air. Then he pushed the guilt aside like he had always done: nothing mattered anymore. There was no turning back.

"Charlie!" she screamed, but the saltwater leapt into her mouth. She spit it out, forgot to use her legs, and was quickly pulled under the water. She kicked furiously to relish the top once more. "Charlie, help me!"

"Belle, you're fine. Just swim to me. See, this is what you were going to do anyway."

"I'm drowning! I'm drowning!"

"You're fine. Just kick your legs. Get your stomach on top and push forward."

"I can't. I can't."

At first he thought she might drown, but then he saw her do exactly what he said. He was amazed. Within seconds she made his point.

With all her might she lifted her body above the furious water, lay with it horizontally, and began thrusting toward the boat. She kept her legs together so she could glide through the water. The tide was with her. She came up for quick breaths then back down. She had her eyes opened just a tad for depth perception. She kicked forward, keeping her legs close together.

Bran was shocked by how quickly she was moving through the water. She was about to reach his boat when he jolted it ten more yards. She dropped her weight in the water, her legs went under and now she was back to bobbing up and down. She wiped the saltwater from her face only to see he had pulled away from her.

"Great job, Belle," he said. "Keep it up. You're almost to the beach."

She kept treading water but was tiring. She looked to the beach and realized she could make it there, but she wasn't sure if she had the strength to do it. Overhead she saw a ring of Storm-petrels gliding above her. They hovered over like theater-goers, first row seats to her and anything around her. Belle knew their sudden appearance wasn't the result of mere curiosity. These birds looked hungry. They circled the way an animal does before a meal. They saw something in the future she did not.

She tried to stay focused on swimming. Her legs were jelly and her arms throbbed from fatigue. She was moving them at angles never before approached. She wanted to give up and sink below until she remembered the gray object in the water.

She thought about it and forgot it just as quickly. She didn't have time to look around for it. She was concerned only with reaching the boat. She swam, the effort to get herself horizontal with the water a gargantuan struggle, but she did it. She was on her way.

As the mist was coming in from the sea and heading for the mainland, Bran saw a grey boat, long and narrow with an emerald light in the fog, slicing through water. At first he thought it was an eye, like a supernatural being floated over the sea. It was headed west of him, but nonetheless, he couldn't do this with someone else out here.

He squinted. The more he looked the more there really did appear to be a green eye! He was dumbfounded.

"Come on, do it," he muttered. Belle resembled perfectly a tiny, helpless seal. He looked around the ocean for a fin. Nothing.

"Do it."

The green light was getting closer. It was just two-hundred yards from his boat. He had to pull Belle aboard. He turned the boat around so the bow was facing the island and walked to the stern. When Belle saw him there, she bolted the last few yards and met his hand at the boat. He tried his best to pull her aboard, looking back to sea as the green light changed course and closed in on him. He waited for the boat figure to appear in the mist. In another ten seconds, it would.

When he pulled Belle aboard, the strangest thing happened. Left below the returned water from her dripping body was a massive head.

Deeper, he observed the outline of a second white head.

Two great whites were staring up at him.

The second head disappeared. The first head glided past him, and he saw what very few people have ever seen. Behind that black mass of an eye, just an inch inside it, was an actual eyeball. White and spherical with a black pupil and an iris, it was all too human. He had seen the eyeball perfectly, and it was fixated on him – that, along with the smile plastered on its half-protruding house of daggers. Bran felt as though the shark had meant no harm to Belle. Maybe it even helped push her through the water to the boat.

As it too slid down to the depths, its half-mooned tail kicking up water, the boat suddenly took off, and Bran was thrown overboard, actually landing on top of its silver scythe.

Belle decided not to wait. She used her mind, a photographic memory of what she remembered from watching him steer the boat, to turn it around and head back toward the open ocean. The farther she was from him, the better.

She drove off into the mist before his head emerged.

"Belle!" Bran screamed, but the saltwater flowed in his mouth to silence him. Though she could not see over the steering wheel, she let her instinct guide her. Bran wanted to break a smile for her cunning. She had won.

He had hope for himself though. He looked out to sea where the green light to the boat he had seen had been heading for him. He sent his arms up in the air, but the mist was thick.

328

The green light had disappeared. The boat must have made a turn somewhere.

Bran imagined the pain of the first bite. What would it feel like to have one's legs sawed off? How scared would he be when he saw that enormous mouth and those reddied gums coming up to swallow him?

And then he saw the emerald light return. It was a light on a go-fast boat. The boat was small. He didn't figure it would last in the waves.

He went to scream for help, but what he heard caught his scream.

"Belle!" the person screamed. "It's Dad!"

Bran knew it was Conrad, and the boat was drifting directly toward his splashing.

Conrad saw the object go beneath the waves, and for a second he thought he had lost her. He put the throttle into neutral to slow, then reverse to stop. He looked over the starboard side where he saw the splashing. Something was down there, moving. He looked closer. A hand suddenly jutted out and pulled him in the water. He managed a scream before plowing into the coldness.

Belle had heard her dad calling for her moments before. She returned to the area with the trawler. She called for him. He was nowhere in sight. She learned to work the throttle by testing it. The boat looked like a go-cart around the island, constantly switched speeds then halts. She continued to call for him, but the fog was too thick to see until she heard a scream.

Belle powered through the waves that crashed above her. She headed for the shrieks and saw two men, both of whom looked like each other, clawing at each other's faces, drawing magnificent amounts of blood. One was her dad, and the other was Charlie.

She looked about the ocean. The go-fast had capsized near the rocks. The only boat out here was hers.

She had an idea, but it would require luck and her total control. She stood on her tip-toes so her dad could see her. Charlie had her father's head in his palm and he was forcing it below the waves. She could tell by her father's efforts that if she didn't act soon, his head would stay there.

Conrad burst through the blue one more time: "Help me," he muttered, and over Bran's head he saw Belle's eyes just above the steering wheel. She was steering right for Bran's head. Conrad needed to get out of the way, but Bran had him vice-gripped around the neck. Bran was stronger, and he was feeling the full weight of his strength.

The trawler was now ten feet from them. If Conrad didn't move, it could kill them both. When he caught another whiff of air, enough for him to speak, he looked above him to catch Bran's attention and said, "Hey Bran." Suddenly Bran stopped fighting him. "Behind you."

Bran could only turn around to see the trawlers' bow as it moved in. Conrad dove under water and swam as deep as he could out of reach. Bran let out a mortal scream as the bow came in and crushed his face.

Belle heard the bumps along the body as she rode over it. When she turned, Bran lie inert face up in the water.

Her father was not out of harm's reach. She drove toward him, struggling to get the portside even with him.

Conrad was no longer just scared of the sharks. He was scared of freezing to death. The water was no more than forty degrees. He grabbed the portside, but getting up was nearly impossible because of his arms. They were too cold, and his hands couldn't grasp anything hard enough to maintain a steady grip. Belle pulled and pulled, but she was too small.

"Daddy!" she screamed. In front of him, a massive

330

dorsal fin came charging.

"Oh, no! No!" he screamed. He held onto Belle and the boat, closed his eyes, then felt tearing of his skin. It took his breath.

He didn't open his eyes for a while. He waited, feeling like he had been transported into another world.

His body hadn't been taken. He opened his eyes to see where the animal had bit him. There was nothing but flaky pieces of yellow. The shark had brushed along his right leg, scraping it and disfiguring it, but leaving it functioning.

"It doesn't want you," Belle said. Conrad had escaped it. The dorsal fin was heading for Bran's motionless body.

Conrad still had to get out of the water. This time Belle grabbed onto his shirt. They pulled together on the count of three, and his rib cage fit nicely on the edge of the wall. His ribs cracked when he came down, but they held him there. He gave one last push, and Belle tugged him forward. The sidewall of the port cracked violently, but neither Conrad nor Belle noticed. Conrad lay over the wall on his waist. He let Belle pull his numbed legs overboard.

It wasn't over. Conrad looked out. He could see Bran floating in the water, a fin investigating him. And as Conrad expected, Bran woke.

"Let's go," Belle said.

Conrad knew better. "I have to see it end," he said, and encouraged Belle not to look.

Bran could see the beach from where he treaded. He could even see imprints in the sand left by the elephant seals. He had no choice but to head for it.

When he caught sight of blood trailing off in the tide from his body, he spun frantically in a circle, expecting to see the huge gray fish rise above the surface and pull him below. It was

331

his nose, bleeding from the impact of the trawler, sending his blood into the water and eventually through the nostrils of his predator.

He had to move quickly. He used all of his strength to pull his chest above the waves and swim. He failed in his first two attempts but was successful on the third and began swimming in an even way so not to attract too much attention.

He knew sharks were mesmerized by sound and blood. He had two strikes against him and had to try and control one. With the tide on his side, he made fifty yards quickly. He let his legs dip below the surface to rest. The sight of the brown island gave him confidence. Sand was just twenty feet below him now. He was almost there. He was going to make it.

He began thinking of ways to get back home from the island. Could he make it in time to intercept Conrad and Belle?

The Storm-petrels came, flight rings in the sky. They made him stop.

He took a deep breath, submerged his face, and opened his eyes. What he saw stopped his heart: A great white, the teeth pulled back like a snarled dog, came vertically. Its tail kicked as it rushed from the deep and swallowed his legs to his abdomen. He was brought out of the water freakishly. The rush of water looked like a torpedo hit. The shark clamped down on his abdomen like it would a seal, spinning 'round, taking a look at the world that existed above it. Its eyes were white until they slid over black on the way down. The pool of red was significant enough to indicate Bran's lower torso had been consumed.

After a few fluttering movements below the water, another shark emerged in the red swirl and with a few gulps, swallowed the other half too.

Conrad hid Belle's eyes during the attack.

"Can we go now?" she asked.

Conrad smiled. She was a kid until the end. "We can go now," he said.

He tried to stand but was immediately shot with pain traveling from his ribs into his neck. He held his chest. His ribs were broken. He could feel them, actually grab them. To make matters worse, the shark had badly injured his right leg with the abrasion. Too much skin had been scraped off and he was in severe pain.

Conrad heard a helicopter overhead, but he was certain they couldn't see him because of the fog.

"We need to drive out of this for them to see us." He tried to stand again, but it increased his pain. He fell back down, clenching his ribs.

"I can drive it," she said.

"No, Belle," he said.

She looked at him intensely. "I can."

Conrad looked back at the Farallones. The waves were crashing all around. The wind had picked up too. He nodded to her. This place wasn't meant for people.

She stood, back on her tiptoes, and headed out to the open sea in the direction of San Francisco.

EPILOGUE

"Dad," Belle said.

Conrad looked up at her, still holding his chest. He was saturated in saltwater.

"What do we do?"

"Stop the boat," he told her. He sat up and looked around. "Look over the side for me."

She did and reported to him what she saw. Conrad did not realize that his pressure to board on the port side made a crack so massive that it penetrated the bottom, giving passage to the Pacific Ocean. They were sinking.

Conrad used all his strength to sit up and look out to sea. He was hoping, praying that he would open his eyes to that beautiful image of the Golden Gate. Instead, he looked out to fog, as if they had never left.

The boat was already beginning to submerge port side up. He could sense the imbalance.

He grabbed the flare guns he had and instructed Belle to put on her life vest. He took the gun, told her to hold her ears, and fired it off into the fog. He knew he needed to wait a minute, that flares set off at one-minute intervals meant distress. But time was of the essence. He waited as long as he could and

334

fired. Bright red smoke ballooned in the air.

The water was coming in quickly. They would be under in a few minutes.

"There's only one life jacket," she said. "I can't find yours."

He looked out at the waters. They were too rough for someone without a life jacket, and there was no way he could tread water with his ribs broken. He was concerned only with keeping Belle safe.

She began sobbing. He grabbed her and held her head into his chest. "I love you more than life itself," he said. "I will be with you until the end."

"You can hold onto my life jacket. It can hold the two of us."

"No, it can't," he said, and kissed her on the head.

The boat was creaking. The port side was beginning to tip over. Soon they would tumble into the sea.

And as if God spoke, thunder came down from the foggy sky. It came louder and louder, spiraling madness. It closed in on them, and then punctured the soft white mist. It was a helicopter. The pilots looked down on them. Their faces were all business.

Conrad looked around, for a shark gliding forth, Bran rising from the depths, anything to derail their rescue. But there was nothing. The boat hadn't even sunk before two members of the coast guard jumped into the water and swam to them. The remaining pilot landed the helicopter safely on the water twenty yards from them. Its propellers blew Belle's hair into Conrad's.

The officers took deep cuts through the ocean to reach them. The younger officer took Belle, placed her in an inflatable dingy, and paddled away as her hand broke free of Conrad's. The other officer, older and full of confidence, swam to Conrad. He had a thick mustache on him and spear-blue eyes. He
335

grabbed Conrad, almost held him like a baby.

"You're safe, sir," the officer said, and held him until the second dingy came. Conrad looked at the man and smiled to the sky. The officer was confused. "What is it, sir?"

"We've met before," Conrad said.

"I see," the officer said, thinking the episode might have made the man lose his mind. "Where?"

Conrad spoke softly and slowly. "Here," he said, looking at the officer's name badge.

It said Briggs on it.

"It was here."

www.ingramcontent.com/pod-product-compliance
Lightning Source LLC
Chambersburg PA
CBHW062022170626
46813CB00001B/254